PENGUIN BOOK

WIDTH OF A CIRCLE

David J. Hirst is the author of nine management books, including the best-selling *How to Communicate with Anyone.* He was born in England and has degrees from the University of Stafford and Christ Church College at Canterbury in Kent, England. He currently lives in Malaysia which, after twenty-three years, he calls home. He has a tenth degree Sifu licence in Malaysian Wing Chun and a Master Practitioner Licence in Neuro-semantics, which allows him insights into human behaviour that give his characters their vibrancy. He regularly attends the MYWriters Penang writing community's meetings and on most stormy afternoons he can be found on his Penang apartment balcony with a chilled glass of something nice, working on his next novel.

Width of a Circle

David Hirst

PENGUIN BOOKS
An imprint of Penguin Random House

PENGUIN BOOKS

USA | Canada | UK | Ireland | Australia
New Zealand | India | South Africa | China | Southeast Asia

Penguin Books is part of the Penguin Random House group of companies whose addresses can be found at global.penguinrandomhouse.com

Published by Penguin Random House SEA Pte Ltd
9, Changi South Street 3, Level 08-01,
Singapore 486361

First published in Penguin Books by Penguin Random House SEA 2023

10 9 8 7 6 5 4 3 2 1

This is a work of fiction. Names, characters, places and incidents are either the product of the author's imagination or are used fictitiously, and any resemblance to any actual person, living or dead, events or locales is entirely coincidental.

ISBN 9789815127966

Typeset in Garamond by MAP Systems, Bengaluru, India

www.penguin.sg

Part One

If you gaze for long into an abyss, the abyss gazes also into you.

—F. Nietzsche

1

It was 8.30 a.m., and the tropical heat was already making its way into the plantation bungalow—my new home for the summer. My loose, faded red T-shirt was clinging to me like my sulky younger brother back in the UK. How come he got to stay? But if I'm being honest, I think I know why.

I also wore a pair of beige leggings and a pair of yellow stressed shorts, which were a little tighter than I remembered.

As if conspiring against me, the ceiling fan in my bedroom groaned and scraped its way to an objectionable halt.

'Really?' What's wrong with these people? Why don't they have air-conditioning?

'Lucky,' my friends had said. 'Tropical white-sand beaches. Snorkelling among shoals of multicoloured fish. White water rafting through lush rainforests with proboscis monkeys swinging from river-bank trees. Shops with the latest tech stuff.'

Yeah, right.

My phone's signal strength read 'No Service'. So much for hi-tech Asia. For the time being I was stranded, cut off from civilization. It had only been my first night and already I was in trouble with my 'creative imagination' being brought up again like an undercooked paella.

I looked in the mirror at the black figurine design on the front of my shirt. She never says much, but her conversation is a lot better than most of the people I meet. She seemed to be telling me to chill. She's wise like that.

I stared at the shadow under my eyes from a restless night with bizarre images. I said to the girl on the T-shirt, 'I told the truth. I know what I saw. What more do they want?' But she was her usual quiet self. I could learn a lot from her.

My name is Zola Tapp but most people call me Zo. My best friend, Alyssa, calls me 'Arry' after the *Game of Thrones* character she says I'm like. I'm a Kenyan-Irish-Brit, fourteen, and an absolute fun person to be with, unless you're a Thrope—my word for people who have an IQ below room temperature in winter. My hair is nightingale-brown, shoulder length, and right now sticking to the nape of my neck because of the blanket humidity that covers this place.

My room was basic but comfortable. It looked like they had taken furniture from a cowboy film set and put it in an IKEA store. There was a single, springy bed which squeaked at one end, two windows behind threadbare curtains which overlooked the plantation, and three similar watercolour paintings hanging on faded primrose-yellow walls. The furniture wasn't much better and I had an ancient hardwood dresser with three large drawers on either side and an equally old desk and chair which would have impressed the Antiques Roadshow. The door didn't lock properly so I used my giant rucksack to ensure privacy. What I did like was the wooden floor which was worn smooth and nice for bare feet. Shoes—including my treasured Birkenstock sandals—had to be left in the porch. The sandals were a present from mum to keep my mouth shut about something I'd seen. She hadn't needed to do that but I guess it made her feel a bit less guilty. It also dragged me into something I didn't want to be a part of. Still, to paraphrase Jaqen H'ghar, 'A girl needs nice shoes.'

I'm staying with my distant relatives—the Junketts—over the summer holidays. They are two kind old wrinklies who have a faint smell of hamster about them. They are nice hamsters though, especially Aunt Margaret, who is Chinese-Malaysian and even looks a bit like a hamster when she eats, her cheeks bulging when her false teeth wrestle with a particularly tough morsel of food. Uncle Donald is a bit weird in an oddball, odd socks, retired army Captain kind of way.

They are 'distant' because I'd never met them before yesterday, and because my dad makes 'they're crazy' finger signs when we receive their Christmas card, one of the few non-digital ones we get.

I screwed up, which is why I'm here in the middle of nowhere with an intermittent one-bar signal. Okay, I did smash everything I'd ever cared about and set fire to my room. But what did they expect? It was the constant fighting coming through the walls. Did they honestly think we wouldn't hear? The lack of sleep, my anxious younger brother begging to come in my room all the time, and then the painful silences at breakfast.

Do I regret it? Honestly, I don't even remember most of it. It was an emotional lightning strike that took over all logical thought. I needed to get out. I'd wanted a new life so they gave me one.

I miss my guitar.

And after only fourteen hours here, I need to face another breakfast filled with dread. I had screwed up again.

The girl on my T-shirt was wrinkling her nose at the strange pong from under the door. It was as if the stench was calling me out to face the humiliation which I knew was coming.

2

Fourteen hours earlier

I had been staring at an elongated shadow that looked like a large animal. I'd put it down to jet lag but I felt an icy shiver crawl up my spine and goose bumps on my arm despite the ever-present heat—it was one of those shivers that tells you something is deeply wrong. Adding to the dread was a strange scent of spice mixed with the smell of damp earth and rotting vegetation.

I'd been walking for forty-five minutes on a meandering path through the estate, trying to clear my head and plan my next blog post, when an unusual shape in the darker undergrowth caught my eye. It wasn't moving but I was still cautious. *Was it dead?*

I knew I should walk away because, let's face it, what were the chances that it actually was a mysterious and rare animal that I could post pictures of on my growing Instagram page? More like another sunbaked and twisted oil-palm frond. Besides, the sun was now making a race for the horizon and I most definitely didn't want to be out here when it got dark. But my curiosity was not going to let it go. It wanted to know what animal it was and what happened to it. That's why I had to look to make sure, even though the thought of anything dead was gross.

There was no smell of death, only spice. Once you smell death, you never forget it.

My eyes went up and down the silhouette again, desperately searching the gloom for any detail of what I was looking at.

They stopped at one end and my heart started pounding. My stomach churned. Instinctively, I took a step back.

I was staring at two flashes of garnet at the end closest to me, trying to make sense of things. Blood? I could feel its presence, and another shiver ran right through me. The air felt thicker and laden with menace.

I think it just moved.

Part of me wanted to find something to prove that my 'overactive imagination' that got talked about so often was based on real life. I didn't make half the stuff up that they said I did. That and the fact it would help take my mind off the storm I had left behind in the UK. And the shame.

The other part of me, the sensible part, was telling me to get the hell away from it.

The light was receding, and the shadows were getting longer. It was almost seven for Christ's sake. Didn't it ever get any cooler here?

It was still there.

The high-pitched whining from the swarming mosquitoes wouldn't go away. They were saying, 'Get out of my plantation.' I regretted wearing a light blue T-shirt and white shorts. I smacked my left arm. There was a black and white mosquito crushed on the heel of my hand and a smear of blood underneath. A small vengeful smile crept across my lips.

I began to regret my adventure and remembered Uncle Donald's caution about giant spitting cobras and the wild boar which roamed through the plantation.

'Last year one of the workers was gored in the leg; missed the artery by a hair's width,' he'd said. Then he got into regimental storytelling mode about an ancient tribe of alchemists—called the Indra—who needed to eat human flesh to keep their youth. 'They would trade their forest secrets and heal the sick for a pound of flesh and blood, which had to come from a healthy living soul.'

That was enough for me. I was staying in my room. However, Aunt Margaret had other ideas and ushered me out of the bungalow, saying that the old grouch was living in a fantasy world and that it was perfectly safe in the plantation. But should I trust a person who thaws out frozen food in an old tumble dryer?

The high-pitched rattling from the cicadas was getting louder, and the incessant croaking of the frogs in the irrigation ditches was making it harder to think. So much for a relaxing exploration of my new home before dinner.

For a moment I considered going back to report on what I thought I was looking at but then I realized how the conversation would go.

'Uncle and Aunty Hamster, I think there's a large mysterious animal in your plantation.'

'Is there, Zola? That's nice, dear. Cup of tea?'

Yeah. That conversation was not going to happen.

My heart jumped at the sound of a dark-olive plantain squirrel racing along a thin track next to me. Its large, bushy tail chasing the rest of it. It stopped and stared. Its eyes were shiny black pearls—wide open and glaring. They were saying, 'Get out of my plantation.'

A thorn bush rustled loudly to my right. My comfort zone was shrivelling faster than stretched shrink-wrap.

'Hello? Is anyone there?'

Silence.

My nerves were being shredded on a cheese grater as I stared again at the shadow resting between cut palm fronds and bushels of brown palm-nuts.

I pulled out my phone. The soft plastic cover felt reassuring.

Decision time—stay or go.

I moved closer, turned on the torch and craned my neck to get a clearer view.

Oh, crap with a hedgehog.

Reflected in the light were two lifeless eyes on a boy's face. He looked older than me, but not by much.

Then I saw a dark crimson stain over the left side of his chest.

This can't be happening. I bit my lip and it hurt. *Yup, he's real.* I was not imagining this. The odour of spice was stronger now.

Is he still alive? I should check for a pulse. Mine was stratospheric.

Is the killer still out here? Any sensible person would run and get help. Yet, half of me still didn't believe, or didn't want to believe, I was looking at a corpse. I couldn't afford to get it wrong this time.

Something grabbed my ankle.

When I watched horror movies, it was rare for me to yelp or scream, and I generally sneered at those who did; but when I felt his hand grab my ankle, I shrieked like two eagles spinning in a death spiral. He had a strong grip for a person who was supposed to be dead.

'I . . . need to tell you . . .' His voice was soft and rasping. He had thick, matted black hair—matted from sweat or blood—but his face was smooth and his features striking. His eyes flinched from the torchlight.

I moved the beam down and looked again at the stain on the boy's chest. Glinting back was what looked like the tip of a small blade where the knife handle had snapped off. 'No. I'll get help,' I blurted. 'You're badly hurt.' A little voice inside my head said, *'I think he knows that, duh.'*

The boy tried to raise his hand. 'No, there's no time.' He coughed up a bubble of pink phlegm.

Not good.

My leg was free. Time to run.

The boy tried again, 'No, please . . . listen . . .'

'Wait, wait here,' I said.

Really? Where's he going to go?

I added, 'My uncle owns this plantation. His house is nearby. You need help.'

The little voice spoke again. *'You need help if that's all you can come up with.'*

I was struggling with the sensory overload. 'What's your name?'

'Daud. You don't understand . . . you must help me . . . please. I'm begging you.'

Daud's breathing was becoming shallower.

'Yes, yes, okay. I'll help. Whatever you want. But I've got to get you an ambulance.'

I went to move but he grabbed my ankle and I yelped again. You'd think I'd be better the second time.

Daud let go and pointed to his dark red trainers. With much effort, he used his right foot to push off the left one. 'You'll need this.'

Something fell out of his shoe. A small, thin card. 'Take it . . . my brother . . . give it to my brother . . . promise me.'

I bent down and picked it up. As I did, I heard, 'They're watching.' Then I saw his eyes close.

'Who's your brother?'

No reply.

Not good. Not good at all. I stood and tried to move, but my legs felt like two anchors stuck in the soil.

A breathy, expressive voice said, 'He'll be okay.'

I was becoming excellent at the startled jump. They should make it an Olympic sport.

'What the . . . ? Who said that? Who's there?'

I spun around and noticed a girl no more than ten metres away. How did I miss seeing her?

My hackles rose. My fists clenched. 'Did you stab him?'

'No.'

Her upper lip rose in contempt and she pushed a puff of air from her nose. 'I have no need to be so crude.'

It was the type of response I wished I could think of and I wondered which Marvel character she'd stolen the line from. I asked, 'Who the hell are you? What're you doing here?'

'Maya, but you will forget that name, and you will forget our meeting.'

I didn't think so. But the earthy tones of her voice were mesmerizing. It sounded like maple syrup dripping from a light breeze.

She was smaller than me, but not by much, and was wearing a light green dress with small lotus flowers embroidered in gold. It would have suited a posh party, but it certainly wasn't anything any normal person would wear in a plantation. She looked anywhere between thirteen and nineteen, yet her voice sounded much older. Her angular jawline, high cheek bones and narrow eyes matched her short dark hair. And she radiated an elfin magnetism that hung around her like a cloak.

She pointed to my hand. 'Give me that. I'll look after it for you.'

'Not going to happen. You're not the brother—' I was going to say more, but my vision was blurring way beyond jet lag.

'You must give it to me. Listen to the gentleness of my voice, listen to the genuineness of my request. You are tired. Trust yourself to relax.'

Palm frond shadows danced across my face and I felt exhausted. Her voice felt wonderful to my ears. It was like the softest of pillows for a weary head.

Fight, I told myself. *Focus on the injured guy. He needs your help.*

The girl took no more than two steps as if she were sliding on ice, and there she was, right in front of me. Her eyes were changing colour from a vibrant hazel to a shimmering gold as she spoke. All I could think of was that the colour matched her smile perfectly.

I knew zombies didn't exist, but that was how I felt. I couldn't move, talk, nothing. I heard a light humming sound as Maya looked me up and down like a zoo exhibit. I felt a tiny electrical current sizzling all around me.

I was zoning out fast.

She leaned forward and all I could think of was that we'd known each other for years. Her lips parted and I saw a flash of sharp, white polished teeth. Kissed or bitten, I didn't care. I was a continent beyond caring.

A sudden, ear-splitting 'koo-el' sound screamed into my zombie brain, sucking me back into the real world. To my right was a large black koel perched on a frond less than five metres away, staring straight at me. It screamed, 'Get out of my plantation. Now!'

I looked back to see that Maya's elfin charm had been replaced with a menacing glare. Her lips were pulled back in anger and her sharp pointed teeth flashed in the remaining light. 'You cannot escape me. I will find you again.'

I jammed the card into my pocket and ran like a hunted animal.

I was gasping for breath when I reached the house to raise the alarm. Uncle Donald grabbed a large torch and his old hunting rifle—that he called Reginald—from the shed and we set off.

Less than forty-five minutes had passed between me leaving Daud and Donald and I returning in his battered blue jeep, but the body had disappeared. I was sure I'd taken him to the right place. I felt awful when he looked at me with his 'I'm too old for this' expression. I searched all over but couldn't find Daud and ended up feeling like an overly-dunked digestive biscuit crumbling into a mug of embarrassment.

Yes, I had been exhausted from the flight. And sure, there would have been jet lag. But it had all seemed so real. People with serious injuries don't suddenly get up and walk off. He was real. *Or am I really losing the plot here?*

Later, after a shower—at least they had hot water—I sat on my bed and tried to put the pictures in my head back in chronological order, but I couldn't. There was a mish-mash of individual snapshots, yet no coherent series of events. It was like an itch that needed scratching. It was there, but just out of reach, almost as if the memories had been partially erased. Another picture flew into my muddled brain, and I went to the hatstand where my clothes hung like limp roadkill.

I put my hand in my shorts' pocket. Yup, there it was. The card. I took it out and ran my fingers over the flat surface. It was thin but heavier than it looked and had a solid, classy feel to it. In the dressing table light, it looked more blue than grey and had tinges of a darker blue towards the edges. And there were two embossed circles, one within the other.

Evidence.

I went for the door handle to tell the Hamsters but then quickly figured that it would be a waste of breath. They wouldn't believe me. Why should they? To them, it would be a scrap of rubbish I'd picked up in the plantation and made up a story about—my famed overactive imagination on display again. Besides, they'd been through enough for one night. I had to get more proof if anyone was ever going to believe me.

I toyed with the card, turning it over, expecting to see a mirror image. However, what I saw froze me to the spot. Staring back at me were two words that scared the hell out of me. I quickly put the card back in the pocket of my shorts and took a step back. *Did I really see that? Am I imagining things again?* It took me a good minute before I could move. Perhaps I was mistaken and jet lag was playing games with my head. I pulled the card out again and the same two words stared back. Now I didn't have a choice. I had to find out what had happened to Daud.

3

Present time

'Good morning, Zola dear. Did you sleep well?' Aunt Margaret enquired with a sympathetic smile. 'About last night . . . You must have been tired. Jet lagged, that's what it was. The plane must've taken at least two days to get all the way here. You looked tired when we picked you up from the airport. Would you like a nice cup of tea?'

I moved away from the bubbling witches brew on the gas cooker. 'It's much faster than that these days, Aunty. Eleven hours.'

Aunt Margaret gave me a look similar to one Alyssa does when I say something stupid.

Uncle Donald's voice rumbled like a looming thunderstorm from the front deck. 'Lord's legs, Margaret, what on earth are you concocting in the kitchen? Are you planning on poisoning the neighbours again?'

What? They poisoned their neighbours? Who are these people?

Margaret offered me a kind smile and said, 'Ignore him, my dear, he's an idiot at the best of times. Don't believe half the things he says. He only does it to get attention.'

She called out, 'I'm making Rosmah's breakfast, which is your job, Donald, if I recall.'

I decided to give it one more try. 'About last night. I know what I saw,' I said with as much conviction as I could manage.

Margaret looked at me with caring eyes, her once pretty face now furrowed by fifty-one years of marriage to an eccentric plantation manager in one of Kuala Lumpur's fast-diminishing oil-palm estates. 'I believe you saw a scary shadow, maybe it was one of the huge monitor lizards which come over from the swamp to eat the rats.'

'Rats? You have rats and giant lizards running around?'

'Yes, dear. They're nothing to worry about. They never come into the house as Rosmah chases them away.' She then turned her attention back to the gaseous gurgling coming from the stove.

I let it slide.

I went back through the hall and out to the front deck where Uncle Donald was sitting in his favourite rattan chair, going through a few papers. I eyed their ancient dog with suspicion. It was a light-brown patched cross between a St. Bernard and a Bassett. I doubted it could chase its tail, let alone a rat. I made a mental note to check under my bed later.

Rosmah looked back at me with a lazy expression and wagged her tail. She then attempted to climb on to an old wicker chair but got stuck halfway. Her two front legs rested on the seat and supported her head while one rear leg waved helplessly in the air as she tried to find another part of the chair to help push herself up.

A rather feeble welcoming toot from an orange Repsol motorbike grabbed Rosmah's attention and she turned around to bark at it.

'Where's my gun, Margaret? The postman's here again.'

'Stop showing off in front of Zola, Donald. You know the man's simply trying to be friendly.'

Donald leaned across to me as if he was going to share a secret. 'Mad as a bag of monkeys, that one. Don't tell her I said that though, otherwise I'll be in the doghouse again. Be a dear and fetch those letters, would you? Onwards and forwards.'

I mean, what do you say to that? Anyway, I did as I was asked and walked down the dirt pathway, collected the postman's offerings, and handed them over to my eccentric uncle.

'Woohoo, breakfast's ready,' Margaret called in a cheery voice.

'Yes, dearest, we'll be right there,' Donald said. 'I'm checking the post.'

'Not you, Donald. Rosmah's. Yours and Zola's will be ready when I've finished writing on the eggs.'

My eyebrows rose as if to question what my ears had told them. *What would you write on eggs? Which planet are these people from?*

I watched a lost squid's tentacle of slobber dribble down Rosmah's lower jaw. I'd never seen such a sorrowful expression on a dog before. I knew how she felt. I'd been there before too.

'Don't look at me like that. I'm not eating it. Go.'

With a resigned yawn—swaying underbelly, and drooping tail—Rosmah waddled towards the kitchen.

'There you are,' Aunty called out in a baby voice. 'Here girl, I have a special treat for you today.'

I thought I heard the dog whimper.

'That reminds me, Zola,' Donald said, looking up from his letters. 'I've got a surprise for you that I think you're going to like. If you're sure you're up for it, that is?'

'Yes, Uncle. I feel fine, honest. What is it?'

'Onwards and forwards, then. Well, even though I'm sure you think we look like a pair of old trout . . .'

Hamsters.

'. . . we understand your need for mobility and getting around. You'll want to go to town and make friends there, I'm sure. Therefore, feel free to borrow the motorcycle one of my workers has left in the shed over there. You can also drive it to the hill in the plantation if you want to access that infernal internet thing which you young people like so much. There's reasonable reception up there. Now and again, that is.'

Wow! Fantastic. I was over the moon and said, 'Thank you, Uncle. You're a lifesaver.' I wanted to give him a hug, but looked at his military expression and thought twice.

Things were starting to look up. *Would it be a Fireblade?*

No, duh. Out here? Be realistic.

A PCX 125? A Lexmoto Echo?

Transport would change everything. Now I could get a signal, contact civilization, and discover more about what I'd seen the previous night. I'd never ridden a motorcycle before, although I'd been on the back of one a couple of times, and it all seemed pretty straightforward. A bit of practice and I could get up that hill. I'd leave going into town for a while, and besides, I didn't have a licence. Not that it seemed to be a problem out here.

Excited and with considerable expectation, I pulled the shed door open and then immediately wished I hadn't.

4

My lower jaw fell with the grace of a drooping banana skin. What the hell was this, and was Uncle serious about me riding it?

Gawking at me was the oldest, most beaten-up wreck of a motorcycle I'd ever seen. The seat was torn with brown foam bursting out like a shaken and frozen-in-time coke. Wires sprouted like weeds, and the plastic leg protectors had snapped off at strange angles. It was also covered in dust-laden spiders' webs criss-crossing their geometric rudeness.

I hate spider's webs.

There's always the question: where is the spider? In the UK that's no biggie, but out here I'd read that there were poisonous ones.

I got a stick.

I knew one thing though. If I didn't get connected to the internet soon, I'd grow to hate this place and my life, and then the whole cycle would start over again. It was a no-brainer.

One of the faded red side-panels had a few sun-bleached letters on it. 'Honda C-70'. It may as well have read 'You're mad' for all that meant to me. But it was this or nothing. The decision wasn't even close.

After a good breakfast of scrambled eggs and a mug of strong milky tea that the Hamsters described as *Teh Tarik*—pulled tea—I wheeled the ancient eyesore out of the shed. It smelled a lot like the fertilizer they used for the oil palm, so I wiped it down with a heavy-duty cloth and a bucket of water with a large plop of washing-up liquid. Then I tried to figure out the controls. The labels, like most of my common sense, had long since disappeared. But it wasn't rocket-science and soon the bike farted into life with a prod of a button which doubled as the horn. It was a wannabe, a hard-ridden, rural run-around. I called her Rachel. *Alyssa will get a good laugh out of it when I tell her.*

The bike was easier to get the hang of than I'd expected. There were a few rules: avoid potholes, drainage ruts and black USOs—unidentified shitty objects. They were sunbaked cow pats that had hard surfaces, but once that carapace had been broken, it would send the front tyre skidding off and send me to a slimy, smelly end. Not a good look for me.

No one in the plantation wore crash helmets, besides it was too hot for one anyway. Plus, it felt rebellious. It's a growing streak I've developed, and I liked the feel of it.

I took easy paths at first to get the hang of the beast. It was like riding a heavy electric bicycle with a twist-and-go grip. Easy. The cooling breeze, once I'd got going, was paradise. More importantly, I needed to get answers to a whole host of questions swimming around the fishbowl of my brain. What had happened to Daud was the first one.

Ten minutes of cautious riding later and I was at the spot where I had seen Daud's body. First glance revealed nada. *What had I seen?* Bodies don't get up and walk off, unless they were zombies, which I was still pretty sure didn't exist.

I pushed the kickstand down, turned off the engine with the key—which stayed stuck in the lock—got off the bike and then searched the area.

The plantation was filled with sounds. A few felt welcoming, but most were unfamiliar. After the breeze from riding, the hot air felt heavy, as if you were breathing steam through a wet flannel.

I felt a trickle of sweat down the nape of my neck. Not for the first time, I felt very alone. But rather than let myself get dragged down into the soft underbelly of self-pity and worthlessness, I opened my ears to the incredible variety of birds trilling exotic songs. They provided a cheerfulness I'd missed for a long time. There were other noises too. Dying oil-palm fronds rustled eerie whispers in the light gusts, and the undergrowth crackled caution. The plantation was alive and pulsing to its own rhythm. I'd expected a plantation to be lifeless. It was what I'd been writing on my Instagram page—one of the few constants in my life. One with a growing readership.

I'm way off from being an 'Influencer', but I have started to receive 'PR' gifts to talk about on my page. One of the gifts they wanted me to talk about were said to be 'forest friendly'. PR's not always as easy as it sounds. One of the moisturizers I'd been sent had a faint scent of a restaurant washroom. And one of the shampoos had the consistency and aroma of a burger sauce. Various other stuff was okay, but nothing that stood out. I was not going to sell my soul for followers or gold. Well, not yet anyway. But then, 'A girl needs a new phone.'

My blog was now long overdue an update and I figured an interview with my uncle to get his side of the story would be fantastic. I'd tear it to shreds, of course. The crazier the hamster, the better the story. Reforestation is my key theme.

I looked around the area. It was different in the morning light, but I divided the ground into areas and took my time. I came across a piece of torn palm frond and held it to the sunlight. There it was. A dark, almost black stain.

Blood.

I didn't imagine it.

Moving another frond out of the way, I saw a mass of insects swarming over a dark leaf shape. I got a stick and prodded the thick gooey mass.

Red fire ants raced up the stick to squirt their hydrochloric acid at me. They were fast, but I was faster, dropping the stick before they could sink their fangs in.

For a moment, part of me thought about bringing my Uncle Donald out to see what I'd found but then decided it would be a waste of time. He'd be dismissive. I put on his army voice 'Well, my girl, it could be anything: animalian or plantarian, but it's not human. I won't allow that sort of thing in my plantation, I'll have you know. Onwards and forwards.'

For the first time in ages, I laughed out loud. It felt good; it had been too long.

A sharp cracking sound grabbed my attention. I looked around but couldn't see anyone. I hoped it wasn't a wild boar. I moved closer to Rachel for a quick getaway.

I got the sensation that I was being watched.

'Who's there? Daud, is it you?'

Nothing.

Then I noticed the silence—the birds had stopped singing. The plantation had fallen silent.

My senses went on high alert. My bladder did the same.

I heard a bush rustle to my left.

'Are you a wild boar?'

Now I'm talking to an imaginary wild boar. I'm becoming as crazy as the Hamsters. The sound of my voice was strangely comforting though.

I looked around for a weapon but saw nothing more usable than a large stone. It would have to do. I threw it in the direction of the earlier crunching sound and heard it fall with a thud on a patch of sunbaked earth in the undergrowth. I waited for the sound of hooves running away.

Silence.

I froze on the spot when I saw the same stone fly back in my direction, landing with a thump at my feet.

Either the wild boar here are exceptionally gifted, or I'm not alone.

My sensible self said '*Get out. Now!*' But it was daylight and curiosity won again.

I called out, 'Who are you? Stop playing around. I'm not joking. My uncle owns this plantation.'

The silence was getting to me. All I could see were rows and rows of dark green and grey palm trees interspersed with piles of dead, sun-bleached fronds, dry undergrowth and the occasional thick clump of coarse green bushes.

The rustling sound came closer, but I couldn't see anything. A sudden chill wrapped around me like a hospital gown. A trickle of cold sweat ran down the inside of my shirt. My breathing became faster.

I remembered Aunt Margaret saying that cobras would always move away and that I'd never see one. Yeah, right. Tempting as it was to prove her wrong, the sensible side of me won this time.

My senses were screaming for answers. I reached Rachel and sat on the old towel I'd put over the torn seat. My eyes left the plantation to find the start button for less than a second but it was all the time he needed.

A strong, rough hand grabbed my shoulder and pulled me backwards. Rachel crashed to the earth, stalling as it fell. I could feel the man's powerful arm slithering around my throat, pinning my back to the front of his body. I wanted to fight but felt weak and feeble. My legs started shaking. I felt his hot, earthy breath on the back of my neck. It was getting harder to breathe as his arm crushed my throat. Sweat stung my eyes. Panic was taking over.

Another powerful hand forced its way into my shorts' pocket, ripping the stitching at the sides.

Oh, shit! The sound of the fabric tearing sent a new wave of fear through me.

He pulled out my small pack of tissues, house keys and then my phone from my back pocket.

I squeezed out what breath I had to beg. 'Stop. Please. I can get money.' I hoped to God it was money he wanted.

His hands went into my remaining pockets and, with his focus elsewhere, I grabbed a breath. 'Who are you? What do you want?'

'Who I am is not important,' a deep, growling voice replied in slightly accented English. 'What is important is that you hand me what you were given yesterday.'

'What? I don't know what you mean.'

'I'm not in the mood for games. Let me tell you what's going to happen. You hand me what he gave you and you go free. If you don't . . .' He left the words heavy in the air like a circling vulture.

'I saw you last night. What did he give you?'

Then I got it. The small plastic rectangle. It was back in my room at the bungalow.

'I don't have it.' My vision was narrowing and I felt paralysed by his strength.

Then my world got a whole lot worse.

The man shifted his grip and spun me around to face him. His hand went back to my throat.

Oh, crap with a hedgehog!

Now I could recognize him again, which, according to all the crime novels I've read, spelt a whole new world of trouble. The risk of being harmed or worse had now quadrupled.

Then I noticed how young he was. No more than a teenager, like me, and his grip was firm but not painful anymore. His expression held more urgency than anger. Fear shifted into confusion.

'What was it? What have you done with it?' There was desperation in his voice.

I remembered a podcast saying that muggers were less likely to cause harm if they had a personal connection with their victim.

The little voice in my head said, '*Make friends with him. Charm him.*'

'It's back at my uncle's bungalow. I can get it for you, no problem.'

He had a boyish face with supple, tanned skin—a bit like mine, but darker.

He exuded an aura of power but he seemed unsure about what to do next.

My shoulders relaxed a little.

'I need whatever documents he gave you.'

'What documents? Who are you?'

There was a long pause before he said, 'Zak, Zak Abraham. I'm Daud's brother. Did he give you a pouch, a key, papers? What was it?'

It took me a moment to get my head together, then I understood and said, 'He gave me a plastic rectangally thing.'

He let go of my throat.

The situation was moving more in my favour. He was becoming less threatening by the second. I noticed that his faded jeans had a tear on both knees which looked more designer-stressed than real, and he wore an open-neck white shirt and expensive-looking Teva sandals. His English was faintly accented but excellent. He'd been to a good school. I hadn't intended to, but I also saw the ridges of stomach muscles showing through his clinging shirt.

I hoped he could answer why my name was written on the back of the card. I'd never seen Daud before. How did he know my name or that he would be able to give it to me? And why wasn't his brother's name there instead? Nothing made sense. Now was the time to get some answers.

'Why was my name on the card? How does he know me?'

There was a long pause and Zak's eyes shifted to the left and then up.

'Oh, er, yes. He er . . . I couldn't do anything. *They* were there too.'

Clearly, he didn't know either.

'Who's they? And where is Daud? Is he okay?'

Before he could answer, we heard another motorcycle in the plantation. I hoped it was one of the estate workers.

'I gotta go. I need to see what he gave you. Don't trust anyone. They'll be after you too now.'

'Who? What have I done?'

I saw that he was becoming stressed, which, in my experience, was what would make him unpredictable. I didn't want him giving any problems to my aunt and uncle. 'Okay. Meet me on the hill over there,' I pointed. 'Tomorrow, same time.'

'Sorry for your shorts. Don't say anything to anyone else. I'll tell you everything tomorrow.'

I watched as he disappeared between the bushes. Well, that was weird. And should I trust someone who says 'Don't tell anyone else'?

5

The other motorcycle was coming closer, which reminded me to pick up my own bike. I still felt weak; my hands were trembling. It felt heavier than before and slid back down to the ground. I needed to stop being pathetic.

When I looked up again, I noticed the other bike was coming towards me. It carried two huge men who were more like baby hippos than human beings. Their greasy shirts, old trousers and dirty sandals gave me the impression that they worked on the estate. Both had enormous stomachs which bounced like two oversized water balloons. The one driving had his dark brown shirt rolled up over his stomach, which made it look as though it was several sizes too small. The pillion passenger looked like an identical twin. They made their bike look comically smaller than it was. I felt sorry for it.

They stopped near me and I noticed then that they were both carrying large machetes. They had to be farm workers.

The pillion passenger asked in broken English, 'Hello, what you do here?'

'Hello. My uncle owns this plantation. Do you work here?'

'Maybe. Again, what *you* do *here*?'

'Err . . . learning how to ride Rachel.'

'Huh?'

Looking at this guy, I realized that explaining the bike's name would blast supersonic over his cultural understanding.

'I help you,' he added.

'No, it's okay. I can manage, thanks.'

'Can help, *lah*. No problem. I help you, you help me.'

It was less than halfway through the morning and too much had already happened.

The pillion passenger blubbered himself off the back seat. 'You find something here?'

Not again. This can't be happening. I could feel a cool breeze on my scalp and reverted to my life-saving motto—when in doubt, lie. 'No, I haven't seen a thing.'

The problem with this sage advice was that I started thinking of Daud coughing blood . . . and the huge stain on his shirt . . . and the rectangular card he gave me.

I'd get away with this if I wasn't feeling so hopelessly guilty right now.

'It's hot out here, isn't it?'

Agh, that sounds pathetic.

The man picked up Rachel with one hand. The other held on to his machete.

'Here.'

'Thanks. I'd best be going then.' *God, which century am I from? Perhaps I should curtsy to put sour cream on the cake of pitiful excuses.*

I went to take the handlebars, but he held on and locked his eyes with mine with a stare that said, 'I know you're lying.'

He leaned forward and I smelled a strong odour of alcohol and oily sweat.

'You find anything, you give me.'

The situation was quickly turning creepy.

The man added, 'We see you yesterday.'

Being caught in a lie was not good. My defence was to bow my head and let the tirade or whatever wash over. Or I used puppy dog eyes. Neither was going to work here.

His machete came up to my face. Today was not going well. Still, he looked more mouth than menace.

'Boy give you card. Bring here tomorrow. No problem. No bring. Accident happen. No-one know anything. You choose.'

He let go of the motorcycle.

'Sure. Yes. Tomorrow. Will do.'

'I help you remember.'

I'd been sure he wouldn't use his knife on me.

I was wrong.

6

'You poor dear . . .' Aunt Margaret said.

I stood there with mud on my face and knees, a torn pocket, and a missing clump of hair. Almost a typical school day. Home away from home. I could see her staring at the uneven hairline but not able to figure out what she was looking at.

I put on my brave-but-I-don't-mind-a-little-sympathy face. 'I'm fine, honest. A little fall, that's all.'

Things were not okay, and my bruises were the least of my worries. It was nice Aunty Hamster cared, though, and aimed at Uncle Donald an expression that could wilt flowers.

'Donald. You should have shown Zola how to ride that contraption before letting her go out on her own.'

'It's fine, Aunty. I told Uncle Donald that I'd ridden one before. It's not his fault.'

'Hmm.' Margaret leaned closer with a wry smile and whispered, 'It's always his fault one way or another, but don't tell the old trout . . .'

Hamster.

'. . . I said so. Mad as a shopping trolley full of baboons, that one.'

After a refreshing cold shower and a change of clothes, I looked at the ragged gap where my hair used to be. I felt like having a small cry, but I was too angry. *People don't do that and get away with it.*

The sound of my hair being cut and the shorts pocket ripping played over and over in my head. Images of it happening flashed like an out-of-body experience. At least now I could remember without trembling anymore. Were my senses numb, or was I changing? I wasn't as tense as before. Determined, yes. And angry. I looked in the mirror again. For a moment, I thought I saw a different person looking back. I blinked and she was gone. I needed a stylist.

I also had a couple of other problems to deal with. My parents. Always arguing and fighting and me living with the constant threat of them splitting up. Who would I end up with? I hoped it was Mum. Would I have any say? But this was a future problem. The current WTF issue was here and now.

I unclenched my fists and slowed my breathing. I was in a serious shit-storm with lots of hedgehogs. But, like I always say, when life gives you shit-storms, make bigger ones. And I had an idea.

The potting shed, where Rachel spends the night, was filled with musty shelves, trinkets, and unwanted presents from over fifty years of my aunt and uncle's inability to throw anything out. Then I saw what I wanted—an old hotel key-card. I got a pair of wire cutters from the shelf and cut it down to about two-thirds of its original size. Then, I took a tin of dark grey wood-tar creosote my uncle used for painting fence posts to prevent rot and dipped it in that. When it was almost dry, but still a bit squidgy, I took the screw top from a plastic bottle and the cap from an old tube of hand cream and gently pressed them into the creosote to create two concentric circles. The finishing touch was a polish with an old rag and it was good to go. Or at least the best I could get it to be. It felt weird writing my name on it, so I left it off.

Next, I needed to talk to people who would believe me about all the crazy stuff going on here, people with whom I could share. The answer came in the form of a cup of tea.

'Thanks, Aunty. By the way, I need to contact my frien . . . err . . . ought to contact my parents and friends to let them know everything's going well here. Do you think Uncle Donald could drive me into town to use the internet? I suppose I could take the bike, but . . .' Out came the puppy dog eyes. Oldies love them.

'You most certainly will not. Not until you've had a lot more practice at the very least. Let me see if I can't persuade the old goat . . .'

Hamster.

'. . . to get me various supplies from the local supermarket. He loves going to the hardware shop anyway. Never buys anything as far as I know. For the life of me I don't know what he does there. Donald!'

'Yes, my little honey badger.'

'I want you to take Zola to town and pick up a few supplies for me. I'll write a list.'

'Will do. Carry on.'

A stress-filled grappling hook released itself from my shoulders. Time to get busy because I guessed my access to the internet would be limited. I wrote out most of the texts I'd send and shortlisted the sites I wanted to catch up on. I then wrote out and saved a post for my Instagram page with photos of the plantation and a teaser about the interview with an estate manager—no-one had to know it would be with my uncle. I'd upload it as soon as I got a signal.

A short while later, I was watching the dark clouds looming on the horizon while Donald and I bounced along the rough track in his old Suzuki Jeep to the main road. The feeble air-conditioning in the car wheezed out a stream of air which was only a little cooler than the baking outside temperature. At one point, when we got up a bit of speed, I thought about asking him if I could have the window down, but one look at the concentration on his face told me to leave him alone with his own concerns.

I let out a happy yelp when the bars on my phone went to five. I felt better already. The car swerved a little.

'Sorry Uncle.'

'Carry on, my dear. Onwards and forwards.'

When we reached the edge of the town, Donald pulled over at a leafy, open-air café with a big sign reading SGR and parked the battered blue Jeep.

'Well, my dear, how about you order a juice or a coffee or whatnot and I'll join you in a short while. I need to pop into the hardware store down the road for a little while.'

The café was amazing and totally Instagramable, with cute signs hidden among large potted plants. Small stone quadrants lined with bricks formed the walkway. The main seating area outside had wooden tables with benches and heavy metal chairs. It was already half full with the coffee-shop crowd: students who should've been in school, older university types and an older couple with a big age and salary gap who looked like they needed to get a room.

My bum had barely hit the seat when a young girl came over with a well-used menu that had curled corners and thumbed edges. She threw it on the table and cooed in her best pidgin English, 'What you want?'

Her name tag read Ms Ann. I almost laughed out loud. Remember what I call idiots?

'Can you give me a minute, please?' I can be so British at times. My Kenyan side would have got her to chew on my *rungu*.

'You order at counter. You go queue. Queue start there.' She pointed to one other person at the counter.

Okay, English isn't her first language, but I don't understand why she's being so curt.

'Far queue?' I asked.

She just stared blankly at me for a while and gave me a tight nod that signaled her departure.

She left me to my five-bar signal and the healthy buzzing of incoming messages.

The next time I looked up, there was another girl smiling like a lost kitten. Her lips were thin and ever-so-slightly pursed to try and hide the teeth behind them. Her short black hair and delicate gold chain earrings framed a nice-looking, pixie-like face with a soft skin tone. She could have been anywhere between thirteen and thirty.

I shivered and felt a sense of déjà vu. 'Have I seen you before?' I ventured.

'No, you think you've seen a lot of people before, but you haven't.'

That's so true, I thought and browsed the pictures in the tatty menu.

'You should have the toasted avocado and honey sandwich and a mango juice.'

'Yes,' I agreed without thinking. I looked up at her again. 'I'll have the toasted avocado and honey sandwich and a fresh mango juice please,'

The girl was still smiling and staring.

'Err . . . is that okay? Or do I order at the counter?'

'I will bring your order. You are pleasant to look at, for a foreigner. What is your name?'

'Zola.'

'I like that name. It sounds . . . tasty.'

Did she just lick her lips? *Whoa. This is getting dark depths of Mordor weird.*

'Err . . . I've never had it described like that before, but thanks, I guess.'

Is she hitting on me?

I looked down to pick up the menu to hand it back, but the girl was already halfway towards the old shop-house entrance. Her movements were quick, and her head stayed the same height as she glided away. *I've got to learn how to do that.*

For a short while, I sat lost in a contented daze until I remembered why I was there. I picked up my phone and communicated with the civilized world.

Almost an hour and two fresh and tangy juices, a mouth-watering toasted sandwich, and considerable free Wi-Fi usage later, I was feeling great. My friends 'got me'. Their support was encouraging and my confidence was almost back. What a difference a few emojis can make.

'Hi,' a voice called out.

I looked up and saw a niceish-looking white guy about fifteen or sixteen with a full mane of jelled-back black hair. He wore loose, light-blue jeans, black and red Asics, and an expensive looking T-shirt the same colour as my juice. He was carrying a book. A nagging feeling at the back of my head told me that he had carefully selected his clothes. Malaysia is a shorts and loose shirt place. The heat decided that for you.

I wondered what another foreigner was doing out here. Another shit-storm thrower? Cool.

'Hi.'

There, introductions over. Now tell me your shit-storm and I'll tell you mine. Instead, I said, 'Are you on holiday or do you live here?'

'Holiday, kind of. You?'

'Same.' I thought that better than saying it was a choice between being hung, drawn and quartered, or banishment. I added, 'I'm Zola. What brings you out here?'

'Daniel. I was about to ask the same. My Dad's looking at investing out here. You?'

'Where do I begin? Want a coffee?'

Daniel arranged his book on the table and scraped an iron chair over.

We were both aliens in an alien world. Normal rules of shyness go out of the window when needs override musts. We were both needing to share. That's why we're human, right?

Ms Ann (Thrope) came to take his order of a long black, which is what I order if I need a coffee fix with friends. Lattes and cappuccinos are great but the milk makes me want to clear my throat all the time, which is uncool if you are trying to make a good impression. *Does he want to impress me?* So far so good.

My take on boys is that they're annoying most of the time, but when they're fun, they're outstanding. I have had a few guy friends but one was also into guys and the others were not my type, whatever that is. Besides, I like them more as friends.

Just to recap, school sucked and also didn't suck in equal measure: that was school. But Mum and I were cool together. She was a graphic designer and I loved it when she told me about the storyboard of what she was working on. Sometimes she'd take my ideas and put them in her projects when she worked at home. That was great. I felt like I was a part of something.

She would also use her designs to create imaginary worlds in for which me and my brother would take turns to build stories together while she got tea ready for us. Those were fun times.

Then one of her colleagues started coming back to the house, Andrew. He was easy-going and comfortable to talk to. I felt I could tell him anything and, more importantly, he made Mum smile. Did I know they were having an affair? I didn't think about it. Often, ostrich is the best gameplan with adults.

My Dad is more down-to-earth. He's an engineer and a practical type. He's always trying to get Simon—my brother—interested in fixing up old cars. Mum was mine and Dad was Simon's.

Overall, he's a good dad. It was the meetings and the deadlines keeping him back in his office too often which was the problem.

One evening, a nuclear holocaust took place in the lounge, and Simon came sobbing his eyes out into my room and stayed the night.

The next morning was as if a major fuse had blown and all the light bulbs in the house had shattered. Overnight it had become a cold dark place.

The stories stopped and I never saw Andrew again. But the arguments kept going. It was driving me nuts. And Simon wouldn't leave my room in the evening. My synapses crashed.

Looking back on it, I don't know why I did what I did. It felt like the only thing I could do. The lack of sleep, the knowledge that the fighting was what I had to look forward to each evening, the icy mealtimes I didn't want to be a part of. I guess they thought it was 'for the best' if they tried to pretend things were normal. They assumed. *Why couldn't they have asked?*

I was in sensory overload and I went full volcano. Mum said I was screaming like a Banshee when Dad broke the hinges off my door and dragged me out. When I went upstairs the next morning, I saw picture frames, books and broken glass everywhere. My guitar was smashed. My drawings and musings had been ripped to shreds. And my bed and desk had been burnt from the fire I'd started. Long charcoal scars rose from the walls to the ceiling. Everything was either burnt or broken and then soaked from the fire extinguisher Dad had used to put out the flames. I needed space. And they needed to give it to me.

Since then, it's all been a bit of a blur. The summer holidays came up and I got flown out here with the Hamsters.

I gave Daniel an edited version of my shit-storm. I realized the full, X-rated version painted me as a psycho. I didn't want to frighten him away before getting to know him a bit more. I looked at his book, which was angled towards me. Was that for my benefit? I knew what it was from the cover illustration anyway. *World War Z.*

Maybe he's into zombies.

I nodded towards the book.

'What do you think?'

'It's great. Lots of zombies.'

'What do you think of the story?'

'Easy to read. What're you reading?'

'Easy to read', yes, except that there was another story to it. About how easy it was for things to fall apart. Had he even read it?

I answered, 'Divergent.'

'Cool. How long will you be out here and will you be travelling soon?

Not interested in books, then. I thought it would at least generate more of a chat—they were a rare treat in my chaotic life. Did he have his book as a prop? I liked books, but I didn't want people trying to read me like one.

I answered his question. 'I've not thought about it. I'm still settling in. I'll travel later.'

I was about to ask a question of my own. It's called turn-taking. I do it well. It's what separates us from the 'mouth breathers', as Eleven would say. However, I didn't get the chance.

'By any chance, do you live with the old couple on the Antara Gapi Estate?'

'Yes. Why?'

He ignored my question.

'Isn't it dangerous out there? Do you have dogs or CCTV?'

Where is this conversation going? He didn't look as though he could burgle his own trousers, let alone an estate manager's bungalow. I was starting to wish that he would take himself and his acne away from here.

'Why do you want to know that? Planning to burgle the place?' I asked with half a smile.

He chuckled. 'No, I've been told it's dangerous out here in the wilderness.'

I guessed he was referring to the jungle but trying to sound cool, nonchalant, or like a dick.

'I've found people very friendly,' I lied. The knifed kid in the estate, the threats from the two thugs, and six-pack Zak came to mind. Maybe he had a point.

We chatted a bit longer, which felt more like an interrogation, but I did find out that his dad was in real estate and that he was hoping to be cut in on a deal he was working on. That, and his spots were breaking out, and the fact that he wasn't into gaming. Not great conversation. And why was I getting the creepy feeling that our meeting was no coincidence? Had Uncle Donald arranged for him to meet me, thinking I needed company my own age to talk to? No, couldn't be. My suspicious nature was shouting at me.

I could see him wrestling with a question. This often happens when a boy wants to meet up again and hesitates over how to ask. *Just ask, duh.*

'Take care. Maybe see you again.'

He paused again. *Here it comes*, I thought. Instead, what he said freaked me out.

'Don't go out at night.'

7

My mind was in a mare's nest when another distressing thought ran through me. I had no local money to pay for things.

As if telepathic, the waitress Ann, who had been hovering in the background with her fixed smile, came over with a scrap of paper. On it were scribblings of my order and the bill that an Impressionist painter would have been proud of. The girl's smile said, 'Pay up. My shift is over.'

Oh, crap with a hedgehog.

Uncle Donald said he would be here by now. *Where has that crazy old hamster gone to?*

I put on my best lost dumb foreigner expression and asked, 'You don't take pounds by any chance, do you?'

'Take what?' she questioned.

'Never mind. My uncle is around the corner in the hardware store. He's got my, er . . . local money. I'll go and fetch him.'

'Cannot. You pay.'

I noticed how Ann's smile hadn't changed, but her eyes were narrower, more menacing.

'Look,' I said. 'I can't pay you until I find my uncle.'

'You pay now.'

A vision of being locked up in a bamboo-walled prison with only a hunchbacked cockroach as a friend filled my mind.

'I can explain. I've recently arrived from the UK and haven't had any chance to change any money yet,' which, I thought, would be what I would say if I wanted to do a runner.

The manager came over.

Oh, double crap with two hedgehogs.

'Everything okay, *ah*?' the man asked in a heavy Chinese accent.

'Fine, thanks. But I need to get my uncle who's in the hardware store as I don't have any local money.'

'Your uncle, ah? Name Junkett, ah? *Sikit gila, ah*?'

I had`no idea what that last bit meant, but I definitely heard my uncle's last name. 'Yes.'

'No problem, *lah.* You stay can. You find, also can.'

I looked at the waitress. The eyes and the smile were back in coordination. All was right with the world.

With that problem solved, I quickly sent another update to my new 'Malaysia' forum. The feedback had all been overwhelmingly positive with heaps of encouragement. So, when another incoming message vibrated in my hand, I opened it with positive expectation. However, what I saw was scared me half to death. The sender was 'unknown', and I stared in disbelief at the screen.

> You're in serious danger. Leave now. I know where you live, Zola. Leave Malaysia or face unmanageable danger. Get out before you get hurt.

The phone fell from my hands on to the table, and my eyebrows furrowed. Who would send a message like that? Why would they want me to leave? I haven't done anything wrong. I tried to take a screenshot and then cursed the fact that I hadn't gotten the function fixed since it had been knocked out of my hand in a school argument. I tried to find out who it was from, but all I had was a UK number which had a familiarity about it. I couldn't imagine any of my friends sending such a thing. And even if I was being 'trolled', how would they know where I lived or get my number? I went back to the message. There was an odd element to it too, but however many times I looked, I couldn't get what it was. I went in search of Uncle Donald.

Outside the hardware shop, I stopped, looked through the plate glass, and saw him hand over a thick brown envelope to the man behind the counter. He was tall and thin like one of the planks of chipboard in his shop. If this were a horror film, he would make an excellent vampire. And what was that envelope for?

The shop owner noticed me looking in and the maps and drawings on the counter were hastily folded away.

What are you up to?

'Ah, hello Zola. I was . . . err . . . telling my friend here . . . err . . . that you are here from the UK, so to speak.'

You look so guilty. What are you up to?

'Err, shall we, um, get those groceries for your Aunty Margaret then . . . ?'

Groceries could wait. I had a more important problem to deal with first. 'Uncle, have a look at this.' I opened my WhatsApp and pointed my phone screen at him.

'Yes?'

'Why am I getting such a threatening message?'

'What message?'

I turned the phone around and stared at a blank screen with '*This message was deleted*' on it. 'But it was there. It said I'm in danger and I need to leave Malaysia. They knew my name.'

'Nonsense. You certainly do have a rich imagination. Now, stop making things up and let's get on.'

'But . . . I saw it. I'm not making things up.'

'Alright, Zola, show me the next time it comes back.'

Donald continued talking to the shop owner. 'Claims she saw a dead body in the estate too. Must be the jet lag. Parents don't help much. Always fighting. No wonder the poor girl's a bit . . .'

'I'm still here, you know.'

'Yes, dear. What is it?'

'Do either of you know a boy called Zak Abraham?'

'Why?' the shopkeeper and my uncle replied together.

They didn't like that question, did they?

The shopkeeper stooped a little and smiled without his eyes narrowing. 'Funny you should mention him. He was in here this morning. Nice boy, but he's had a lot of bad luck lately. Well, more than that. First his parents were killed in a car crash last year and then last week his brother was abducted. The word is that a triad gang was involved. My guess is that it was to do with money his father had borrowed. Lives up the road in Ulu Yam, but that's another story. How do you know that name?'

I ignored the question while mentally arranging this new information into bite-sized jigsaw pieces.

'Nice boy,' Donald added. 'You ought to meet up with him, now that I think of it. Decent chap. About your age too.'

The shopkeeper gave Donald a stare which I interpreted as 'That's not a good idea.'

I thought it best not to mention that we'd already met, and that I wasn't entirely sure he was such a 'decent chap'. I waved my phone around the shop to get better reception and try to recover the message I'd seen earlier. Doubt wormed its way into my thoughts. Had I imagined it? A lot of weird stuff had happened recently.

'Look,' Donald advised. 'There's a storm coming. Time to get a move on. Onwards and forwards.'

We observed the dark, foreboding clouds gathering above, blotting out the sun. The heat remained. Treetops danced in the strengthening zephyrs.

Thirty minutes later, the groceries were packed in the footwells of the backseats and I went to pay the coffee shop bill.

As I walked through the leafy entrance, my skin started zinging again, and I sensed my heart pumping harder. My eyelids felt as if they had weights attached. I let them fall into a slow blink. When I'd refocussed, the strange waitress from earlier was standing right in front of me. She moved closer and a cool breeze ran up my arms.

She glanced at the money in my hand. 'You can leave that here,' and pointed to the table next to me.

I did as I was told. Whatever she said was always perfect.

'That's nice,' she added, pointing to the small pendant hanging around my neck. 'I wish to see it.'

The magnetism she had was captivating. Before I knew it, her hand had reached up and rested on my neck, cradling the shining lapis lazuli stone in her palm. It seemed to glow.

'Your heart is fast.'

'Oh . . . er . . . must be the rushing . . . to get the shopping done. Well, I should get going. See you next time. I'm Zola.'

'I know.'

'Oh, yes. Sorry. I forgot. What's your name, then?'

'I am Maya. You smell nice. What happened to your hair?'

Okaaay. Where's this conversation going? And again, this nagging feeling that I'd seen her before stuck in my throat, refusing to reach my brain.

'I err . . . they . . . the thugs cut it.'

Maya reached further up and felt where the clump of hair had been cut away. I could have sworn her eyes flashed bright gold.

'It won't happen again; I will watch over you.'

I tried to brush my hair back, but Maya switched her grip to my hand and stared into my eyes. She said, 'You want to be good friends with me, and I accept.'

'Yes . . . I . . . err . . . yes, of course. I honestly think we've met before.'

All I could see were swirls of hazel-brown with bright gold specks in Maya's eyes. The longer I looked, the calmer I felt. And more trusting. I could feel myself falling and not being able to stop it. Would she catch me if I fell? I wanted a hug. Her hug.

My mind was over the hill and far away when my hair suddenly stood on end and my eyes were blinded by a flash of brilliant white light. Then a huge explosion shook me back into reality.

I yelped—I've been getting a lot of practice at this. A fraction of a second later, pelts of stinging, heavy wet globules came hurtling down. Torrential tropical rain. I stood there holding my pendant. Alone.

Had I been dreaming? Did I lose time? Where did Maya go? And why do I feel like I want to be with her? I prefer boys, I think. No, I'm sure. Then, why am I intensely fascinated by her? It was all getting too much too fast.

An old colonial voice brought me back to reality. 'Don't stand there getting wet, Zola. Get in the car. Always move forwards, never surrender! Let's get going, what?'

I ran with Donald to his car just as the skies unzipped and the sky became one huge waterfall.

The jeep's headlights illuminated a wall of water. The wipers looked like two helpless fish swimming their way against an unstoppable tide as they fast-paced their way across the swimming pool of a windscreen. The car smelled like a wet dog which had rolled on the forest floor.

'Carry on,' Donald barked with regimental glee as the jeep fought its way through the wind and rain.

It was almost impossible to see more than twenty metres ahead. More worrying than that was the wind, which howled and buffeted the car into the oncoming lane every now and again.

My mind was filled with an image of Maya's face and an outbreak of questions.

'Not too bad, what?' my uncle shouted above the noise of the rain hammering down on the thin steel roof.

'Don't worry, Zola. I've driven in a lot worse. And we need the rain. Been bone dry for ages.'

I always worry when I hear 'don't worry'.

Since Donald refused to have the air-conditioning on while we were still damp, the car started to steam up and the rising heat increased the mix of interior smells. I cracked the window an inch and stuck my nose up to get some fresh air and smatterings of chilly rain.

My uncle shouted above the noise, 'Full steam ahead.'

Which planet is he from?

Although we were not travelling fast, an extra strong gust of air smashed into the light jeep, taking it careening off the road and on to the grass verge where the wheels bogged down in the mud. I yelped in fright—*I need to get this new habit under control.*

'Now, this is an unusual pickle,' my uncle said, as the jeep's rear wheels spun in the sludge. 'Never surrender, my dear, we have a four-wheel drive. You need it out here. Ah, but there's one slight issue. I need to go outside to swivel the callipers on the front wheels.'

Not to be beaten, Uncle Donald jumped out defiantly into the now weakening storm.

As sure-footed as a newborn fawn on an ice-rink, and with hands waving quicker than a Wright brothers' early invention, Donald pirouetted his way face-first into a soft pool of light-brown mud that, in a previous life, may have come from a cow.

'Could've been a lot worse, I suppose,' he spat as he pulled himself up to his knees and winced.

Poor old hamster. I got out to help him up, getting freshly soaked in the process. 'Are you okay Uncle?'

Covered in mud and tufts of grass, he looked miserable. 'Lords leeches, Zola. I think I may have twisted my knee. Be a dear and turn the other calliper, would you? Never surrender.'

No sooner had we extricated ourselves from the mud, the downpour faded to a drizzle. Blue skies with brilliant, glaring sunshine transformed the countryside. The sun increased the humidity to that of a sauna with steam rising in vapour swirls to form a swaying mist on the roads.

'Good evening, Margaret, sweet pea, we've had a spot of bother, you see.' Donald said as he leaned against the porch trying to take the weight off his injured knee. I held up the dripping shopping bags.

My Aunt examined the scruffy pair of devastations in front of her and decided it wasn't worth arguing. 'You two are becoming quite the pair. I suppose I'd better put the kettle on.'

8

The bungalow where I was staying was large with a high ceiling to give it a Tardis-like effect. It was spotlessly clean and I suspected that Aunty Hamster spent a lot of time dusting and fussing. Most of the furniture looked as though it had been bought from a period film set and, weird as it seemed, it seemed to match the overall vibe of the place. The chairs around the heavy hardwood dining table were a mixture of rattan and mismatched wood. The wall separating the lounge and dining area had been knocked through, allowing more natural light to reach the inside of the bungalow, emphasizing the feeling of openness. None of the inside doors had locks and were usually left open. I compromised and left mine ajar. The lounge had an ancient cracked brown leather sofa and one matching armchair grouped around an empty coffee table. Two large sliding glass doors led to the patio which, as with my uncle, was fast becoming my favourite place. It was a welcoming home and one which was a longed-for change from the messed-up atmosphere in the UK. Despite all the weird stuff that was happening around me, I felt the place fast growing on me.

After another restless night, and I have many of them, I put on a green and white batik shirt my aunt had bought me as a welcome present and a pair of jean shorts. The shirt was more obligation than choice, but then who cared out here.

Sleep had always been an issue, made worse by what had happened. Once I was asleep, it was fine. It was getting there that was the problem. The usual 'just do this, just do that' advice ranged from an almost sensible 'hot milk and bananas' and the bizarre 'put these healing stones under your pillow' to the extreme 'smoke this, sis. Sure crash.'

I tried the lot. And the winner was not a good choice. Xanex took me to a calm, dreamy state and then sleep. When I woke, I felt relaxed, almost exhausted, but chilled and happy. It became addictive. And, because I got it at school, expensive.

Unfortunately, one evening, I threw the aluminium foil away in the bathroom rubbish bin without thinking. Mum found it and we had 'one of those' chats. I was made to see a psychologist who looked like a reject from a 1980s disco and had a voice so monotone, I'd zone out after the second sentence. After several sessions that did little for my sleep or self-esteem, I wanted something that worked and saw a psychiatrist. I thought the psychologist was weird, but this guy was off the scale. He looked in such a terrible state, so much so that I asked him if *he* was alright. Wasn't it supposed to be the other way around? After a short while and a bizarre explanation that he'd been trying out one of his drugs, I learned a lot from that guy, including the fact I suffered from Mysophonia—a rare condition where certain sounds caused my brain to explode. I also got some non-addictive stuff to help me sleep better. For a while my life improved beyond anything. *Should've gone earlier.*

Having put off the idea of going to meet the mysterious Zak for most of the morning, I finally decided it would be better to get it over with—hand over the card and get back to my blog. Sure, I hoped his brother was okay, but there was no way I was going to get dragged into a family feud. I had enough on my own plate with parents. And if the thugs with the knives came back before Zak did, I'd give them the fake. If that didn't work, I'd give them the real card and get back to sorting out the rest of my life.

Their problem, not mine. The fact that my name was on the card still bugged me though.

Rachel fired up first time, as if encouraging me that I was doing the right thing. Yet, the closer I got to the rise in the plantation, the less I believed that Zak, with his six-pack, would still be there. But then again, he had said that he desperately needed what his brother gave me.

Rachel's engine was keen to rev today and the single rear-view mirror blurred anything behind. I was getting to like her the more I rode her.

At the rise, after a few extra circles around it to check for any unwanted other people, I came to a stop. I stayed on the bike in case I needed to make a quick dash for it. The hill had a small clearing on top, and I could see for at least fifty metres all around. Then there was scrub, a few small trees and then the palm began. Although there was a nice cooling breeze, the strength of the sun had me drive up to one of the old rubber trees for shade.

Numerous livestock and motorcycle trails crisscrossed the dry grass where I sat astride my bike. I watched as a small boy herded a single-file line of cattle with whistles and yells while typing a text into an oversized handphone. His rag-tag appearance had me wondering how he could afford such a thing. Farming must pay great out here.

I was still cautious, but my confidence was returning and, for reasons I couldn't put logic to, my thoughts went to Maya with the belief that she was being honest when she said that the thugs wouldn't bother me again. Yes, she was toothpaste short of a brush, yet she liked me. Also, there was a magnetic charm about her which was addictive. She was a Pandora's box full of contradictions and mystery. It was as if she could hear what I thought.

Do I trust her?

No. I don't trust many people.

Am I drawn to her?
Yes, more feeling than logic.
Her presence is super-strong.
I'd like to have that kind of presence.

My phone vibrated incoming messages as three intermittent signal bars flashed on the screen. I got off my bike and walked over to a fallen and dried out tree trunk which provided for a good perch in the shade. Forty minutes later and I was pretty sure Zak wasn't turning up. And since I'd promised to help Aunty Hamster with Sunday lunch while Uncle Donald rested his twisted knee, I said to the warm breeze, 'You've got twenty more minutes, mate. After that, I'm off.'

With my mind back to texting and making a couple of hilarious Facetime calls where friends' faces would stick in bizarre expressions when the signal failed and then came back, I failed to notice the two large men from the previous day riding up from the edge of the plantation.

'Nice we see you again. Why you don't wait down there, *ah*?' the man who had cut a clump out of my hair asked. He got off the bike, and I thought I heard it sigh with relief.

Caught off-guard, I froze and then hated myself for not being more aware. 'I er . . . thought it was here, wasn't it?' The lie felt pathetic.

'Where is it?'

Maya came back to my thoughts and I immediately felt more confident. I could also see that the pillion had a limp which I hadn't noticed before, and both were plumper than the cows that had passed through earlier. I could outrun them, maybe even their bike with them on it. My famed curiosity said it was time to find out more about what I'd seen. I got the impression that Daud, Zak, these thugs, and Maya were all connected and the cardkey was the answer.

'Where's what?'

'Don't play *bodoh* with me,' the man still sitting on the bike said, raising his index finger to emphasize the warning. It was a short, fat, stubby thing and I would have loved to ram it up his squashed-wide nose.

'Look, I wasn't given anything. Why would I come out here to meet you if I was lying? Tell me what you're looking for and why you need it, then perhaps I can help.'

They didn't like that.

I added, 'You should leave here or I'll tell my uncle. He has a gun and is way crazy enough to use it.'

'You blackmail us, *ah*?'

'No. I'm saying leave me alone, that's all.' I backed up towards Rachel.

'No more chance. I slice you like watermelon.'

The thug pulled out his machete from its sheath. 'Give what we want or I make face get big scar. Clown scar.'

He stepped forward and brandished the blade in front of me and said, 'Maybe I do that first.'

I had choices. I could run. Yes, they had a bike, but I still fancied my chances. I could jump back on Rachel and, if she behaved herself and started first time—which she had done so far—I could outride them. Then curiosity kicked in again. I'd give them the fake card and see what they said about it. If they weren't fooled, I'd give them the real one. Zak had had his chance and screwed up.

What was I thinking? These dudes would drown themselves in a car park puddle. No issue. I really should be more scared. *So why wasn't I?*

The thug with the knife looked me up and down. 'Maybe I cut your other hair. See what you can do.'

'The hell you will.' It felt like an ignition switch had been pressed inside my head.

While these thoughts were synapsing in my brain, the atmosphere had changed. Humpty and Dumpty were still staring, but their expressions were no longer anger. Their creased brows were still there, but their eyes were wider. Their lips had opened and stretched: I knew that expression from my brother when our parents went at it.

Fear.

They weren't staring at me; they were staring through me.

I turned around to see a slender figure wrapped from head to toe in loose folds of mahogany-red cloth. A fold of flowing material at the top of her head, like a ponytail, danced in the gusts. There was a narrow, uncovered slit left for her eyes. The newcomer's silhouette shifted from shapeless to form-fitting as the breeze tugged on the elegant garment.

She came closer to the three of us and uttered a few words in a language I'd never heard before. Her tones had the earthiness of a sleeping dragon mixed with the higher melodic vibrations of a solitary jungle animal. The two tones folded into one mesmerizing and beautiful sound.

The sound of its eerie voice was disturbingly familiar. I'd had heard it before; it was on the tip of my tongue.

Her strides were long, graceful and effortless; her movement enhanced by the loose-fitting clothes.

Strangled sounds were coming from behind me. I turned to see the thug with the machete struggling against an invisible force, which was turning the knife blade until it faced him. He was fighting a battle to keep the blade away from himself and losing. The alien force edged the knife in his right hand closer, while his left hand tried desperately to push it away. The other thug saw what was happening and grabbed his friend's right hand. It made little difference as the knife moved inexorably closer to the man's face.

I heard more mysterious words coming from the figure. Her eyes were a bright golden-yellow with two small black irises shining like iridescent pearls.

The thug with the knife cried out. It was now inches from the man's right eye and moving closer. His friend hung off the man's right arm, doing all he could to make it stop.

I watched as the blade reached the man's eyebrow and cut deep into his flesh. Blood and tears flowed down the man's face. He was shaking uncontrollably as the knife sliced down towards his eye. He screamed a rising, shrieking sound, which I'd never forget.

'Stop!' I yelled.

Instantly, the knife dropped from the man's hand, and his friend fell to the ground in an exhausted heap. They helped each other up, their fear hurrying their actions, got on the bike, and rode away as fast as it would take them.

I turned to face my rescuer.

'They will not bother you again,' she said.

Her voice, even more beautiful than before, sounded of a rolling cloud on a bed of whispering breath.

Despite what she had done, I felt no threat from the mysterious person in front of me. I asked, 'Your eyes and voice. I know them. Who are you?'

'We are the Indra. I must go. You are safe now.'

This time she sounded more defensive, and there was a sinister edge to her tone.

As she turned to leave, a stronger gust of wind jerked one of her cloth folds free.

For a fraction of a second, I caught a glimpse of her face. I froze, petrified with shock.

9

There are things you can't unsee once you've seen them, however hard you try. The vision is permanent. It was the first time I'd ever wished that other people were right about my dreaming and making things up.

'Hi. You're shaking. What happened?'

I hadn't even noticed Zak arrive. His tone was more matter of fact than caring.

'Where have you been?' I snarled back. I don't snarl that often, but my friends knew to tread carefully when I did—the situations that pre-sleep re-enactments are made for. 'You were supposed to be here.'

'Okaaay. Nice to see you too,' he replied frowning. 'Yeah. I got held up at the hospital. My brother's in an induced coma.'

Maybe I was being a bit harsh. After all, I didn't know the dude well, and he was trying to be kind. I said, 'At least he's alive. That's good, right?

'He's alive but in a coma until his autoimmune system is strong enough for him to breathe without all the tubes. Doctors say he's got a fifty-fifty chance. What happened to you?'

I had a fit of the shivers again. I sat and rested my chin on my hunched-up knees and rocked a bit. It felt good. He sat down on the dusty earth opposite and rested his hand on my shoulder. It was a nice gesture.

'You didn't see it. And you won't believe me anyway. No-one does.'

'What? What are you talking about?'

'The thing that got rid of the thugs.'

'What thugs? Hey, look. You got to begin at the beginning,' Zak moved to sit next to me. Also nice.

I replayed the events and listened to myself telling a story which I would find hard to believe if it came from one of my friends. I stopped when that image came into my head again. Imprinted forever.

Zak waited patiently while I took a few deep breaths. He even said, 'Look, you're struggling, aren't you? It's cool if you want to chill a bit.'

That was nice. But I had to get it off my chest. At that moment, I felt that if anyone was going to believe me, it would be Zak.

'It wasn't human,' I blurted. 'It was . . . Christ, I don't even know what it was.'

He nodded and gave me an encouraging smile.

I felt the smile.

He added, 'Describe it a bit . . . what you think you saw.'

'I *know* what I saw,' I snarled again and then regretted it. I had a lot of different emotions fighting each other for control. I needed to sort it.

'For a moment I thought it was a girl about my age. In fact, at first, I thought it was a girl I'd met before, at a café in town. Her voice sounded familiar. But it couldn't be her. This thing was slender with longer arms. As her face turned, I saw a side profile. It was pure demon. Her lips and cheek had been half eaten away. And I saw animal teeth—thin teeth like a dog's but sharper and more needle-like at the front and curved like a scimitar. Behind them were a row of brilliant-white smaller pointed teeth like miniature mountains. They were evenly spaced and . . . perfect.'

'Perfect?' Zak's eyebrows rose.

'If you were going to have animal teeth,' I tried to explain, 'these would be . . . perfect. Look, I can't clarify any more, okay? That's what they were.'

'My bad. It doesn't sound scary if you can say "perfect" though.'

I realized how bizarre I was sounding, but it felt good to get it out of my system. To talk about it and to describe it, made it less threatening.

'Her jaw was longer, like a snout, but smaller, narrower. A bit like a squirrel's. And her nose was dark like a cat's. And her eyes . . . They were brown before, but they changed colour. When the scarf was blown off, I saw they were bright yellow-gold and the iris shrunk to a small, shiny black dot.'

'I know I shouldn't say this, but she still doesn't sound terrifying. Was it a werewolf-type thing?'

'No, nothing like a werewolf. They don't exist. She was in pain. I felt it. How can that happen?' I hadn't finished what I wanted to say, but I needed a moment while I processed the words.

Zak was being a great listener and giving me time. I appreciated it more than he could know. I had a lot of questions buffeting my thoughts with the main one being, what was it that I saw?

I could feel my heart pounding and my body tensing, but I had to get the next bit out. I took another deep breath through my nose and let it out slowly through my mouth.

'The girls face, it was shifting, changing from one face to another, but partially human. I don't know what it was. And the scariest thing was that, for a moment, I thought part of the face was familiar. I knew that face from somewhere. Then I saw bone and skin peel away from raw muscle. It was the most disgusting thing I've ever seen.'

'You know what you've described?'

'A demon.'

'A devil? Maybe. An Indra?

'Yes, yes. That's what she . . . it said.' *He believes me*, I thought, and relaxed a bit.

'It talked to you? But Indra are simply make-believe monsters to frighten little kids into eating all their dinner because leftover food attracts them, or to clean their room to stop them hiding there. Look, I don't know what you saw, and before you say anything, I get it, what you saw was scary and weird, but Indra are stories, nothing more.'

I wasn't so sure. Then his face lit up.

'I'll tell you who it was. There's a guy who lives not too far from here. Had an accident when he was young and got horribly burned. He has a bit of a reputation for dressing up in girl's clothes. More than a little strange, that guy. Likely it was him.'

I wanted to argue, but a tidal wave of tiredness was taking over. I was exhausted. The images he'd placed in my mind were pushing the old, scary ones out. My logical side wanted to believe him. Monsters are real, I know, but they're always human.

Zak's voice was nice and easy to listen to; deep and resonant: honey dripping over distant thunder. And his English was so easy to understand. I became aware that he was holding my hand. It felt good. I was tired and wanted to sleep. The images of the demon were disappearing.

I must've been mumbling aloud as Zak said, 'Huh? What was that?'

'Nothing,' I lied. 'Thinking out loud.'

I forced my mind back into the present. I didn't know anything about this dude who's holding my hand. *It's nice though*, with the right amount of 'mhmms'. *He can keep doing it.* But the questions I had were gnawing through the thin cord of my relaxation. I asked, 'Who are you? What's going on? And how did you get here? And how did Daud disappear?'

'Whoa.' Zak raised his other hand towards his chest in a surrender pose. 'All in a moment, I promise. But first, did you bring whatever it was my brother gave you?'

I told him I had and pulled the small plastic card from my pocket. My hands had stopped trembling.

I could feel the tension lifting off and, for the first time, my eyes got a good look at my new friend. He was at least an apple taller than me, and his thick black hair hung in loose curls over his ears. He wore a baggy white T-shirt and red, slim-fit shorts, which stopped an inch above his knees. Beads of sweat glistened on his forehead. He most certainly wasn't a worker from any plantation. He was beautifully tanned or, more likely, it was his natural skin tone. *Nice.*

'Is this it?' he asked.

'Yes. I thought you'd know what it was. And why is my name on it?' I turned the card over and saw that he was as surprised as I had been.

'No idea.'

'Ask your brother when he wakes up. And how did he manage to get out of the plantation anyway?'

'I managed to find him and carried him out to my bike which was on the dirt road next to this estate. He won't be waking up soon.'

How does he know that? Why did his intonation fall like he knows? And how did he know Daud was coming to this estate? He's creating more questions than he's answering.

We went into the plantation, where it was much cooler, then found a piece of raised dry ground under a tall palm and sat together. I felt his knees touching mine; his natural scent was nice, and I was melting into a friendship.

'What's it related to?' I asked.

'Deeds. Our parents died in a car crash.'

'Oh, I'm sorry.'

'It's fine.'

It's fine? You can't have liked them much.

'When my brother turned eighteen earlier this year, he inherited the land our father had invested in. When he passed you whatever this thing is, you became their focus of attention.'

'Can't you go to the police?'

Zak smiled with a look which said that it was a dumb thing to say. 'They're more corrupt than the crooks. Nah, I wouldn't mind betting they're involved already. They can smell a free stack of money in a river. Malaysia is not the UK.'

'You've been to the UK?' I asked.

'No, but I went to a UK international school in KL. The problem is that the man borrowed a small amount from an *Ah Long*—an unlicensed money lender—who wants his money back plus a large amount of interest, which he knows we can't pay.'

The man. That's distancing language. Why didn't he say 'father' or 'dad'?

'Now the *Ah Long* wants the land instead. My brother said that there's no way that's happening. At first, we thought we'd mine it for tin or marble or whatever minerals were there, which was our first choice. However, when we had the land surveyed, we found that it's on the edge of a swamp on one side and thick jungle on the other with oil palm on the rest. It needs a huge amount of work to do anything with it. But it has potential. We're thinking of either replanting or building a hunting lodge.'

Now was not the time to get into an argument about the environmental footprint of palm oil. Not yet. Instead, I went for 'Wow. You've got things sorted, I guess.' It was a safe reply. As well as being a good listener, he was also easy to listen to; it was as if we'd been friends for ages. I moved a little closer.

'The real problem,' he continued, 'is that we need to get our hands on the deeds and then file our names as the owners. Whoever gets their hands on the deeds can file first. That's why those thugs were giving you a hard time because they think you have the documents.'

I wanted to change the subject and leaned sideways a little until our shoulders touched. It was like a soft muscle pillow and I immediately felt better, safer. I looked into his dark brown eyes. 'You were telling me about your land.'

At this point, a regular guy would forget all the land stuff and kiss me. But he continued as I'd asked. *I must be losing my touch.*

'Yeah. According to our uncles, this is the only clue our father left as to where the deeds are. He knew he had to be secretive and keep the documents away from any prying eyes, but also from our other greedy extended family.'

We stared at the embossed circles in the plastic rectangle in front of us. 'Where are the deeds then?'

'Not sure. This is the key to finding those deeds, but he never said exactly where.' He looked into my eyes. 'Any ideas?'

I was caught off guard since I was checking out the rest of him. I mean, a girl's got to see what she's getting into. I fluffed a reply, hoping my lack of blush was still working.

'Huh? Me? Err . . . no. I'm afraid not.'

He put his arm around my shoulders. 'We'll figure it out.'

Ooh, that's good. His muscles felt like that memory foam stuff on expensive mattresses. This guy was dope.

I had an idea. 'Let me take another pic and re-send it out to my 'Gram. The answer's out there somewhere.'

As I pulled my phone from my back pocket, I remembered about the text I'd received the previous day.

'Another thing,' I said. 'I got a text yesterday afternoon telling me to leave Malaysia or I'd be killed. "*You're in serious danger. Leave now.*" They knew my name and where I lived.'

My heart was starting to punch harder in my chest again. More stuff I have no evidence for.

'Can I see?'

'That's the thing. The message was deleted moments after I'd read it. It's like it didn't exist, but I did receive it.'

'Was it a joke from one of your friends, maybe?'

I gave him the look he'd given me earlier 'No, duh. I don't have friends who would do things like that.'

'Okay, who's your provider, your telco?'

'Celcom, I think'

'Can I . . . ?' Zak held out his hand for my phone. 'I have a friend who works in Celcom. Mind if I call him? Maybe I can find out the name of the person who sent it.'

'Sure.'

Zak stood and punched in a few numbers as he got up and moved to one side.

I followed eagerly, putting the card back in my pocket, and listened to the way he switched from perfect English to Malay and back. Nice. I wanted another hug.

Good with languages and tech. And everything looked nicely proportioned. Excellent.

He turned to me and said, 'We have to wait a minute. He has access to the mainframe and can trace any call if he has the number called and the rough time of the call.'

I nodded and stole another furtive glance at his profile. I put on my I-need-a-hug face. For the first time I considered whether I wanted a 'special friend' out here. 'It's a rite of passage', my friends from back home had said. 'Everyone does it.'

My phone buzzed and Zak answered. 'Okay, *terima kasih* anyway, bro.'

I saw the expression on Zak's face and knew the answer before he said anything. 'It's fine,' I said. 'Thanks for trying. I'll check my TikTok and Instagram lists and friends' numbers later.'

'Call.'

'What? Yes. No. Wait. I need to think and figure out who the number belongs to first. I need to know before they know I know.'

'Sure. Up to you.'

What was it about the number that was bothering me? I saved it and filed the mystery for later. I needed more head space to work on it, which reminded me. I checked my watch.

'Look, Zak, I need to head back before my uncle and aunt send out a search party. I really appreciate you talking with me today. Oh, I almost forgot. You'll want this back.' I dug deep into my pocket and retrieved the mysterious card.

'Thanks for your help, Zola. Enjoy the rest of your holiday here.'

He proceeded to walk towards the plantation.

What? Where's my hug? Where's he going?

'Maybe we'll meet again?' I said, knowing that those were the lamest words I'd ever uttered. I tried a risky recovery, 'You've helped me too.'

That didn't sound much better either. What's a girl got to lose? Self-esteem? Huh! That went out the window with 'Maybe we'll meet again.'

'How do I contact you if one of my friend's finds out what the card's for? I mean, I feel involved now and . . . after what's happened today, I'd feel safer if you were around. Maybe we could meet up again?'

It could've been better delivered, but at least he got it and said, 'If you're sure you want to, fine. Give me your number and I'll give you a missed call later. I want to spend a bit more time with my brother in hospital over the next couple of days. How about meeting up here after that?'

'That's great,' I said, perhaps a little too eagerly.

He asked, 'Can I hitch a ride back to the side road where I left my bike?'

'I think it's safer if you drive.'

As we bounced along the rough tracks with an early afternoon breeze cooling our hot skin and white cotton-wool clouds boiling in the sky as a backdrop, I wrapped my arms around Zak, and felt happier than I had in a long, long time.

10

I sat on the end of my bed having showered and changed into a well-worn T-shirt and lilac pyjama bottoms. I'd gone through the entire list of my UK followers and friends but still couldn't find who the number belonged to.

The quick of my nails was starting to show blood. I mustn't go down that rabbit hole again.

The message played over in my mind; each word burned into memory. There was still a question mark hanging over the phrasing.

You're in serious danger. Leave now. I know where you live, Zola. Leave Malaysia or face unmanageable danger. Get out before you get hurt.

What was it? What was wrong? I looked across to my bedside clock and noticed it was getting late. Early morning in the UK. I knew I had to find out who'd sent it, but also dreading it at the same time. What if it was a friend I trusted or liked? Or was it a prank? Who would send such a message?

My little voice told me to cut the indecision and get on with it.

I pressed 'call' and recognized the voice on the other end of the line instantly.

'Hello?'

'Hi Dad.'

'Zola? How did you get this number? It's my clients' direct line. Look, Zola, I'm kind of in the middle of a meeting here. Can I call you back later?'

'But Dad. Why did you send that text telling me I had to leave, saying get out or face the consequences?'

'Don't be silly. I never sent such a thing. Why would I want you to do that? I have enough on my plate here without you adding to it. Did your mother put you up to this?'

'No, no. I don't understand . . .'

'Well neither do I. This type of behaviour is the reason why we have been driven to where we are now! Stop making things up. I've had enough, Zola. Stop it, do you hear? Why do you think you were sent there?'

The line went dead.

I dropped the phone, pulled up my knees and rocked gently on the bed.

Look what you've done now. You're beyond stupid sometimes. No, not sometimes. Always.

The message played over in my mind. One of the sentences still bothered me. '*Leave Malaysia or face unmanageable danger.*' I said the words aloud and stumbled on one. Then I saw it. How obvious. Why didn't I see it before? *Shit, shit, shit.*

Knowing how fussy my dad was about word choice, he would have never have used 'unmanageable' when he would have meant 'unimaginable'. The message was never his. I would still have called, but I would have phrased things better. Regretting what I had said didn't begin to describe it.

But, if it wasn't from him, who *had* it come from?

I wiped a trickle of blood away from the base of both thumbnails, curled up under the sheets, and, while my demons looked on, cried myself to sleep.

11

In the middle of the afternoon, anywhere in Malaysia, it is a cross between a sauna and a bonfire, which is why the cool air-conditioning of the hair salon made me feel comfortable to the point of almost zoning out. All my worries had vanished in the exotic scents from the perfumed shampoos and conditioners which enveloped me like my favourite nightshirt. Soft, caressing fingers examined my hair. I felt like drifting off to the soothing, pulsing, lounge-jazz beats playing in the background.

'Someone make your hair very messy. You try cut by your own?' the hairdresser asked in a soft, lilting English.

'Err, no, it's a long story.'

And one I didn't want to relive right now. I had not felt this relaxed for such a long time. This would definitely have to become a regular experience. Much better than the slop-scrub-slap of UK hair salons with the pervasive feeling that you were doing them a favour by being there.

The hairdresser was caring as she teased out the knots from my tangled mop. With me not replying to her broken English, the room was quiet and all I heard was the sound of the rhythmic scraping from her soft plastic nails working the shampoo into my scalp.

'Moment please,' the girl said.

I let my heavy eyelids slowly close. Less than a minute later, the relaxing massaging returned, except it was firmer.

'A little less strong please,' I requested.

'Yes,' the voice said. It was different but familiar at the same time.

Seconds later, the scraping became stronger.

'Please! I need it softer,' I demanded.

I felt a reassuring hand rest on my shoulder. I opened my eyes and glanced down to see what plastic fitments the girl had changed to. What I saw were real nails. The thumb and the fingers were long, the backs covered in tufts of thick white hair.

It took me a fraction of a stunned second before I gazed into the mirror to see the reflection behind me. My body went rigid with fear. My heart raced, then missed several beats and pounded. Cold perspiration escaped from every pore.

The creature which had saved me from the thugs stood behind my chair. Piercingly white conical teeth shone from a small pixie-like—but menacing—face. A firm voice said, 'No need to be frightened, Zola. You must come to me willingly.'

I felt its sweet breath on my neck and watched paralysed with fear as the creature sunk its two curved and slender canine teeth into my yielding shoulder muscle. I couldn't even lift a hand to protect myself.

I tried to scream, but nothing came out. I tried again, more forceful this time and heard my own voice crying out from somewhere in the distance.

Coughing and sweating, I saw daylight streaming through the thin curtains and into my room. My throat felt constricted and I gasped for air, each breath was never enough. My heart raced to keep up, and the feeling of it exploding inside my chest triggered further panic. My stomach was cramping up, and I needed the loo. It was the last realization, a simple body function, that helped me focus. It was a nightmare. Everything was okay. That was too real though.

The nightmare faded like the condensation on a pane of cracked glass. With nerves still on edge, I reached across to the bedside table and looked at my phone. Nine o'clock! Wow, I must've been exhausted. The memory of last night's call to my dad and his angry reaction came rushing back. '*Leave it*,' I told myself. '*Focus on the good things. You're happy here. You're having fun. Kind of. You like Zak, especially the way his hair falls in thick curls which, on anyone else might look too feminine, but his face is all man with a firm rounded jaw and cheekbones with dark, almost black eyes. And his strength. You feel safe with him. Think of your arms around him again. Besides, you've got your Instagram posts about the environment going viral over two platforms. You've got over triple the four thousand views necessary, and your subscribers are well into triple figures. The money has already started. Stay positive. Focus on that.*'

Still in my boxers and oversized white T, I got up and went down the hall to the loo, everything was back under control. I made a mental plan of the direction I wanted to take my next blog with ideas taking shape. In the middle of that, I had a flashback of sitting on the back of my bike with my arms wrapped snugly around Zak.

The past few days had dragged like an anchor through a sewage farm. The call still haunted me and I missed company my own age. If I was being honest, I missed Zak.

Confession time. I never thought I'd become that attached to a person in such a short space of time. He was a first. The more I thought of him, the more I felt that he was the one person in my life I could depend on. Apart from the Hamsters, of course. But then again, I remembered going through their bookshelf and finding two well-used paperbacks: one on 'Self-dentistry' and the other on 'Head Shrinking for Beginners'. I mean, who reads stuff like that? Nevertheless, mad as they were, I was becoming increasingly fond of them too.

With my mind still flitting between thoughts, I wandered into the kitchen.

'Good morning, my dear. Did you sleep well?' Aunt Margaret asked as she prepared breakfast. 'We heard a scream. Did you see a swamp rat?'

Ah ha, so they do come in the house.

'No, I was dreaming. Sorry.'

'No "sorries" in this house, Zola. Think no more of it.'

Aunty is now officially my favourite Hamster.

'We thought we'd let you lay in a bit to get over the jet lag. Tea?'

Jet lag, still? I didn't have the fight to argue the fact it had already been over three days since I'd arrived. And what was it with these people and tea? Crazy, with a clown's hat on top, the pair of them.

We heard a commotion coming from the front deck and went to investigate.

'Damn the blighters!' bellowed Donald at the top of his baritone voice. He tried getting up from his place on the front deck, but winced in pain and fell back in his chair.

'What is it, dear?' Margaret soothed.

'It's bizarre, my merry mantis. One of the farm workers informed me yesterday that the harvesting had almost been completed for the palm oil nuts and that we should arrange transportation today. Fine, so early this morning I asked him to go around with a couple of the boys in the truck to start loading up and said he found at least a quarter of the bushels had been stolen.'

'Was it the rats again, dear? They're terribly hungry at this time of year.'

'Margaret, sweet pea, you're not listening to what I'm saying.' Donald's face boiled red with anger. 'Thieves have grabbed my bushels, and with my knee like it is, I can't do anything about it.'

I saw my uncle stewing in his fury and wondered if I should tell him about the two men from earlier that week and the plastic card they were looking for. And Zak. Had they stolen the bushels as a warning to Zak and me? Would they give them back if I handed over the card? Then again, would they think I was making up another story and not believe me? No-one ever seems to, except Zak. *God, I miss him.*

'Morning Uncle, what's happened?' I asked in my best calming voice, while my aunt went back to the bungalow.

'It's those bast . . . err, blasted people from the Land Office. They sent me a notice by express post yesterday telling me that I have to show the plantation is working to certain standards or they will reclaim the land. It's no coincidence, I'll bet. That letter coupled with the theft means that they plan to get their hands on my land by any method possible. But "Never surrender" is what I say. I've worked far too long and hard to have my plantation taken away from me now. Our whole life is here. And they won't win. I have a plan.'

A new thought crashed into my head. The strange kid from the café, Daniel, he mentioned that he was in a land deal. Did he have anything to do with the theft? He did warn me not to go out at night. I bet that he knew something more. The café in town might know more about him. Then Maya came into my thoughts. Sure, she was a toothpaste short of a brush, but she had a lot of answers to unasked questions. Maybe she's seen him around. And it would be good to use their fast internet again. I was about to reveal my suspicions but then reminded myself that my track record in believability was not on my side. I tried to resist the desire to blurt. It didn't work.

'Can I help?' I blurted.

'Well, now you mention it, Zola, you can.'

'Great. I'll head into town and ask around to see if anyone knows anything.'

'That's all well and good, my dear, but I have another role for you and I'm afraid you're going to have to play your part while you're here.' Donald pointed to his knee. 'It still hurts like hell. The doctor said it was torn ligaments, but if you ask me, a duck would speak more sense. If it doesn't get any better soon, I'll need you to collect a few leeches from the swamp. That'll do the trick.'

Leeches! What century is he from? He's gotta be joking, right?

'Anyway, I'll talk you through what to do regarding the documents I've received. Should be a piece of cake.'

'Oh,' I said, disappointed. I still thought the café would be a better use of my time. Instead, I said, 'Wouldn't Aunty Margaret be in a better position to—'

'No, afraid not.' Donald lowered his voice. 'Mad as a gaggle of gherkins, that one. Love the old bat . . .'

Hamster, she's a hamster.

'. . . to bits though.'

'I'm afraid you're the only one left with a level head on their shoulders.'

Subconsciously, I straightened my posture.

As if to confirm my uncle's suspicions, Margaret called from the kitchen, 'If there are burglars about this morning, I'd better put an extra tea bag in the pot and get out my crimson lip gloss.'

'I'd like to help where I can,' I began my polite refusal, 'but . . .'

'That's settled then. First, I need you to visit the Land Office. Best do that tomorrow, first thing. I'll brief you later this afternoon. Now, I'd like you to go out and shoot the thieves.'

'What!'

'I'm joking, my dear, but I would be grateful if you could drive me around the plantation. I want to see the exact amount that's been taken myself.'

'But I can't drive. And I don't have a licence.'

'Nonsense, Zola. About time you learned. These are all private roads in the plantation anyway. Onwards and forwards, my dear. Never surrender.'

12

Earlier that morning, in the dead hours, when even most fish were sleeping, Anush Rhammar rounded up his gang of failed drug pushers and wandering lowlifes. He wore a pair of rough baggy trousers and an old grey T-shirt with an oil stain on the front that resembled the African continent.

They squashed themselves sardine style into an aging and sun-blistered grey Proton Wira and a sixty-year-old, rickety, open-backed Mercedes lorry loaded with two *kapchai*—mopeds.

At their destination, they spilled out on to the dirt track like an overturned barrel of snakes. Despite the initial chaos, Rhammar soon had his crew in order. The two mopeds were wheeled down a steep grass bank, lifted across a swampy ravine and up to the simple wire fence at the back of the Antara Gapi oil palm estate. With the fence providing little resistance, the bikes were soon on one of the well-used plantation roads. Extra silencers were pushed into the exhausts and clip-on tow bars were fitted with a mini-trailers which could hold six to eight bushels of palm nuts.

The riders and pillion passengers made their way to where the bunches had been stacked in readiness for collection with each of the two teams making easy work of heaping the loads on to the trailers. The bushels were then transported back to where a loose line had formed to manhandle them across the swamp to the lorry at the side of the road. Hours went by until the first rays of light crawled over the horizon.

Rhammar looked at his watch. 'Okay boys, time's up,' he said in Malay. 'Let's get back to town. You three take the lorry up to the Sungai Buloh Estate and ask for Botut Cheong, the operations chief. He'll give you the best price for the bushels. If anyone asks any questions, mention my name and that it was arranged a long time ago. Anything else, pay "coffee money", *lah*.' He handed them a fifty-Ringgit note that would cover any bribe necessary. 'The rest of you pack everything up and get out of here. Those of you not with me, meet me back at the Brickfields office later at ten.'

A little after 8 a.m., Rhammar went on his own for breakfast at a *roti canai* shop in nearby Taman Seputeh, where he was to meet his paymaster. Up until that point, all communication had been conducted on the phone in *Bahasa Melayu*, the Malay language, so when he was addressed by a *matsalleh*—a foreigner—a boy at that, his mouth fell open in surprise. Before him was a teenager dressed in sandals, loose beige shorts, and a casual collar-shirt with the sleeves rolled up.

Daniel had wondered what to wear for his first contact with the Malaysian underworld. He didn't want to appear too smart, yet he had to show authority. Likewise, too casual a look and Rhammar wouldn't take him seriously enough. In the end he settled for a halfway house approach. Half of him was curious about the meeting, the other half was petrified that he would end up at the bottom of a canal. He had always tried to avoid dangerous situations and running away from violence had always been his favoured tactic. But there was too much money in it for him to back out. The money mattered. Had his father's car accident been fate? No, the roads had been wet and greasy from the storm, and the outcome had been cast in rusting steel, crumbling rubber and cracked black vinyl.

Bumpers had fallen off; a boot had swung open; a headlight had hung by its wires like a gouged eye; and a radiator grille had sloped lamely at a forty-five-degree angle, steam hissing from its side. It had squeaked and groaned like the participants at the end of a Weight Watchers' exercise routine. The buckled bonnet of their car had wrinkled with disgust and, already having had a hard time as a rental, with bits glued and taped back on, the collision had been the tipping point. The car had reached the end of its long and hard life.

Daniel remembered seeing his father slumped over the steering wheel, blood dripping from his nose and the corner of his mouth; the airbag and seatbelt having failed.

Later that afternoon, in one of KL's growing healthcare-tourism hospitals, Daniel had seen an exhausted but welcoming smile on his father's face as the nurses wheeled him through to a private room. It was there he'd heard the full plan of the hostile land takeover. It was good and sounded like a plan he could extract a nice large fee for. He was trading in his holiday; this was payback. He'd do the run around stuff and his dad would do the rest by phone. He'd been given the promise of one thousand reasons to help out. Besides, it had been this or go to the shopping mall with his mother. He'd rather eat his own socks.

'Mister Rhammar?' Daniel asked with the reverence he reserved for those he admired and feared. He looked at the gangster's expression and wasn't sure if the man was going to say 'hello' or put him on a stick and roast him like *satay*. Nevertheless, he knew he needed to get on the good side of the gang leader.

'Who are you?'

'My name's Daniel. I understand my father's land agent, Mr Chow, was liaising with you. I have a payment for you.' Daniel took out a folded brown envelope from his trouser pocket. 'But first, we'd like a progress report, please. How much of the oil palm did you manage to get?'

'Who "we"?'

Daniel had been told to be firm or the man would walk all over him. But then again, his dad wasn't the one facing one of the hardest and roughest people Daniel had ever met. 'Err . . . my father is in hospital and asked me to find out how things went.' Daniel held up the envelope. 'He asked me to pass this on to you.'

Rhammar took a moment to process the words. He had expected an older person. But his money-mindedness considered the bony specimen in front of him. 'Put down envelope *bodoh.* You speak Malay, ah?'

'No, but I've been told you can speak English.' Daniel was starting to feel more confident. He wondered what *bodoh* meant.

'Ah, *sikit-sikit, lah*, okay. We take away half oil palm,' the lie coming with ease since the truth was nearer to a quarter of the cut stacks.

'Nice, my man,' Daniel said and thought he was doing well and grinned. Mixing with the hard crowd. Oh, yes.

'I not "your man".'

'No, err . . . yes, right. Sorry.'

Rhammar glowered at the squid of a boy before him. He wondered whether the boy would squirt ink if he shouted. His eyes darted to Daniel's hand.

'Ah, yes. Six thousand Ringgit in one hundred denominations as promised,' Daniel said. He would have liked proof of the man's work but saw no other option and held out a moist palm clutching the paper package. He had done the calculations earlier. It was over a thousand pounds for one night's work.

Rhammar glanced about him with the eyes of the guilty and grasped the moist, fingerprint-marked packet. Without looking, he felt the thickness of the contents and, as only an expert could, knew it was around the correct amount before pocketing it. He would not lose face to a 'boy' by counting it out.

He looked again at Daniel and decided that there was the possibility of extracting a little more money out of him. Rhammar leaned a little closer to Daniel and lowered his voice for added menace. 'We wait before next raid. Two weeks can, *lah.*

Daniel took a step back. He sensed the situation was moving way out of his control, and Rhammar's garlic-and chilli-laced breath was only adding to the vile threat.

'Well, Mr Rhammar, let's see if we're s-successful with this raid first and then consider if we have to r-risk another one.' He could feel his old stammer bubbling under the surface of his speech.

Rhammar glowered at the wimpy teenager in front of him. His angry brow gathered into contours of cruelty. He stared down at the quivering boy and thought about slicing off a fillet. He held Daniel's eyes captive. 'We do again two weeks. You pay or I look for you.'

13

'Stamp on it like you would one of the swamp rats, Zola. That's the ticket. Now push the gear lever up. Ha, onwards and forwards. Doing marvellously, my dear.'

I have a new respect for my uncle. Driving was the most fun I'd had since learning how to ride Rachel. But it was a whole new level of fizz.

The little blue jeep bounced along and I thought I felt it lurch on two wheels when I turned the corner a bit fast. I assumed I'd be in for a bollocking, but instead, he said, 'That's the stuff, Zola. Never surrender.'

He's cool. Crazy, but cool. My second favourite Hamster.

'Wow! I never thought learning to drive could be this much fun, Uncle Donald.'

I saw the farm hands accompanying us on their *kapchais*—other types of Rachel—scatter in all directions as I wrestled with the steering wheel on the rough, pot-holed plantation roads.

'This is how we learned before they brought in automatic gearboxes and power-assisted steering. The proper way. Turn left up ahead.'

I turned, concentrating on changing gear.

'Okay, let's try the other left this time and left again. Carry on.'

'Onwards and forwards,' I shouted above the engine noise.

'That's the spirit. Bring the beast to a halt up by that junction, if you will.'

I brought the car to a gentle stop, and the engine died.

'You have to remember the clutch pedal, my dear.'

'Sorry Uncle.'

'No problem. Never concede, always move forwards.'

'You are such a good teacher, Uncle.' I gave him a hug and a peck on the cheek which brought out red cheeks and a fluster. And brought a smile to my face.

I made a mental note to self that I'd found a soft spot in case I got into real trouble.

Donald opened the passenger door of his jeep and gingerly stepped out to survey the empty indentations in the soil where bushels of his palm oil crop had sat waiting for collection. His shoulders slumped and his face carried a long-suffering expression.

'I estimate about a quarter to one-third of the cut bushels have been taken, Zola. People don't steal crops out here unless there's another motive. There's easier money to be made in town. The amount spent on labour and fuel hardly makes it worth all the effort.'

I jumped down from the driver's side and walked around the car. 'Are you okay, Uncle?' I asked. I could see he was hurting.

'I suppose I've got to go through the formality of the paperwork. I'll ask one of the workers to go to the police station to drop off a report for insurance purposes.' His shoulders slumped, and he looked older. 'The payout will be a long time coming, and we'll never recover the true amount.'

I didn't know what to say, which is often a good sign that I'm thinking with a degree of sense and logic. Then I saw him smile. *He is a resilient old hamster.*

'We need to look on the bright side, Zola. And the bright side is, err . . . that we don't have to worry about thinking about the bright side.'

Crazy? I bet he howls at the moon when it's full.

One of the farmhands tutted and stared at the motorcycle and trailer tracks which led up to the perimetre fence. 'Boss, I got motorbike track. Maybe thief. Come!'

'Lord's lounge lizards, Zola. Go and have a look. We might shoot one of the blighters yet. Here, take Reginald.'

I found an ancient rifle thrust into my hands. It was heavier than it looked. While I had no intention of using it, I hoped that if any other thugs were about, they would see me with it and not cause me any more trouble.

I followed the farmworker over to the other side of a small hill.

'Boss girl, look see where come here.' He pointed to the broken fence and the trail through the swamp to a side road.

'Oh. We thought you could see them—the thieves.'

'Oh, no, boss girl. I see them, I call you.'

'But you . . . never mind. And my name's Zola.'

'Yes, boss girl Zola.'

'Anyway, perhaps you should go and report back to my uncle. Take Reginald back with you.' I handed over the rifle and turned to look at the tracks through the swamp.

The farm hand looked at the rifle, not really understanding this strange new girl, rested it against a palm tree in case the boss girl needed it and jogged down the hill in his flipflops and green sarong to where Donald was now sitting in the jeep resting his knee.

A short while later, I went back down to the jeep too and overheard uncle berating the labourer.

'What are you doing here? You should be up there!'

'I here because I not there.'

'Yes, yes, I know that, but why aren't you there?'

'Because I here, *lah*.'

'But you should be there.'

'I cannot there.'

'Why not?'

The farmhand looked exasperated at his boss's lack of logical reasoning. 'Boss, you no understand. If I there, I not here and I not see here.' He bent down to pick up a thin, serrated steel pipe, half hidden by a palm frond. 'Baffle,' he said with certainty.

'Yes, me too,' Donald replied.

'It is baffle.' The farmhand rolled his eyes.

'I know. I'm baffled too.'

'You no understand.'

'Yes, alright. No need to rub it in.'

'I tell you is baffle.' He let out a heavy sigh.

'And I'm telling you that if you don't stop with this nonsense, I'll dock some of your pay this month.'

'Is motorcycle baffle, boss. Silence for noise.'

Donald looked at farmhand. 'Why didn't you say so? Horse's arse, the lot of you.'

The farmhand rolled his eyes.

It was clear to me that they had all grown to accept the crazy couple who employed them. Their bonusses would always make up for the eccentricities they had to put up with.

Donald turned over the piece of metal to see 'Property of Rhammar' scratched on the side.

'Interesting. I wonder if the police have anything on him. Time to make a report methinks. Never surrender! Right, Zola, time for part two of your lesson: let's reverse back to the house.'

My eyebrows rose with surprise. 'What, all the way?'

'How else are we going to get back?'

'By driving forward?' I said the words with care, as if each one of them might explode.

The farmhand looked down and shook his head as if I were a lunatic.

'That would be ridiculous, Zola.'

'I thought it was, "Always move forward; never surrender."'

Out of the corner of my eye, I noticed the farmhand now had his right hand covering his face in despair.

'Quite right, of course. But since we've come from the house, we should reverse ourselves to it. If we move forwards, we go to a different place, a new place. It's all simple logic, Zola. Makes me wonder what they teach in schools these days.'

'Oh, yes. I suppose, when you put it like that, but . . .'

'And how are you going to move forward without reversing first?' Donald pointed to the jeep with its front facing a solid looking palm tree.

'Yes, yes. I thought you meant . . .' I watched the farmhand behind my uncle making a cross with both hands, willing me to stop. The message was clear: the day had a limited number of hours.

'Well, come along, then. I need to get back to give that postman a good whack with my Papua fighting stick.'

'Is that absolutely necessary?' I asked, dragging out the last word. 'I know he brought bad news, but he's only doing his job.'

'Don't worry, my dear. This time I'll use the soft end. Onwards and forwards.'

Later that afternoon, and with much anticipation, I rode Rachel up the dirt track leading to the rise. I'd been looking forward to seeing Zak again every day. There was a twinge of excitement, wondering whether we'd take the friendship further. Driving lessons aside, the thought of him had been a peach sundae to the chili-padi stress of what had happened over the past few days. It had kept me going.

He'd texted a message earlier saying it was urgent that we meet up and I'd replied that I'd missed his company too and put a hug emoji at the end of the party ones. The fact I didn't get one back, I put down to the reasoning that boys were sometimes slow when it came to decoding stuff.

The buzz of the little motor matched the nervous tingle of apprehension I had. I tried to recall his face and mannerisms. I wondered if I'd feel the same way about him as before.

He was already there when I arrived. *Good, a quick learner.* However, when I saw his face, a feeling of cold fear ran through me.

He stood there wearing knee-length loose khaki shorts, trainers and a light green T with the name and outline of a Malay band I'd never heard of. Both his hands were resting on each hip. His expression was pure arrogance.

His first words cut into me like a chef's knife slicing through a ripe mango. 'Why did you do that?'

I kicked the side stand down, got off the bike and approached Zak. 'Do what? What have I done?'

'You know exactly. Don't bluff, *lah.* I suppose this is a game to you, isn't it?'

My happy anticipation avalanched into sadness. I hadn't a clue what he was on about and said, 'Zak, in all honesty, I don't know what you're talking about. Please, I thought we were friends.'

He shrugged. 'So did I.'

I guess he must've noticed the blank look I was wearing and asked, 'You genuinely don't know, do you?'

'No I don't, and I was looking forward to today.' I could feel my eyes swelling and watering. One blink would be the tipping point. I tried to get the anger back. 'Today was going to be the highlight of my week. Instead, it's another piece of shit in the toilet bowl of a life that I have.'

Even though I tried to convince myself he wasn't worth it, I still blinked. Two burning, salty tears fell down my cheeks and into the edges of my mouth.

'The card you gave me. It's a fake.' Zak pulled the item from his pocket and threw it at me.

I caught it as it landed at my waist. Even with blurred vision, I could tell from the texture of the plastic what he meant. I'd screwed up. *Again.* Quelle surprise.

'I didn't plan on giving you this one, honest. I don't know how it happened. You must believe me. I want to help. I do.' The floodgates had opened, and I felt like a dam full of misery.

'The best way to do that would be to give me the real one then, wouldn't it?'

His words cut like the tiny 'machine gun' thorns found in the plantation which ripped into your flesh and didn't let go. In *Sheng*—a mixture of Ki-Swahili and English used in Nairobi—we called them *waitabit* thorns. The sluice gates closed and I folded my arms. A full arm barrier. He deserved it.

'Look, I'm sorry, okay? I made a separate one as a backup to give to the thugs. It meant that I could keep the real one for you. The other one, the real one, must still be in my room.'

'Let's go and get it then.'

'Sure.' *Screw him.* Then, when I saw his body language, I asked, 'What? Now?'

'Unless you have something better to do,' he said with a contemptuous half-smile.

I weighed everything up. *He gets one last chance.*

'How's your brother?' I asked, giving him a reason to at least be a little bit nice. Okay, I did screw up yet again. But come on, it was an accident.

'He'll be fine. Thank you.'

He dragged out the last two words like they were poisonous tentacles. And it didn't sound right. The guy was in a coma. What gives?

'That's good news.' I meant it. 'I guess I expected you to be happier.'

'I am happy,' Zak said smiling but was still looking and sounding angry.

I looked at his face. It was the type of smile I put on when I get pestered by people I don't want to be with. Why had I been so stupid to trust a guy after only a couple of meetings? Naivety doesn't even begin to describe it. *What a sucker I've been.*

'Do you want me to drive?' The contemptuous half-smile appeared again.

'No, thank you. I've got the hang of her now.' I gave him his shitty 'thank you' back with a double reveal of the finger.

'Huh,' he scoffed. 'Typical. Drop me off at the treeline. You can go get it and bring it back to me.'

I was pissed. 'The second word is "off", now guess the first. You can wait here and I'll be generous and consider bringing it back.' *Jerk.*

I gave up and resigned myself to yet another stupid misjudgement. All I wanted now was to get this over with as quickly as possible. I glanced over to where Rachel was waiting, with her front pouch now hanging open. Then I heard a branch crack and a shadow flashed past where the neat rows of oil palm began. I ignored it and said, 'I'll be back soon.'

When no reply came, I turned around to see Zak staring at me with a shocked expression.

A fraction of a second later, I saw why and went rigid with fear.

14

'What the f—?' I watched a small crimson patch grow on the side of Zak's shirt. He pulled it up to assess the damage. Blood was flowing from a graze, a trickle rather than a spurt.

There was the sound of another crack in the air and a small shrub exploded next to his feet.

There was nowhere to hide. The rise was bare except for a few gnarled bushes. We were sitting ducks.

I felt Zak reach out for support as he fell towards me. Now he wants friendship? *Too late pal.* Besides, I didn't think that the wound was that bad; more of a scratch than a deep injury. I tried to steady myself, but his weight was limiting my movement. His powerful hands gripped my shoulders. I couldn't move; his strength was too much. Then it finally sunk in. He wasn't asking for help; he was using me as a shield from the shooter.

The sound of an angry turbo-charged wasp rushed past my ear followed by another loud cracking sound.

I twisted and swivelled my way out of his grip—my Aikido training paying off—until he was exposed again. This time he ran backwards, making sure I was between him and the shooter. He shouted, 'Make sure you get me that card tomorrow, or you'll be in a pile of shit.'

I was thinking I should've kicked him in the boy's brigade and left him to the shooter. Yes, there are times I like to focus on the hate. It's my way of dealing with arseholes like him. But I now had bigger problems: I stood there in front of the shooter like a lone cocktail stick in the last piece of fruit salad.

Oh, crap with a hedgehog.

My ears waited for the next sharp crack and the bullet which would have my name on it. The next few seconds felt like a snail making its way through superglue.

Nothing.

Another few seconds passed. The sounds of the jungle started coming back: the trilling birds, whining insects and the playful sounds of macaques playing among the fronds.

Whoever the shooter was, they weren't interested in me. But why should they be? What had I done? But, if it wasn't about me, then I guessed it wasn't anything to do with uncle's land problems. Whoever it was, they had a mare on with Zak. *Serves him right.*

I don't like wishing people dead. And tempting though it is, I'm not going to start now. But I'm hoping the pathetic graze he got hurts more than severe sunburn in a steaming hot shower. Anger sometimes becomes me.

I rode Rachel hard back to the bungalow, my head filled with questions which bubbled away like boiling mud. *What the hell is really going on here?*

By the time I'd made the short ride back to the house, I'd had the opportunity to channel my disappointment into pure anger towards Zak. I hoped all his shits had porcupines in them. I was a bit surprised that Rachel didn't break down given the abuse she received. She was aging badly and couldn't take too much of the rough stuff.

At the bungalow, I saw Uncle Donald and a younger guy on the front deck deep in serious conversation. Another Honda like Rachel was on the main dirt track. I didn't think it was possible that there could be a bike in an even worse condition unless I'd seen it with my own eyes. But there it was. Leaning against it was a slim, tattered golf bag with a couple of ancient clubs poking out.

Anger gave way to curiosity.

I parked Rachel next to the potting shed and went to meet the new arrival.

Before I said my 'Hellos', I slowed my pace to get a good look at him. He wore a light blue, long-sleeved shirt with a stiff raised collar, and loose-fitting slacks, which looked as though they would benefit from the washing machine. His sandals were wafer thin and I half expected them to crackle every time he moved. He had a dark complexion with a weary expression that aged his face, and he was slim to the point of looking malnourished. His small, rough-skinned hands looked as though he worked outside a lot. Yet, when I walked around the front of the deck and got another angle, I saw that he was young enough to be in my year at school.

I thought myself lucky, and that doesn't happen often. He looked sad. Like Elio staring into the fire in *Call Me by Your Name.*

'Ah, Zola,' my uncle called. 'I'd like you to meet one of my neighbours from up the road in Ulu Yam. I think it would do you and him good to get out with company your own age.'

He's the same age as me? I doubted we had anything in common. Instead, I said, 'Sure.'

'He's a year older than you,' Donald continued.

Don't you mean a decade?

'And I thought you two could team up when you went to town. Or you could ride up and see his plans for an eco-lodge.'

Or I could ride in the opposite direction.

'Like you, he's into environmental stuff. Thinks I should ditch this plantation and reforest.'

One box ticked, I suppose.

'He already has his head in the clouds. However, unlike most of those hairy, bearded green types, he also sees things from a farmer's perspective. His ideas are quite remarkable.'

I'll build a fire for him to look into and divine the future then.

'He says you and he have a lot to talk about . . .'

Presumptuous and sad. A double whammy.

'Margaret and I have asked him to stay for dinner. I'll leave you two to it, then.'

Oh, no. Please don't go. I'll even go to the swamp and harvest your leeches, if you promise to stay.

'I must look for my rifle. There's a rumour the Jehovah's Witnesses are in town again, and Rosmah's too slow to get them like she used to. Saves on the inoculations from the vet though. Onwards and forwards you two. See you later.'

What? He inoculates the dog from biting the JWs? Hmm, hang on, he's starting to make sense.

Time to put on my sociable face. I can do that. *But if this new kid starts telling me about his pet goldfish dying this morning, I'm off.*

On the bright side, I was sure he didn't have one. I was also aware that I needed to put out another post on my Instagram. And as he was the first local I'd met who cared about the environment, I decided to give him a chance. *Here goes nothing.*

'Hi, I'm Zola. I write an Instagram page on environmental issues, especially the protection of rainforests. It'd be cool to get your thoughts.'

He paused for a moment before a smile dissolved the worry lines on his face.

'Hi. Yeah. Can. My brother and I follow you.'

That sounded creepy, but I hoped I got his real meaning. Cool. Two followers in Malaysia. He suddenly leaped into my 'interesting' inbox. And I was relieved his English was better that his clothes. It could have been even more strained otherwise.

'I need to sort out few things with uncle. And the guy at the hardware store in town say you mention me. Hi. I'm Zak . . .'

Not another one.

'. . . Zak Abraham.'

'You can't be serious!' I blurted.

Blurting and yelping. I could make a kids' TV programme with these characters. But this feels like too much of a coincidence. *What gives?*

I said, 'I was with a "Zak Abraham" a moment ago at the rise in the plantation. We were shot at.'

As soon as I'd said the last bit, I realized how it would sound. My creative licence uploading again.

He looked straight into my eyes and said, 'No, you were not.'

I could feel my anger bubbling away. A little bit surfaced. 'Actually, we were.'

When I use 'actually' at the beginning of my sentences, it means 'listen you stupid idiot.'

'Yes, I know the shooting.'

O*kaaay. Where's this going?* I added, 'And I know who I was with.'

'Yes. He is not Zak Abraham.'

I thought, *he's got to be lying, hasn't he?*

This guy was fast becoming a sus my life didn't need right now. I put both hands on my hips. 'How do you know?'

New Zak stepped off the porch, went to his bike and pulled out what looked like a club from his golf bag.

Only it wasn't.

15

My knees became weak and all over the place. In Zak's hands was an old hunting rifle pointing in my general direction. I was glued to the spot. I wanted to call for Donald but all I could manage was a croak. My legs wouldn't do what they were asked. He took a step closer and there was nothing I could do about it.

'Chill,' he said, raising his hand. 'The answer to your first question is "Yes." The answer to your second question is also "Yes", and the answer to the third question will be a long story. But I need your help. Okay?'

I fixated on the rifle, pointing more at my feet now. 'Were you shooting at us up there?' I tried gesturing with my arm, but it flopped back to my waist like a lifeless fish.

New Zak waved his palm in a circle. 'Next.'

Flustered with confusion and angered by the arrogance of this wannabe gangster, I was getting my mojo back and snarled, 'You shot him. You do realize you could've killed me, or him, or both of us, don't you?'

Zak's expression remained the same. He waved his palm in a circle again and said, 'Next.'

I couldn't remember what answer he'd given for the third question. And I was getting annoyed with his little game. I asked, 'Why?'

'Anger. Hatred. Revenge. You choose. I needed to stop you two from meeting but when I saw I was too late, I had to do something, and my rifle was with me.'

'You hit him. He was bleeding.'

'Yeah. Luck is on my side. This thing . . .' Zak waved the rifle around, '. . . is crazy inaccurate. I got lucky.'

Got lucky? Not another one from Planet Hamster.

'Wait! You're telling me that you shot in our direction with a, and I quote, "crazy inaccurate" gun? Are you off your effing head?'

'It was spontaneous.'

'How about "Excuse me, can I see you before you meet with . . . whoever the hell that was?"'

'Ha. Your uncle said you were funny.'

'Does my uncle know about you shooting whoever that was?'

'About now? No.'

'Then I intend to tell him.'

'Good one. He knows you well. "Imaginative," he'd said.' Zak laughed.

Although furious at this cocky twat of a person, he was right. My uncle would have said 'What? The devil got away? Well shoot him again, then.' I wrestled my snarling to a manageable growl.

'Well, I'm glad everyone is having such a great time. Care to let me in on what's going on around here, or are we done?'

'Not done. And, as I said, we need your help.'

'We?'

'Your uncle and aunt's future is tied up with mine. That's the "we".'

I went back to snarling.

'I needed to stop you from handing over the safe key. But it doesn't matter anymore, right? You gave him the card, didn't you?'

'I gave him the wrong card. That's what he wanted to see me about. I still have the real one.' Then I remembered. 'And why was my name written on it?'

Zak's shoulders visibly relaxed. '*Bagus!*' Even his voice sounded less constricted. 'We need it. The rest I'll explain during dinner.'

'Can you give a hand please, Zola?' Aunt Margaret called.

I looked at my phone. Almost forty minutes had passed, and I hadn't noticed any of them. Get it together. You can do this.

Heavenly aromas of rich gravy and herbs floated around the bungalow from the pot roast. Donald carved, and Margaret served a huge helping on to Zak's plate while I brought the rest of the dishes out from the kitchen.

Despite being one of my favourites, I had little appetite.

'Zak's had a stretch of bad luck,' Donald began. 'In fact, it's worse than that.'

'It's okay Uncle,' Zak used the Malaysian 'Uncle' as a common term of respect. 'My older brother Daud—you met him before he was taken to HKL—he was the target of a Chinese triad. He is in an induced coma. The police are not interested unless it involves money.'

I felt my anxiety building. It was all too familiar. *Am I shifting between different Astro-planes? Am I in a real* Stranger Things *existence?* My breathing and heart rate were rising, and my stomach was twisting. I glared at Uncle Donald, who was nonchalantly tucking into the roast. 'You,' I was almost shouting. 'You, tried to get me to believe I made it up. Now you're saying you knew all along?'

'Zola!' Margaret said loud enough to get everyone's attention. 'There's no need to raise your voice like that around the dinner table, a little courtesy for our guest, if you will. Howsoever do you expect to find a husband with such outbursts?'

'I'm fourteen!'

'Precisely my point. Time to practise on a few toads. More toads than princes these days. And you can pour me another tea, please.'

It was a quick lesson: never argue with the crazy.

'Yeah, well what do you expect. Next time, mix a pinch of salt with dry chilli flakes and pour it on another open wound. Garnish it with lemon, why don't you?' Then I realised I was starting to sound like them.

Margaret smiled politely. 'Yes, dear.'

Donald, who was uncharacteristically showing the patience of a long-term visitor to a mausoleum, noticed my death-ray glare and said, 'In fairness, Zola, it was not until Zak came over that we found out. It's not our fault, you know. If you had told us about the other imposter, things may have been different.'

'But you'd never have believed me.'

'I wouldn't swear on a Pangolin's rear end, but we are liberal and progressive thinkers, aren't we, my Nightshade Ninja?' he looked at Margaret.

Aunty gave a little murmur of agreement and added, 'Yes, quite progressive. For example, the other day I designed my own website.'

Zak nodded his support while cramming a huge portion of food into his face.

I was caught out by the non-sequitur, although I was also impressed. I wasn't sure that I could do something like that without help from a geek. My anger evaporated. Even getting Boomers on anything other than FB was a result.

'Wow, Aunty, that's great. I'm impressed. Can I have a look later?'

'With pleasure,' Margaret said, showing a little self-pride. 'I'll dig it out of my sketch pad.'

'Sketch pad?'

'That's where I drew it, dear. Do pay attention.'

Crazy? No, way beyond. It must be the tea.

Zak broke the silence that followed. 'Daud was caught by thugs. He was waiting for me at our farm. But I was late. It's my fault. He was thrown in the boot of their car to drive him to their boss in KL. Then the car got a puncture. When the thugs opened the boot, Daud hit one with a tyre iron. He fought with another thug, but the man stabbed him with an old knife that snapped in half. Daud saw your uncle's plantation and tried to run and lose them. He was much fitter than the thugs, but the wound got worse every time he moved, so he stopped to write your name on the card.'

'Why? Why didn't he just keep running?'

'Maybe he thought he couldn't make it. He had a small marker pen from measuring in our new bungalow. And your uncle told us you were coming here. If he threw the card on a path in the plantation, it would look like it was yours. If thugs found it, they wouldn't care. If an estate worker found it, he'd hand it in.'

'But it was in his shoe,' I said with suspicious eyes, looking for any telltale signs that he was lying. I was still angry that he hadn't apologized for the shooting earlier.

'Zola!' Aunty said sharply. 'Do let him finish. Good things come to those who wave.'

I was going to correct her, but actually, she was probably right. I waved. I blame the tea.

Zak looked at me as if I was crazy. I wanted to tell him that I wasn't the crazy one, aunty was, but then I figured that's what a crazy person would say and kept quiet.

'Anyway,' Zak continued. 'When he stopped running, the wound stopped bleeding and he felt better. But just in case, he put the card in his shoe. However, he said that when he tried to stand up again, he blacked out. Then you found him.'

'When you came back, the thugs had caught up and carried him back to their car. Daud was in a bad way, and no use to them dead, so they took him to the hospital.'

I still had loads of questions, but Zak wanted to continue.

'Before my parents died in a car crash, my father borrowed some money from the *Ah Long,* a money . . .'

'. . . lender.' I finished his sentence. 'I heard the same from the other so-called Zak. He wants this.' I placed the plastic card on the table. How could such a small and innocuous card cause so much trouble? I was glad to get rid of it. And this time hand it to its rightful owner. I attempted a self-congratulatory smile.

'Who was that imposter jerk, then?'

'Abidin. He's the Malay orphan adopted by the *Ah Long* who wants my land,' Zak explained.

Donald leaned towards me and raised his glass of *toddy*—a fermented drink made from the palm-heart. 'Most excellent, keeping that card thing. And . . . err . . . sorry about not believing you before. No hard feelings, eh? Onwards and forwards?'

I couldn't keep any anger towards the Hamsters. Drift with the current. 'Never surrender, Uncle,' I said and flashed him a resigned frown.

'Fried bananas, anyone?' Margaret asked.

Before he left, I gave Zak my number and he returned a missed call with the agreement that we would meet up the following afternoon to get the property deed from the bank together. I felt, no, I needed to see this through and make the situation right.

He was closer to the Hamsters than me, and way more rational. There was a lot spinning around in my head with much to digest. The other imposter remained lodged in the back of my mind like an annoying pimple that couldn't be burst. How could I have been that trusting? How could he have lied to my face like that?

Sleep took a long time to arrive.

16

I'd had a restless night and woken at least twice. Once when the outside window shutter started to creak with the strengthening wind, which I fixed with a piece of rolled-up tissue, and again when I had to turn the ceiling fan up another speed. *Is it ever possible to get used to this humidity?*

After I eventually found sleep, I had another weird dream in which I found myself moving along a corridor of rotten black palm fronds interlinked like Venus' Flytraps. As I walked, each one unfolded to reveal a dead body with a knife stuck in the middle of a blood-stained chest. At the end of the row, two fresh green palm fronds opened slowly. Maya was in one, sleeping. I was being drawn in by a gravitational force sucking me inexorably towards the spiky fronds. I tried running back, but no matter how much effort I put in to move my legs, they were leaden and slow, and my arms felt weak and useless. As the fronds closed over me, I screamed and woke up sweating. If anyone had heard me, I'd blame it on the swamp rats this time.

I then spent the rest of the night rolling from side to side, unable to find a comfortable position. Since I couldn't sleep, I listened to the jungle night. It had a low, moody and foreboding sound, broken by the occasional scream of a night animal. It was hypnotic. I also thought of Maya at the café and felt that I should talk to her again. No, I needed to talk to her again. Although we'd barely spent any time together, I couldn't get her out of my head.

It felt like we'd known each other for years. As soon as Maya had entered my thoughts, that was it. She stayed there until it was time to get up. I made a mental note to go back to SGR Café as soon as I had the chance. I wanted to find out more. Was she involved in the landgrab?

At breakfast, I had little appetite.

Uncle Donald took off his bottle-top reading glasses which were shaped like two small cars facing each other. He said, 'Just so we're clear, Zola, are you sure you're up to it? If you are, go through the plan once more for me please to see if I've got everything covered.'

I was dressed in a floral-patterned summer skirt and light cotton blouse. It was the smartest stuff I'd brought with me. I took a deep breath.

'When I get to the Land Office, I should get these forms you've filled out stamped and approved. Then I present them to a Mr Chow, whom I have a meeting with at 11.30 a.m. After that, I . . .'

'You grab him by the throat and strangle every last breath out of him until he signs the last paper showing our plantation is running efficiently.'

'Is it?' I was starting to get wise to Uncle Donald's outbursts. I was also starting to see the funny side of them. He sounded like my brother when he was pissed off. Road rage in the cycle lane.

He calmed down and clarified, 'No, not by a long way. Even before the theft we would have been at around sixty-five to seventy per cent by their calculations. We need to show eighty-five per cent. Now it's much less.'

'What's the land worth if you were to sell?'

'It should be worth well over six million Ringgit, over a million pounds, but the Land Office won't approve the sale if they think they can get their hands on it for free. But that's not the point.

Where would we go? What would we do? Living here has been our life for as long as we can remember. Where would a couple of old cronies . . .'

Hamsters.

'. . . like us go? The city? We'd hate it. And we wouldn't be able to afford anywhere even half decent with land attached for farming and then have enough to live on. I must look after my Margaret, you see.'

I saw his eyes moisten and sensed the emotional drain he was being sucked into. Beneath his stern exterior, he was a vulnerable, old hamster trying his best in a world changing faster than he could cope with. I felt like I could relate. It was hard enough navigating the mercurial changes in my friends at school.

I said, 'I'll do my best.'

'I know you will, my dear. Right then. On—'

'Onwards and forwards, Uncle?'

'That's the spirit. I can drive you to Serendah Station, but my knee's not ready for hoofing it around the city yet. Get out at Kuala Lumpur and you'll find it's just a short distance from there.'

Donald unfolded an old flap of mould-speckled paper. 'Here's a city map.'

I chuckled, 'It's okay Boomer, I have it all here.' I waved my phone at him.

'Boomer?' he queried, his bushy eyebrows rising.

'It's just a term we younger people use for . . . err . . . older people.'

'Oh? Sounds more like the name of a dog, if you ask me. Now you mention it, us older types have a name for younger people like you too.'

'Really?

'Yes. Lazy. Let's get going.'

I walked and he hobbled on to the porch where Margaret was airing underwear on the outside barbeque.

'Lord's leeches and lawyers, Margaret,' Donald called out. 'What do you think you're doing?'

'It's awfully humid at this time of the year, Donald,' she explained.

'Ah, well, right then. Carry on.'

With a small, exasperated shake of the head and a hurried pat on the head for Rosmah, who responded with an excited wag of her tail, we made our way to his jeep.

'Guard the property, you ugly hound,' Donald mumbled.

'Yes dear, as you wish.'

'Not you, Margaret, my little jar of mustard, the dog. I was speaking to Rosmah.'

'Oh, that's nice, dear.'

Mad as a bag of monkeys, both of them.

On the train, I managed to get a seat next to a large Malay lady in the 'women only' carriage. Bored, I decided to play a game by giving the other commuters the name of the animal they most resembled. It was a repetitive game since it was either Mouse-deer or Buffalo.

Bored of that, and with an eagle-eyed intensity, I tried to comprehend the incomprehensible by going through the documents. The key, it seemed, was to get the last document signed. *I can do this,* I tried to convince myself.

Compared to Serendah, the traffic noise outside KL station was thunderous and disorientating, and after twenty minutes of following Google Maps, I felt I was getting nowhere. Roads intersected at strange angles and my path was blocked by walls and fences which shouldn't have been there. Had they grown overnight?

I didn't think it possible, but the heat was even greater here than on the plantation. My hair was damp and my scalp was starting to itch; even the flower patterns on my dress were beginning to wilt.

I gave up and asked for directions from a kind-looking local at an open-air food stall. While I listened and deciphered the mix of English, Malay and what sounded like gibberish, a heavily modified white BMW 535 drove up to the curb. A thick hairy arm came out from the driver's window and smacked me on the bum.

With a lack of sleep coupled with the frustration of finding the Land Office in the heat of Hell's Car Park, I snapped.

Here's the thing about anger. Boomers will go on about how it's a choice. They'll say if you get angry, you look at the person before choosing how to react. If they're heavyweight MMA material, you put on a scowl then move along. If they look weak, you kick the shit out of them.

Yeah? Well, I went full nuclear. I didn't care who they were.

Wewe, unafanya nini jamani?

My Ki-Swahili may be basic, but I find it's the best language for ripping people's balls off. It's all in the tone.

Three, heavily built, rough-looking men leaned out of the car, bewildered. They got out and stared in my direction with an angry intent. The driver said, 'Accident, *lah*. I was signalling.'

I didn't like to swear that much. It's what Thropes use when their minuscule vocab runs dry, but now and again it fits. I told him to get lost using two choice words, and then described what I thought of him using a four-letter word beginning with 'T' and ending with 'D'.

'Yeah? Well, bring it then, huh?' dog turd said.

With a tiny bit more sense than my considerable temper, I remembered that I was in a foreign country with a police force that my uncle described as the official Mafia. I stormed off towards the Land Office, hoping it wasn't an omen for the rest of the day.

Although it took less than fifteen minutes to get to the building, I walked through the front door with perspiration dripping in thin rivulets. I was not happy.

Even the welcoming embrace of the fierce air-conditioning did little to reduce my boiling temper.

I walked through the small corridor entranceway and turned a corner to see a bright circus of an office crowded with people also trying to fight the system. *Ignore them*, I said to myself. *Play the game.*

I dutifully took a number and sat in one of the few remaining free seats on an uncomfortable, perforated metal bench. My ticket showed that I was twenty-three away. *Shouldn't be that long*, I thought.

One hour and ten minutes later, my number came up. At the counter, a huge, fierce-looking woman in a full-length Malay dress glowered at me. Her strawberry-coloured, jelly-like lips spoke in a language I couldn't understand.

'Hello,' I replied.

No response. I thought I could try a 'Moo', but then the woman's various chins started shifting as she reached across the counter to take the papers from my hands.

In broken English, the woman stated, 'You go different office. Get approval stamp to make application for claim. This is payment office. You go the upstairs office.'

I wanted to tell her where she could go too. Waste of energy. IQ of a farm door. But the Hamsters were relying on me, and I was not going to be beaten.

I strode up the wide spiral staircase to my right which wound its way to the first floor. At the top, there were rows upon rows of austere, polished wooden doors. One opened and a vampire exited. At least that's what she looked like with her black clothes and flowing black cape.

'Which is the office for land use stamping please?' I asked while holding the forms up for vampire girl to see.

'In here,' she said and held open the door to the coven.

Everyone was wearing similar outfits and running around from counter to counter. They were either a lot of lawyers, or people auditioning for a new *Underworld* film.

Focus.

There was standing room only, and not much of that either. The vampires rushed here and there, muttering what sounded like evil spells, but no-one stopped to help.

Okay, I can do this.

I approached the crammed counter in front, where one overworked member of staff raced between the caped characters and the back office. A vampire pushed me aside.

'Mjinga!' I shouted in Ki-Swahili.

The room fell into an uncomfortable silence. Capes fell like limp flounders.

'Will one of you please tell me where the claim stamping person is?'

An elderly and sloth-like Malay man emerged from the back, took my forms like they were diseased, scrutinized them for a few long and quiet seconds, then uttered two words: 'Pay first.'

'How much?' I screwed my nuclear-bomb eyes into his.

'Fifteen Ringgit.'

I gave him two notes from my manila envelope.

'No, you pay downstairs, ground floor near entrance; get stamp.'

I know my face can be expressive at times, but I swear that most of the vampires hid behind their cloaks. Corvinus would turn in his grave.

Downstairs, Norhasleazy, or whatever her name was, saw me coming and realized that setting fire to herself would be less painful than asking me to calm down and produced the payment stamp as I approached her.

Back up in the coven, I thundered through fleeing capes to the counter. A lawyer who had not been there earlier tried to push past. Bad move. I grabbed his arm and gave him my best Selene look. He cowered in servility, skulking off to the side. Viktor would have been proud.

'I don't know why you didn't do this online,' sloth-man said and disappeared before my hands managed to grasp his throat.

Another hour and a half later, and I was sitting in the waiting room of the senior vice president of Land Planning. It had a faint whiff of unwashed onions and the soil they grew in. Clusters of small paintings spilled around beige walls creating a bland, forgettable setting—a bit like a custard pudding with a few raisins poking out. The chairs were modern and cheap with shiny chrome tubing. They also had a cloth covered back and a slab of dark, prehistoric-looking leather in-between that could have come from a beach donkey's saddle.

In one corner was the receptionist whose nameplate read Clover Nagamurthi. She busied herself with musty piles of documents while the fierce air-conditioning recycled stale odours and dry, static air.

I waited with the patience of a cat that had lapped a full bowl of Red Bull. My fingers fidgeted with a fraying chair thread.

When all seemed lost and hope drained down into the sewage, I heard the dark ironwood door to the main office creak open like the lid of an ancient Transylvanian coffin. Clover made a welcoming grunt, but it could have been indigestion. I looked up to see the person who, according to Donald, was the key to ensuring his land wasn't taken away. I had to be ultra-nice. Or strangle him.

The man looked to be in his late-forties and was dressed in dark grey business trousers and a blue-striped shirt. He had a receding hairline, tired eyes, a slight build, and a hilarious cluster of feline whiskers protruding from a large black mole on his right cheek. I tried to not stare at the hypnotic mole and the whiskers dancing in the stream of air-conditioning. He came over towards me.

I stood up. 'Hi, I'm Zola.'

'Sorry, who?'

'You wrote to my uncle, Donald Junkett, regarding the asportation of his land.' I enjoyed using my new word.

The man looked at me with contempt. 'Chow,' he said in hushed tones.

'But we've only just met.'

'Haiya! My Chinese name's Chow, but my English name is Vivien.' He presented his business card. 'Yes, I've written to your uncle.'

I said, 'Unfortunately there was a car accident, which is why I'm here to represent him.' I stared at the whiskers.

Chow sat down on another saddle chair next to mine. I followed suit. His squeaked and I wondered if it was a protest from the leather or something else. I sniffed suspiciously. *Was I making him nervous?*

'The facts are these, Miss Zola,' he bleated. 'All will be well if your uncle, Mr Junkett, can produce evidence of land use efficiency as detailed in the land usage laws.' He leaned across to his desk and picked up a weighty tomb. 'It's all here in Section 63 with particular reference to paras eight and their respective sub-clauses with the caveat of a three per cent margin. There's nothing I can do to change the facts. Come back after your harvest with the tonnage stamped by the government officer at the refinery and we can perform a quick calculation as to the operating efficiency of your plantation.'

His saccharine-sweet smile oozed condescension. I got the feeling that he already knew the answer. He should have been a politician.

'In fact, I've already taken the liberty of scheduling a hearing next Tuesday for the return of the land to this office for redistribution should you be unable to obtain the necessary certification of efficiency. I've already sent details to your uncle who will need to attend or forfeit the land.'

'Why the urgency?' I asked.

He shrugged his shoulders. Then it dawned on me. The monotoned moron was in on the deal too.

I felt like a deflated balloon. My confidence from earlier in the day now lay in a heap on the floor. It seemed like the world was conspiring against me. 'What about compensation?' I demanded.

Vivien Chow looked like he was either thinking hard or the leather chair was about to squeak again. 'Yes. The law is clear regarding compensation. You will be entitled to compensation at two-thirds of your final harvest.'

He looked like he already knew that figure too.

I didn't want to talk anymore; I wanted to carve him like a roast.

At the exit door, I paused at a cracked pane of glass and stared through my reflection to the dull grey clouds now blanketing the sky. I breathed a weary sigh. I had let my uncle and aunt down, and there was nothing I could do to make things right.

On my way back to the train station, I passed the same noodle stall where I had asked for directions. The tables were almost empty now, but since I hadn't eaten since breakfast, the aromas coming from the stand made me ravenous. My stomach growled.

While tucking with joy into a bowl of Sarawak *Laksa* noodles, I noticed that the white BMW was still there with its sunroof left open.

Fifteen minutes later I was feeling much better. The meal had given me a new-found energy and determination. I needed to balance things out. And I had a plan.

I put on my uncle's voice, 'By St George, dragons are for slaying' and cracked a vengeful smile.

Then I heard another voice dripping malice. 'No-one believes you but me.'

It sounded like Maya. I spun around expecting to see her. And I thought I caught a fleeting glance of her, but when I blinked, she'd gone.

I rose from the table, paid the stall owner, and before she knew what I was going to do, I went over to the large plastic bucket where the cook had scraped all the empty prawn carcasses, fish guts, and other pungent organic waste. I pulled off the lid to reveal the most disgusting, foul-smelling, gut-squirming slime. Then, using all my strength, I lifted the bucket and tipped the entire contents into the BMW through its sunroof.

'Yes,' I said to the shocked stall owner. 'One dragon down. Two more to slay. Onwards and forwards. Never surrender!'

17

I couldn't shake off the feeling that I'd let my aunt and uncle down. I rummaged around in my dustbin liner of a brain for how I could help. I felt my father's comment 'Trouble seems to follow you' flashing again and again. The Hamsters were going to lose everything, and I was in the way. I had this nagging feeling that the weird kid at the café, Daniel or Spaniel or whatever, was also involved. I made a note to self to go back there and see if I could find out more. If he was involved, there was a good likelihood that he'd be hanging around there. Then there was Maya. She was magnetic. Like a Pringle, I wanted more than one bite.

Zak and I met up at Central Market, near the front doors of the old façade which was still intact, almost. Inside, the shell was like a factory warehouse, although the bustling people and competing sounds from the vendors made it difficult to observe anything more than 6 feet ahead. An artist wanted to draw my caricature. He was dressed in loose folds of beige shirt and cargo trousers. He wore a tie-dye scarf and boater hat. He should draw himself. Then a 'Dude' came up smelling of patchouli oil. He asked if I needed anything. I said, 'The death sentence for dog owners who don't pick up.' He nodded with an absent expression. Sarcasm is not a big thing here.

When Zak arrived, the sellers disappeared.

'What's the plan?' I asked him. *Still in the mood for a fight?*

Zak gave a small mouth shrug. 'We collect the deeds, then go to the Land Office first thing on Monday; it's too late to register it now.'

I seriously did not want to go there again. I said, 'I have lots to tell you about that place. Why not leave the deeds in the bank until Monday?'

'I'll feel happier when the deeds are in my hands The *Ah Long* can get hold of the papers if any staff in the bank owes him a favour.'

'Malaysia sounds . . . well corrupt.'

Zak smiled. 'You have no idea.'

He reached into his pocket and removed the plastic card key. 'This opens the safety deposit box under Daud's and my name. You take it now. If anyone follows us, we split up and meet at the bank. It's at the end of that road,' he pointed. 'They'll think that you've given me the key. It makes me the target. Walk a bit behind and watch if anyone follows me too close. If you see them, you run. Run like crazy.'

I can do crazy. I've got two great teachers. I said, 'Got it.'

I didn't want the responsibility, but my skirt did have a secure inside pocket with a stitched flap of cotton to separate the secret from the less secret. And I am a good runner.

Sticking to the main street, among a throng of other shoppers, we were more than halfway when Zak's path was suddenly blocked by two large, thuggish-looking men. Other shoppers moved swiftly out of the way; none of them wanted to be involved.

I saw a pair of hands going for Zak's arms. He dodged their grasp and backtracked.

'Quick,' he said. 'Down here. We'll lose them in China Town.'

The alley we ran down was narrow with high concrete walls. I had an uneasy feeling, but he seemed to know where he was going, and there were plenty of labyrinthine paths to dart into. They couldn't cover them all.

It was darker in here and rank smells of urine and unwashed bodies attacked our noses. Trees tried to grow where cracks in the walls allowed small puddles of water—mosquito infinity pools.

A thug who looked like one of the earlier ones in the street, blocked our way. I could hear Zak breathing harder. I was okay. I trusted he knew where he was going.

Blocked again. The triplets.

We had to backtrack this time and take another wider alley. Wider is good. I wanted out of the maze. At the end, I could see it merged from a bottleneck into a wider road with traffic and, to my mind, safety.

I heard shouting behind us and glanced back to see the triplets blocking out the light, following at a considerable pace. We had to make it to the end of the lane. The only way out was forward.

Another person, smaller but with more of a muscular shape, stepped into the alley at the far end. He was different. He wore a hoodie and had a young person's gait. He walked towards us, blocking our exit.

I still thought we had a chance. Fifty-fifty. Zak was thinking the same thing because he sped up. I followed. One of us would get past. It needed to be me.

When Zak was less than 3 metres away, he came to a skidding halt.

What? Idiot. I'd been through too much in the past few days to let him get in my way now. I pushed past Zak.

The man opened his jacket.

I didn't care. I was an attitude on a collision course. If it was a large knife or machete, he would be too late to swing it. I'd make it.

It wasn't a knife.

I saw why Zak had stopped, I tried to slam on the anchors and barely managed to stop in time. What I saw scared the hedgehogs out of me faster than the threat of a machete ever could.

18

The gangster held out his hands as if holding a delicate present.

I stared, transfixed at the expanding hood of the cobra in front of me.

'You look worried,' the gangster said. 'But then again, you should be.'

'You!' I shouted, recognizing the voice and noticing his face for the first time.

'Yes, me. You could have made this much easier on yourself. But you're a stubborn little bitch.'

'Who are you?' I demanded. 'And don't give anymore fake shit.'

'The name I'm using now is Abidin, but Zak here knows me well, don't you? Maybe not as well as his brother, but well enough.'

Zak moved forward, fists clenched.

The cobra rose, hissing, its hood wide and threatening.

I always back off from an angry animal. Humans are far less frightening—they're more predictable unless they're off-the-cliff crazy. I had one golden guideline: never mess with the crazies.

Abidin looked like he had one of those stupid speeches that people use when they watch too many gangster films on TV. My guess was right.

'This is a young one, and they're the best if they like you, but the worst if you piss them off. They empty all their venom in one go. The older ones hold a little back. I've cared for him since he was born, which means he's comfortable with me. But you, on the other hand,' he pointed with the snake, which hissed angrily. 'Well, he's not keen on foreigners.'

Well, at least he didn't add 'Would you like fries with that?'

Two can play this game, I thought and asked. 'How's your side? Does it hurt? Did you go squealing to daddy like the sad dog turd you are?'

That felt good but I did wonder if I should be talking like that to a guy with a snake in his hands. It was thin and slithered around his palm. I wondered if it was a substitute for something.

I saw him flinch. Nice. Round two to us. The cobra hissed again.

'There, there, Precious,' he said while caressing the snake's hood.

'Seriously?' I laughed in his face. 'You named it "Precious"? Anything else?' Maybe not the smartest thing to ask, but a vision of him doing rummage rugby in his trousers and calling it precious was too much. I put it down to weird mental relief from the danger we were facing.

He seemed to get what I was thinking and flushed. Anger or embarrassment. I'd been right.

'Yeah, good one. You should be a comedienne. And then again, look where we are. I'm still the favourite son of a powerful triad leader. And you? You're a messed-up kid. Oh, that's right, you were having *feelings* for me, weren't you? What a stupid little girl you are. You think I wanted anything more than the card from you? Total loser.'

He said the last word like it had too many vowels. Cliché putdown. He really should get a job in a fast-food place. 'Little girl' riled me a bit. 'Bitch' I can handle. I was becoming as pissed off as the snake.

Abidin turned to Zak. 'And here's a jerk who's about to lose his brother and his brother's land.'

'What do you mean?' Zak asked, clenching his fists.

'You don't have as much in common with him as you think. In fact, about the same as me. I don't know why you care as much as you do. I wouldn't. I don't.'

He laughed at his own pathetic joke. The snake hissed again. I noticed that it was getting more agitated with our verbal jousts. I also noticed that the rest of the lowlifes around us also seemed nervous about getting too close to the reptile.

Civilization and safety, although less than twenty metres away at the end of the alley, may well have been twenty miles away. The sheer concrete walls added to the feeling of being trapped. Behind us were the other sextuplets, each a differing shade of the same build: broad-shouldered, barrel-chested, potbellied and spindly-legged. And Malaysians say us foreigners look alike. Clearly, they haven't been down many dark alleys in China Town.

'Hand it over Zak,' Abidin said.

'I hid it in the plantation. You'll never find it.'

Wow, he's worse at lying than me. Base it on the truth, always. Lie detector test 101.

'Cut the crap. You're on your way to the safety deposit box in the bank now. Give. Me. The. Key.' He pronounced each word with menace. We watched Abidin push the cobra towards us and back again, this time it opened its mouth and two surprisingly large fangs from such a small mouth popped out from their recesses.

'Do you know the excruciating pain a cobra bite can deliver? No? Let me tell you; it's for you to look forward to.'

Fast-food guy with his slow-worm wasn't finished with his boring lecture. 'First, you'll think it's not too bad, then, within a minute, the swelling starts as the toxins make their way into your bloodstream. The fun part starts when the blisters start forming and the skin turns black and necrosis sets in. I'm told the pain is like putting your hand in an open fire and watching it burn.'

He paused for effect.

I wondered if he was going to ask if we wanted tomato or chili sauce. *My aunt's personality is rubbing off on me.*

'For the last time, where is it?'

'I don't have it.' Zak held up his arms while one of the thugs went through his pockets.

One of the other graduates from the school of waste disposal said something to the effect that he couldn't find it. *School for the gifted? I think not.*

'Beat him.'

A fist slammed into Zak's gut. He doubled over, gasping for breath. Then a hard right hand to the side of his face dropped him like a sack of potatoes. Blood dripped from his nose. Rough hands picked him up and slammed him against the wall.

Things were getting serious. Even my weird sense of humour scurried for cover.

Abidin and his snake moved closer to Zak. 'You think we won't kill you, don't you? Well, think what we did to your brother. You are nothing to us.' As if to prove his point, he stepped back and gave a signal to two of his gang members to lay into Zak; their hands smashing into his ribs and face, until he dropped again. Then they went in with their feet.

I tried to help but two sets of large hands held each of my shoulders and pinned me to the wall. The heavy stench of stale cigarettes, alcohol, and unwashed body odour of the Orks holding me almost made me gag.

The deed was still in the bank. If they let us go, we could maybe get to the bank before them. To do that, I needed Zak alive.

'STOP! Stop. I have it.'

The blows stopped. Abidin's eyes moved from Zak to me.

'Of course, I should have known he would give it to you. You know we would have killed him and the police wouldn't have cared. You also know we will kill you if you're lying. You're nothing more than an inconvenience. The police only care if it's in the news.'

I decided we were not going to die in a rat-infested alley. *Fight another day; don't play the hero.*

I looked at Zak, who was coming to. His face was covered in blood and already swelling. His pleading eyes caught mine. He mouthed the word 'No' and clasped his hands in front of his chest.

The thug by my right asked Abidin something in Malay and then looked straight at me, daring me to say anything. I guessed I was about to be searched, which churned fear into anger.

Abidin gave a half-smile. 'Make it rough.'

'How you treat all your girlfriends then?' I asked. 'Must cost you a fortune.'

One of the Orks crouched down until his face was at my waist. His calloused hands grasped my right ankle and rode up. The further he got, the more he grinned a cruel, lascivious smile.

I tensed before I felt a click in my head. My synapses crashed.

I never remember exactly what goes on when it happens, but I saw my arms pulling free and my fists thrashing at his face, connecting with both.

The Ork staggered back and I saw a dribble of blood from his swollen lip. Then he pushed his face back up into mine.

'You want rough, *ah*?'

The next thing I heard was a cracking sound as a fist slammed into my cheekbone. My head spun, and a high-pitched whistle filled my ears. Initially, my face went numb. Then my legs buckled. Shit-storm girl had left the house and taken all the facial anaesthetic with her. I felt the vibration of myself groaning.

'Hold her,' the Ork said while he lined himself up for another crack.

My arms were held and I was dragged back up from the alley. I was immobile. There was nothing I could do. I watched another fist steam towards me.

'The key, idiots!' Abidin shouted.

The fist never landed.

He brought the cobra within striking distance of my face. 'Where's the key?'

'Pocket,' was all I could get out. I felt my skirt being pulled down as a large, blood-stained hand tried to force its way into the tight space of the inner pocket.

The hand stopped and then pulled away. He held up the grey rectangular card.

Zak got to his feet and tried to reach out but was pushed back against the wall like a rag doll. I could relate.

The Ork with the key stared at it, wondering how it worked. I guess he'd never stayed in a hotel. No surprise there.

I slumped against the wall, now forgotten for a moment.

I pulled my skirt back up, which drew the attention of the Ork. He wanted to do a more comprehensive search.

My face was throbbing royally, but I was gradually getting it together. The whistling had lessened. He put his hand back inside my skirt, but I got his eyes to focus on mine.

'I'm back.'

I kicked as hard as I could between his legs, grabbed the plastic card, and threw it as high as possible into the air. And then I kicked at his cupped hands even harder. All the other Orks looked up, with hands extended to catch the card.

With a strength and speed I didn't think I had left, I grabbed Zak's arm and pulled him towards Abidin and the twitchy cobra. With the momentum, I got into my Aikido zone and sidestepped the cobra's strike. I pushed through, turning as I did, forcing Abidin to spin towards the wall, together with his 'Precious'.

We raced towards the street at end of the alley. Less than ten metres.

I heard the shouts of the Orks behind us.

Seven metres. We were going to make it.

Five metres. I pushed Zak ahead as the alley narrowed into the bottleneck.

Three metres. The Orks were closer but we were almost free. A few more steps.

Two metres. Zak was at the end of the alley. I felt a hand slap down on my shoulder, slowing me.

One metre. The powerful arm was winning.

I turned my head to the filthy hand on my shoulder and bit down as hard as I could. A spurt of warm liquid filled my mouth, and I spat out a lump of skin and tissue. A piercing scream echoed through the alley.

Zak pulled me free and into the crowded street. Shoppers stared briefly and then went about their business. In this part of town, they had seen it all before.

Back in the alley, Abidin looked down at the two marks on the hand he had used to protect the snake from being crushed against the wall.

19

'What have you done?' Zak asked again. I leaned across the solid kitchen table to grab another tissue which I moistened with antiseptic and then dabbed the cut above his eyebrow. The rest of the swelling had started to subside.

'I saved us, that's what. You should be grateful. Now hold still. Uncle,' I called. 'I think this cut might need stitches."

Donald Junkett marched into the kitchen with a medical kit last seen on the Antiques Roadshow and had another look at Zak's injuries. 'What's wrong with him? Nothing more than a flesh wound. I'll get some leeches. Carry on.' He gave me that 'I don't know what the fuss is about' look and marched out towards the garden.

Margaret poked her head around the corner looking anxious.

'How about a nice cup of tea, Aunty?' I suggested.

'Cup of tea?' Margaret repeated as if she would never have thought of it. 'Oh, what a good idea. Yes, I'll put the kettle on. You seem almost cheery about the events Zola, dear. Are you quite well? You may still be concussed.'

She might be right. I was feeling good about the way things turned out. Shit-storm girl did good for once. 'I'm fine,' I replied. 'A bit dizzy still, yes, but okay considering. Besides, we still have this.'

I reached into my blood-stained skirt pocket and pulled out a blue-grey plastic card. I gave my best 'I've saved the day, but that's just me' look at Zak.

'We still have the real key. The other one they took was the fake. It's not over yet.'

Zak looked as though he was hearing things.

'What? Fantastic. I thought . . . Why didn't you tell me? How long you knew they took the wrong one?' Zak asked in broken English, frowning but looking relieved at the same time.

'I did, on the train, but you were out of it and mumbling weird things.'

I was beginning to think that he was an okay dude compared to my initial thoughts. Sometimes you've got to give people time to wash away the stupid.

Donald returned. 'Couldn't find any leeches. It got me thinking though. We've entered the eye of the storm now. We can expect more trouble, not less. Do you think there's any correlation between the *Ah Long* wanting to get his hands on your land and the landgrab going on with this plantation?'

'They didn't mention anything about us,' I offered. Nevertheless, he was probably right. The coincidence was there.

'Any more news?' Zak asked Donald.

'Ah, yes. Well, I'm up the proverbial creek without a paddle. I need to transport what bushels of palm nuts I have left to the main refinery in this area. Then they will send the report of the amount to the courts by Wednesday where I will have to beg for their mercy, of which I'll find none, I'm sure. There's no way I can produce enough palm oil to satisfy their regulations. Not even if it were running at full steam. The way things are, they'll take my land faster than a ferret's fart, and they're not going to give up. These government officials are like rabid dogs; once they get their teeth into something, they rarely let go until they get what they want.'

Donald removed a timeworn handkerchief, which was little more than a white rag, from his frayed trouser pocket and blew his nose.

'And now the evil bastards have stolen a quarter of my crop. And as sure as night follows day, these two events are related. As an old white farmer, I knew I was going to get targeted eventually. I thought I might be able to hang on until I retired and sold the place. Now, I'm afraid, I feel like an old pet at a vivisectionist's gathering.'

Screwed by the system? Welcome to my world. At some stage I knew I had to get my head around the idea that my family was splitting. Take it one decision at a time. I thought about the Hamsters and the affection they had for each other. As crazy as a contortion of unconventionality, they made it work with heartfelt feelings. I sensed the genuine love and concern. The little things—they got the little things right. I felt the urge to give them both a hug.

I don't use the 'L' word often: it's been reduced to a sad cliché like 'nice' or 'like'. Yet, I started doing what I should never do and began wishing my Mum and Dad were more like the Hamsters. I know it's a rabbit hole, comparing. It's like a lot of stuff we shouldn't do. '*Feels good at the time though, right?*' I told myself. I needed that feeling now.

You show emotion and people screw you.

Yet, the Hamsters appreciated each other with such love that they worried individually to ensure the other didn't have to.

I loved them. I loved them to bits.

I had a brain fart. All this emotional stuff got me thinking.

I said, 'I think there might be an answer. It's a stop-gap solution, but I think we can make it work.'

I could sense a beacon of hope fluttering around in Donald's mind like a murmuration of starlings.

'Can't you borrow or buy extra bushels and say they're yours?'

'It would be illegal. Whoever I borrowed from would be taking a huge risk for nothing and I don't have that kind of spare cash to pay.'

'You could pay them back with a little bit extra when you get paid.'

'Zola, my dear, I'd be prepared to risk it, but the danger for the other farmer is too much to ask.'

'Not from a friend.' *God, how much of a hint did I need to make?*

Zak finally got it. 'You can have my harvest, Uncle Donald.'

'Are you sure, my boy?' Donald asked. 'The risks are not small. And even then, there's no guarantee that there will be enough bushels to satisfy those idiots at the Land Office.'

'I don't know either, but at least we can try.'

'What about your land and the *Ah Long*?' Donald asked.

Before Zak could answer, I said, 'One dragon at a time.'

'Absolutely,' Donald agreed.

Yes. Shit-storm girl does it again. *I'm on a roll.*

I sensed a fresh pot of tea was about to materialize.

20

I woke up to bright sunlight streaming through the faded curtains, a cup of tea, and a puzzled look on Margaret's face.

'Time to get up, Zola. The day will wait for no-one, you know. And there's much to be done. My, I would have thought you could have put on some clean clothes though. Didn't you shower last night?'

Only then did I realize that I must have slept on top of the bed in yesterday's clothes. I'd slept very well. I should have wallowed in the joy because afterwards I'm usually ready for anything, but this morning my whole body felt like one giant lead weight that would be quite happy to lay back for another ten minutes or ten days. I slouched my way to the shower and freshened up.

With a clean orange T and loose, black sports shorts, I sauntered outside to the front deck where Zak and Donald were finalizing things.

Donald moved a toy gun and a container of soft crystal jelly bullets he used to get the geckos off the walls to one side to make space for my fresh tea and toast.

'Busy few days ahead people,' he advised in stentorian army-officer tones. 'Zola, would you be a dear and give your aunt Margaret a hand in town with the shopping this morning? Zak and I will get to work here and we'll see you when you get back.'

Excellent. Now I could get to ask around about Daniel. I also wanted to question Lurch in the hardware store. He was up to something. Then there was Maya. *Why do I get a whole-body tingle whenever I think about her?*

Serendah is a quiet town with one main road and a lot of traffic going through it. But get on to one of the small shop-access roads which run parallel, and you could be forgiven for thinking that you were in a different world. It's a quiet, laid-back town, where most people know each other and strangers are treated with suspicion.

As we neared the town, with Margaret looking for a tree with some shade to park the car under, her eyebrows rose as if a new idea had just occurred to her. 'Zola dear, how about we treat ourselves at the hair salon? Your hair could certainly do with fixing and it's been way too long since my last visit. What do you say?'

'You've been planning this all along, haven't you?'

Margaret blinked furiously and stuttered. 'Well, I may have given it some thought when I was brushing Rosmah this morning.'

My hair took twenty minutes, but it looked three hours' better. 'Short enough to allow my neck to breathe' were my instructions.

Hair isn't a big thing for me. It's there and is what it is. It fell into the same place, no matter what I did with it. I figured it was something to do with my Kenyan side. The stylist had done well. I wondered if it would last the day.

As if reading my mind, Aunty said, 'Zola, my perm is going to take quite a while, and it's so much more comfortable here than doing it with my head in the oven at home. Why don't you head back to the café to do your internet thingy. I'll meet you there when I'm done.'

I wasn't even phased by this new revelation of madness. 'Well, if you're sure you don't mind.' I was out of the door before she could think about replying.

I was about to cross the street to the SGR Café, with a list of 'To Do' stuff on the internet, when I heard a soft voice.

'I've been waiting for you. I could sense you were coming.'

I looked around towards a tattoo parlour in one of the run-down shop-lots—*soooo tempting*—but saw no-one. Was my ship of sanity sinking into a sea of madness?

'I'm over here. You're looking straight at me. Your hair looks nice.'

My eyes refocussed to see Maya standing right in front of me. How come I hadn't seen her before? 'Oh, hi. What's up? I was just going over to your café.'

'Let's go then. But let me show you around. I know a quiet corner where the flowers bloom and their scent is amazing. Follow me.'

Her voice had me at 'Let's go', the rest was inner ear waffles with chocolate ice-cream. I had loads of questions to ask, but they seemed irrelevant now. I felt so relaxed. Everything she said fired my senses. I was getting the scent of the flowering trees, the sound of a yellow Oriel calling to its mate, and the roasted coffee aroma from the café.

I couldn't even remember crossing the road. And I didn't care. All the while there was a silky vibration in the air from her voice. I didn't understand what she was saying, but it was intoxicating. *She* was intoxicating.

We walked through the café filled with morning coffee patrons, half of whom were scruffy in their tatty Ts and shorts. The other half were just scruffy. They took no notice of us walking around to the back.

We entered a small enclave with refurbished wooden shelves and large plastic boxes full of restaurant stuff on them. We then went through a heavy wooden door half off its hinges and entered the empty house next door. Most of the roof was missing and all manner of greenery proliferated the floors and the walls. Bright yellow flowers bloomed where the sun reached through. Their heavy fragrance filled the air. To their left was a small stone table with a chrome scalpel and tongs resting on it. Maya picked them up and asked me to follow her along the path leading into the forest at the back.

I drank in another glass of something she said.

'Come.'

I followed like a newborn kitten. I couldn't tell how far we went, but the undergrowth was clearer and the trees were tall and majestic, their bright green canopies filtering the light so that it was much darker and cooler than before.

Maya suddenly stopped, turned to face me and her eyes gazed into mine. She said, 'I've been waiting for you.'

She reached out and touched my hand, 'Enjoy the scent of the forest. I need your heart.'

I heard all the words clearly. They all seemed so normal, so perfect. Of course, she wanted my heart. *Why not?*

I breathed in the whirling fragrances, Maya's scent mixing with the other perfumes. She talked in a strange language using a soft, lilting intonation. I'd heard it somewhere before, but couldn't place it. It could have been Gaelic, but how would she know that language? The sound was irresistible. I felt an overwhelming sense of belonging and value. They were feelings I hadn't felt for what seemed like an eternity. It was the same unconditional love my parents had once shown.

Maya held out both arms. 'Come closer.'

I was floating. Her grip was soft but firm. A frisson of electricity went through my arms. With an urge I found impossible to resist, I inched closer. I couldn't feel my legs moving. All my emotional scars were sealing closed and healing. Bad memories evaporated. No regrets. Nothing other than the now of things. I put my arms around her. I was in a place I never wanted to leave. She was perfect. I felt perfect.

Maya unwrapped herself from me. 'I need your heart. Do you give it willingly?'

I smiled. I wanted to sleep for a thousand years. 'It's yours.'

She locked eyes with me. I sensed she was looking deep into my soul. Her eyes were changing. The tiny specks of gold in the rich hazel were growing. And then it stopped.

I too felt something happening, as if I was being pulled violently from a dream state into a shattering, altered reality.

I couldn't remember getting to where I was in the forest. Maya was still staring, but now with a confused and sorrowful expression.

She said, 'I saw your soul. Your heart is fractured. You are broken. I cannot eat your heart. It would poison me.'

Great. No heart eating today.

Now where was I? Should I stay on this path or take the bypass? Instead, I said, 'Where am I? Where's the café?'

She ignored my questions; she does that a lot. She said, 'I saw the pain living there.'

'Yeah, well, life hasn't exactly been good recently.' I don't know why I said what I did, but it felt right.

'You are the fawn with a broken limb that even a ruthless hunter would want to nurture back to health. There is goodness in you.'

Hmm. I'd like to keep it there.

This is getting beyond weird. Where the hell am I?

Before I could react, Maya had wrapped her arms around me and all felt good with the world again, and this time I was fully conscious, or I thought I was. I needed to get my head around what was going on.

I broke off the hug and tried to fathom out who this girl was and where I was. Maya stood there looking disarmingly innocent. She was slim, with toned arms. Her simple stretch jeans were filled with athletic legs, and her shirt had a boyish look to it. It matched her high cheekbones, delicate nose and other small elfin features. She looked . . . good.

'You are confused,' Maya said. 'Hold me again.'

Part of me was confused, it was true. Another part urged me forward. Last time felt good and, since I'm a fully paid-up, card-carrying hedonist, I gave her another hug. It was even better; lots of little zings happening.

She started to pull away, and I tensed.

'Trust me,' she said. Her breathy voice was like double cream rolling over a chocolate mousse. How can you not trust that?'

She kissed me on the lips.

Here's the thing. I should've, could've, would've backed away, but I liked it. I mean I really liked it. She smelled so good. Her kiss was like the taste of a chilled drink on a warm afternoon after a run; one sip would never be enough.

No boy had ever made me feel this zingy. Their kisses were more like a perfunctory hello before they got more physical. This was more meaningful. We kissed again. I took her upper lip between mine and gently squeezed the soft, delicate hairs under her nose. A tingle of perfect happiness vibrated from my mouth to the base of my spine. I pulled Maya closer and turned my head slightly to move my mouth over hers. The tips of our tongues touched fleetingly. It felt like a warm charge of energy passing through my core. I wanted it to last forever.

Time evaporated. We let our lips glide away.

I struggled to get any words out and when I did, it was a feeble, 'This is not who I am.'

'Then, who are you?'

It was a tough question, but I couldn't lie to her if my life depended on it.

'I'm not so sure anymore. But I do know it felt right. I thought I would resist, but instead it was like a complete release of pent-up frustration. What about you?'

Maya looked pensive. 'I have done that only once before. This was much . . . tastier.'

'That is one weird way of describing it. You are more unusual, special, than anyone I've met before. And strange. And . . . nice.'

Ugh 'nice' is that the best you can do? That most insincere of words.

'And extraordinary.'

Better.

Maya moved away a little and I wondered if I'd gone a bit overboard with the complements.

'I can mend you, if you want.'

'I didn't think I needed it.'

She added, 'Many of you are broken. The system, parents, even friends tear small slices of hope away from you.'

'I don't know how I feel right now,' I said, 'but I know I wanted—no, I needed to do that.'

Maya reached out for my hands. 'There's no need to justify who you are. I learnt that a long time ago. I want to share my story with you. It is a fantastical one. You won't believe it, at first, but I will show you who we are. But I wonder, will you hate me after that?'

'Right now, I feel that you could say anything and I could accept it. I'm floating and I want to share everything with you too. I don't know what this is, but I know I don't want it to end.'

'Me too. Hold me again, and I will share with you something about my past I've never shared before.'

Maya inclined her head slightly and leaned forward to whisper in my ear. 'We are different from other hu— people. I am part of the Indra. There's a lot of sadness to our story. It will be a lot for you to take in.'

'I'm ready, honest.'

She took a step back and wore a more serious expression. 'You may think you are. Let me tell you this and see how you feel after. We need to eat fresh organs to keep our age the same.'

Maya saw my expression of surprise and gave a small chuckle. 'We eat berries, nuts and other things too. But we must be careful.

The wrong food can kill us. When we are young, we crave dishes like liver and bacon, cooked, until we are weaned. Then we desire rare, or what we call bluemeat. If we want to live longer, we need to eat fresh organs. We become younger or older depending on the age of the meat. Human organs are the best, but most of us survive on animal organs. They're a poor substitute and sometimes cause illness. It is the chemicals in the foodstuffs which damage us.'

'Wow. That's a great story. I mean I want to believe you, I do, but then that's some weird, different planet kind of stuff. But whatever you say, there's something about you I don't want to give up.'

'Then I promise to tell you everything. And I will show you how to understand the jungle and its gifts. For now, let me give you something to help you understand us.'

Maya held me again and kissed my lower lip. Her top teeth gently held on to the skin. Other teeth pushed harder like they were independent of the rest. It was weird, a little painful, but strangely zingy, like a loose tooth which needs to come out or the squeezing out of a thorn from the middle of an itchy mosquito bite.

'There, a present. It must be done with love. The chemicals are different.'

I was a bit lost for words. My presents usually came wrapped. To be honest, if they were from my parents, they were often half-wrapped and a day late. This was way better.

'You'll notice a change soon.'

All I could manage was, 'Sure.' I mean, what else do you say to that?

A short while later we were sitting side by side, watching the weird and the wonderful on TikTok and sharing stories. We were being normal, if you could call a human and an elfin Indra sitting together normal. Everything felt right with the world. I looked across at Maya's face; our noses almost touching. I took in every line and curve; the rich hazel of her eyes with the golden specks in them; the curl of her obsidian lashes; and I took in her skin's light honeysuckle scent.

'Has anyone told you that you look a bit like the lead singer of the Sugarcubes, Björk? It's a band my dad likes."

'What is a Björk?'

'Good question.' I played 'Birthday' on Spotify.

'She screams so beautifully. She sounds like one of us, but she is white. She is not like me.'

My phone buzzed like a relentless bee.

'It's my aunty. Look, I have to go, but I need to see you again soon. Sooner than soon.'

'I know. There's much I want to share with you, and I have to do it a little bit at a time so that you might accept me. I want to repair you.'

We held each other again. It felt right; our chins fitting perfectly on each other's shoulders.

'You can tell me anything and I don't think I'll care how bad it is.' I leaned forward for a goodbye kiss. I closed my eyes for the extra-sensory 'mmm' feeling and got the magnetic frisson of Maya's lips about to touch mine. There was the gentlest of touches, like the hairs on a fine art brush moving across my lips. When I opened my eyes, Maya had vanished.

I was alone in the jungle. For the first time I heard the whining of insects, the trilling of birds, and felt a wave of oppressive humidity.

Did I just dream that? *What a trip.*

I followed the main path and hoped I was heading in the right direction. The trees became fewer, the undergrowth rougher.

I came out at the back of the café and looked for Maya. She was nowhere to be seen, so I walked towards the hair salon, still floating. My mind was still high on what had, or I thought had, taken place. It felt like nothing else mattered now I had a best friend with unexplored benefits.

Wait. Is that what I want? I like boys. Some of them. One or two. But that was so good. A bit eww about eating organs, she could have used a metaphor of dreams or emotions. Seriously, what's wrong with people these days?

Margaret was waiting by the entrance to the hair salon. 'Ah, there you are Zola. My, your eyes look a little red. I hope there's no bad news.'

'No, I've just been sharing TikTok with a new friend.'

'That's all well and good, but I don't want any more strays in the house. It's bad enough with Rosmah and Donald.'

'What? No, it's . . . a software app. Never mind.'

'Oh, is that what you call it these days. You should have just said you need more lingerie, dear. I'd rather you didn't go sharing it with other people. Anyway, let's hurry, there's a special offer on lady's fingers at the market. They go so well with my vegetarian mutton curry.'

21

'What a day it was yesterday.' I said, stretching my back. I'd had another excellent night's sleep and felt great, no, better than that: strong. I put on a pair of black jeans and a grey gym top; it was slightly cooler this morning with thick cloud cover.

Yesterday afternoon I'd helped Donald and two of his farmhands load what was left of the cut bushels into a hire truck. The other workers went with Zak to his plantation to collect there.

They looked like they weighed a ton, and it took both farmhands to lift anything other than a small- to medium-sized load. Since Donald couldn't stand well, let alone lift anything, they gave me a pitchfork and pointed at a small mass of palm nuts, waiting for a good laugh when I failed. Never underestimate me.

The old wooden pitchfork felt as light as a feather in my hands and I wondered if it would snap. It didn't, and I hurled the palm bushel way over the truck and into the opposite plantation.

The workers stood there slack-jawed, but I put on my 'everyday me' look. It wasn't a fluke either. I found I could lift large bushels on my own and the workers had difficulty keeping up. Either I had natural talent for plantation work, or recent traumatic events had coalesced into extra strength, or it was to do with Maya's enigmatic 'You'll notice a change soon' bite. I wanted to put it down to the tension of recent events, but I couldn't get Maya's words out of my mind. The romantic me rarely surfaces, but she would have wanted to believe Maya.

Uncle Donald was also amazed, but he too played it cool and put it down to good genes. 'My side of the family, naturally,' he'd said to the other labourers.

Later, I sat with Uncle Donald on the front deck while Margaret supervised the breakfast.

'I didn't know farming was that labour intensive out here. Aren't there machines that could do the job more efficiently?'

'There are, my dear,' he replied, 'but the small size of the plantations and the cheap cost of labour mean you won't get a return on the investment in machinery for years to come. And most of us can't wait that long.'

'But will you support me when I write that the destruction of the rainforests is not worth it? What would it take for farmers to let the rainforest grow back?'

'It's not as simple as money, Zola. I get about five times the oil from my plantation than I would if I were planting soy or coconut. I'd get more, but the topsoil here is thinner than most other areas.'

'Yes, but . . .' I blurted. Then I remembered what my mum taught me about other people using 'Yes, but . . .' at the beginning of a sentence—it showed they were not listening to the other person.

I continued, 'The destruction of the forest means the destruction of the wildlife habitat for orangutans, tigers, Asian elephants and rhinos.'

Uncle Donald put his hand to his chin. 'I understand, I do, but the crops that people would cultivate to get the same amount of revenue would result in even greater deforestation, to say nothing of the loss of employment for much of the local community.'

'Employ them in environmental projects like reforestation, eco-parks and related jobs, like . . . solar energy.'

'Zola, that takes a lot of investment and years to happen and even longer for revenue to be generated.'

I also knew that when adults used your name at the beginning of a sentence, they were getting frustrated.

'Well, do it step by step, then. Make a start. Stop the destruction and start replanting.' I could feel myself digging in. I was entering the Greta Zone, and it was not a good time for a shit-storm. But like a rough piece of skin at the side of a nail, I couldn't leave it alone. I said, 'You're taking the farmer's side because that's what you do, and you don't mind destroying our world because you're old and it's too late for you to do anything else. But we're going to inherit this heated up world and—'

'I'm trying,' Donald said with his palms open. I guessed he wasn't used to this kind of argument. And I felt more powerful than ever. *Self-destruction guaranteed.*

I added, 'But you're not trying hard enough. None of your generation is. The glaciers are melting and it's affecting freshwater availability and creating deserts.'

I was working myself up into a shit-storm zone. Why was I getting angry with him suddenly? He was a nice old hamster, but I couldn't stop myself and my rant continued.

'And there're more greenhouse gasses because of the oil processing. Forests save more CO_2 than palm, and you ruin the land—'

'I agree . . .'

'Then you agree that the world is much better off without palm oil.'

'No, it's not, Zola. But I do agree that things must change.'

'You do?'

'I do. Zak's plantation is more eco-friendly. He cultivates other crops between the palm which rejuvenates the soil and encourages a greater diversity of wildlife. Yes, the oil yield is lower, but he gets a longer life from the palm. And whatever you say, it's better than factories and housing developments. I agree that we have to work *with* ecologists, not fight each other. It will be too late for my plantation if they take the land away, but I was planning to follow his lead before trouble came . . .'

I wore my 'guilty' look.

'. . . with the landgrab.'

Phew. For a moment I thought it was me he was talking about.

I sat there trying to process where my outburst had come from and what my uncle had said. My next Instagram posting would stir the reptilian brains of a lot of followers.

I went over to Donald and planted a thank-you kiss on his forehead. I saw wrinkled creases of happiness on his face. He looked a little embarrassed with the show of emotion.

He picked up a stick which had found its way on to the wooden flooring during the night and threw it for Rosmah to fetch. 'Fetch, Rosmah, there's a good girl.' Rosmah looked up at the stick flying through the air and then at her master. She then slowly twisted herself on the worn outdoor foot mat, doubled her snout over and began to clean herself.

'Oh Rosmah, you filthy mutt from Mordor. Can't you do that elsewhere? I'm about to have me breakfast, don't you know.'

'Breakfast will be ready in a minute, dear,' Margaret called from the kitchen. 'You'll have to hang on till then.'

'Not you, my little jar of pickles. I was talking to the dog.'

'Oh, we're not having dog, dear, it's sausages this morning.'

Uncle Donald chortled and said to no-one in particular, 'God's teeth and tarantulas. What did I marry?'

I smothered a smile.

Donald asked, 'What's your plan, Zola? Thanks to you, all our bushels are collected. Nothing more we can do until we get the results from the processing plant, which we won't get to hear about until we arrive at court. We won't know if we've done enough until then. You could go over to Zak's and help there.'

'I'm going into Serendah later. I want to see if I can find out anything more on who's behind the theft and the landgrab.'

My mind went to Maya. 'And to see a friend.'

'Marvellous. Onwards and forwards, my dear.' He paused for a moment. 'Look, er, Zola, could you pick me up something from the pharmacy there? Been having a few personal problems recently.

I froze. The way he was asking caused my mind to jump. Don't ask me to get you any 'V'. *Eww.*

'It's for my Formula One.'

'Huh?'

'Formula One, Zola. I'm sounding like a race car, but not going anywhere.'

Sounding like a crazy hamster, more like.

'Huh?' I took a sip of tea.

As if he were about to tell me the secret of the universe, he leaned forward. 'Laxative. I need a decongestant.'

I snorted tea through my nose. It was painful but helped me to try and keep a serious face.

'If I tell my Margaret, she'll start forcing traditional Chinese medicine on me, and the teas taste like a cross between monkey's penis and tree bark.'

I wondered how he came to that conclusion but filed it in the mental dossier on crazy hamster and said, 'Yes, Uncle, of course. No problem.'

'Excellent. Zola. You're shaking, my dear. Are you entirely sure?'

A squeaky 'Yes' was all I could manage.

'Marvellous. Onwards and forwards then. See you at dinner. Don't forget about your promise to Zak about Monday. And please be careful this time, or I'll get it in the neck from you know who.'

Later that morning, I parked Rachel outside the SGR Café under the shade of a huge rain tree among several other badly aging bikes. She blended in perfectly.

First stop, because I didn't want to forget, was the pharmacy for Donald's 'Formula One' medicine, which consisted of a box of extra-strength chocolate laxatives. They looked yummy.

Inside SGR were a group of what had been previously described to me as *Mat Rempit*, or Rat Armpit, as I decided to call them, or in English, motorcycle gang members. I had been advised to stay clear if I ever saw them. They looked even younger than me and I doubted they could scare a two-year-old with a burst balloon. I ignored their leering and sat at the same outside table as before. Ms Ann brought a menu. She had a smile and a spring in her step. Pay day?

She asked, 'No-one join you today? No friends?'

She was really bubbling today.

I ordered a coffee and a chicken ham and tomato croissant—the place was *halal*, which meant that no pork was allowed. They sold beer. *Got to keep the local uncles happy.*

I looked around for Maya but couldn't see her. I missed her company.

The local wannabees looked at me then made rude gestures to each other. Jerks. Won't it ever get old? I gave them my best 'go screw yourself' look. Then I wondered if they'd seen the other kid, Daniel or Spaniel or whatever his name was.

My sandwich arrived with the meat looking suitably frightened while the tomato had wrinkles. I didn't care. It got walloped in an instant. My appetite was raging. Must be the heavy lifting yesterday. The coffee was great; the right amount of sourness balanced with the roastiness. It too got walloped.

The puberty pups were now arm wrestling each other and looking over. It was only a matter of time before one of them plucked enough courage to invade my privacy. I buried my head in my phone.

'You speak Malay?' their leader asked. I assumed he was the leader from the fact that he was the biggest and had the courage to call out.

I replied, 'No, sorry,' No point in antagonizing them. Besides, they might have useful information.

I asked, 'Have you seen another foreigner, a tourist guy about my height, dark hair, pasty white?' I almost added 'has long ears, mournful face and answers to "Spaniel"'. 'His name's Daniel.'

'Uh?'

I thought I could hear the cogs moving in his brain.

'Maybe. Why, ah?'

The boss was a big kid. Heavy. If the café was a gym, I'd say good core strength, but it wasn't, and a moment ago he'd polished off an ice-cream with condensed milk. His arms looked powerful.

'He's a friend. I was wondering if he'd passed by here.'

'My bike club is "Blood Rockers".'

Strange, I would have guessed 'The Tinkling Tappets'. I guess he thought he could try and make himself sound scarier.

He added, 'Daniel, yeah.' He nodded as if he was convincing himself. 'We make business together.'

'Really? Not a baby then? *Quelle* surprise.' Irony, sarcasm, and sexy foreign words were from my Irish side.

That didn't go down too well. His other clubettes giggled, which seemed to piss him off. Oops, my bad. I did want to find out what kind of deal they had done though.

I asked nicely, 'What business did you do?'

He gestured around at the empty plates and glasses on his table. 'You pay, lah, or you can wrestle?' He flexed his bicep and I almost laughed out loud. Perhaps not all Neanderthals had evolved.

Given the disparity in sizes and strengths, it was a stupid bet that no one in their right mind would take.

'Okay.' I looked around for a *rungu.*

I don't know what I was thinking, but I had a feeling he knew about my uncle's stolen crop. I hoped that my bushel throwing arms were still in top form. They looked pathetically thin compared to the lardon lad. Maybe he'd take pity if I was nice enough and a gracious loser.

He gave me a look which was either 'I'm a hard dude' or 'I need the loo'.

I went over and smelt the air warily. 'Let's get this over with,' I said to more giggles from the playground.

His hand was large, wet, and squidgy. It swamped mine. I had to grab his fingers rather than his palm just so I could get a grip. I almost ewwed out loud, but I wanted info and that was not the best way to get it.

We squared off and one of the others, who probably had an IQ of a swimming pool, counted 'Three, Two, One, Go!'

There was a cheer from his petting zoo and I expected my hand to get slammed down, but instead he squeezed harder. The idiot was trying to hurt me. By the look of his expression, he was putting everything he had into it. *Mjinga.*

I raised an eyebrow. *I'd make a great 007.*

Boy Blunder seemed upset that his attempts weren't working. I could feel a twinge of pain but nothing more. He was sweating like a spit roast.

I said, 'A deal is a deal. What business did you do with Daniel?'

'Not win yet,' was the reply. He was breathing heavily—a combination of stale cheese and monkey poo. Hadn't he ever heard of flossing?

He changed tactics and tried to slam my hand down, but I held him there since my arms were longer and had more leverage. I tried a little crushing of my own.

I watched the expression on his face switch from evil to anger to fear to panic. 'Tell me now,' I demanded. I felt his fingers and then his knuckles touch, then grind together.

His motorcycle boyfriends could see that their game was not going the way it was supposed to, and one of them grabbed my arm to pull me away. Another made a swing at me. I grabbed his fist with my other hand and twisted it. I was loving my Aikido training. I wondered if his tiny balls were growing from inside his palm since that's what he sounded like. Even *my* yelp was more manly than his was. It had the desired effect since the rest of his playmates left me alone.

'Let go or I do this.' I squeezed harder.

They all heard the crack as boy blunder's knuckles scrunched together. *Oops*. My bad.

I was amazed at my own strength. I hadn't meant to do that. Oh, well. It sounded worse than it probably was, but the effect was worth it. I eased up but held on.

'You were saying?'

'He pay big money. He no smart.' He paused while he thought about what he'd just said. Then he added, 'Take *buah sawit* near here.'

'Take what? Palm oil?'

'Yeah.' He tried peeling my fingers away with his other hand.

Result! 'When?'

'Two days. Crazy *Matsalleh* farmer.' He looked at me and thought about who I might be. You could almost watch the thought bounce around a mental pinball machine before finally dropping into the slot. He made the connection. 'Please, please. I need money. Family no money. No work.'

I let go but grabbed his arm. He clutched his wrist in agony.

'Give the palm oil back.'

'Cannot. My boss take to process.' He rubbed the blood back into his fingers.

I played with my chin a bit. Thinking. If there was no possibility of reversing the problem, what to do?

'Who's your boss?' I asked.

'Rhammar.'

'Where can I find Rhammar and Daniel?'

Spit Roast looked at me, drenched in sweat. 'I need doctor,' he bleated.

'Where?' I snarled.

'Behind you.'

22

I whirled around to see Daniel standing there, grinning but with his tongue moving behind his lips like he was checking for spinach between his teeth. His nose looked larger than before, and he was sunburned. A parsnip sticking out of a rice pudding which had been left in the oven for too long.

He wore large khaki shorts that emphasized his matchstick legs and an Arsenal football shirt. Great combination for an open-air prison here. Lots of local MU and Liverpool fans.

'You!' I snarled. 'You need to replace those bushels or I will report you for stealing them. I have witnesses.' I pointed to the fast-disappearing Tinkling Tappets MC. 'I'm sure you'll make a lot of friends in a Malaysian prison.'

He looked a lot more composed than I thought he would, given that we could now get a lawyer and subpoena the motorcycle clubettes to testify.

'You can try. It won't make any difference. Development will start on your land within the year and there's nothing you can do to stop it. Your farm will show it's not running efficiently and will be taken away.'

Now was not the time to mention about collecting Zak's palm oil bushels too. Besides, we still didn't know if it would be enough to satisfy the courts. Living on hope, information was key, and I wondered how much I could get out of him. I stood up and walked towards him, my eyes glued to his. 'You're putting two old people who haven't done anything wrong on the streets. They'll be left with next to nothing. How can you do that and sleep well?'

He was thinking about what I'd said as if it were the first time he was considering it. 'Progress. The world is screwed. I'm making sure I get a slice of the money before it all goes. I'm sorry for your . . . guardians, but if my father and I didn't do it, someone else would. Your land is classified as commercial, not agricultural.'

'It was doing fine until you paid the Tinkling Tappets to steal a quarter of our crop.' I saw him frown when I said 'quarter'. I wondered if he'd been told more. 'Besides,' I added, 'we have other plans, now that we know what you intend.'

'Like what?'

I could see he was starting to panic and that meant he'd blurt. It was time for him to be on the backfoot.

Daniel started squeezing his fingers. 'You can't sell the land between now and Wednesday. And even if you try or attempt to reallocate, it will have to go through the Land Office, where the well-reimbursed Mr Vivien Chow is waiting to deal with any problems and then reallocate the land to us. We have it all sorted.'

Arrogant arse. I bet he couldn't spell 'reimbursed'. I remembered the name he used and then the face that went with it. I played a hunch.

'We're planning to ask for a court injunction to delay judgment based on the fact that it was my uncle's last harvest and that he already had plans to develop the land commercially.'

I wasn't sure what a 'court injunction' was, but it sounded good, and Parsnip Nose probably wouldn't know either. I saw his expression. He didn't like it.

'You could try, but our lawyer, Basil Van Geezer, said that "Cutting them is a waste of time because they're all fibrous."'

Not gifted. I could have told him that, duh. I noted the lawyer's name too.

'The fastest way would be to use tractors to knock them over, but they're expensive to hire. Then you'd have to dispose of them. And burning is illegal, which is why I'm here to check on things.'

I started to wish that Maya's fantasies about eating hearts were true. This guy didn't need his.

'What? Nothing more?' he asked.

'I was thinking of a heart specialist.'

He looked puzzled and then looked me up and down, pausing at the top of my legs. Seriously? You want to take everything away from the two most important people in my life, two old hamsters I really care about, and you think I'd be interested in you?

I felt shit-storm girl rising wild-eyed, like a submarine from the Mariana Trench of my brain, speeding through unchartered territory, a periscope piercing my conscious mind like a lanced pimple. I burped. It smelled like dragon's breath. I had an idea.

'Look,' I said, putting on my best sad face, 'I get it. You're going to take the land anyway. I'm stuck out here with nothing to do and a shitty life.'

I saw his expression change.

'It's business. Nothing personal. Would you like a coffee?'

He held out a fifty-Ringgit note like he was a Russian oligarch. His personality oozed like sea snot. 'Latte, one sugar, brown.'

I took the note and went to the counter. Less than five minutes later, I obediently came back to where he was now sitting and placed two coffees and a saucer full of thin dark chocolate squares balanced between them in the centre of the table.

Daniel looked suspicious. 'How much were those?'

What a parsimonious prick. 'The guy at the counter said they were "on the house".'

'In that case, all the better.' I watched Daniel grab a handful of the little squares and pop them into his mouth, chewing with relish and rinsing with a gulp of creamy coffee.

'Coffee and dark chocolate; great combination. Aren't you having any?' he asked.

I took a long sip of my latte and put on my best patronizing expression, 'I'm trying to watch my weight.'

'Well, you can't miss it,' he laughed at his own joke.

Daniel walloped the rest of the chocolates, slurped the rest of his coffee down to the foam, then took his index finger and spun it around the cup to get at the froth around the sides of the mug, and licked it off.

Disgusting.

Moments later, a pained expression crossed his face. The sound of a clown making a small animal out of an elongated balloon came from his stomach region.

'Coffee's a bit strong. How's yours?'

I cleared my throat. 'Mine's delicious, thanks.' I allowed myself a little ruthless chuckle.

Daniel's stomach rumbled like thunder on a stormy sea, and I watched with rapt enthusiasm as face-muscle ticks started appearing on his face. Minutes later, high-pitched squeaks accompanied muscle spasms so strong that I thought his stomach might explode.

'Are you okay, Daniel?' I asked, with certain knowledge that he wasn't.

He was desperately trying not to lose face and kept shifting in his chair, but he was losing the battle.

He asked, 'Was that chocolate out of date?'

'No,' I replied truthfully. I was beginning to enjoy our chat.

He must've tried to relieve the pressure and squeeze out a little of the colonic gas as I saw him lean to one side and scrunch up his face. His concentration suddenly changed to shock when he realized that the ensuing wetness had not been part of the arrangement.

'Oh God,' he shrieked.

'Toilet's inside,' I volunteered.

I watched him rush inside. There was considerable banging and what sounded like shoulder charges.

When he emerged, he was even whiter than before. Panic filled his face. 'Where are the staff? The toilet's locked,' he screamed.

The twenty Ringgit I'd paid Ms Ann to lock the toilet door and padlock the gate at the back of the café was now the bargain of the century.

The entire restaurant giggled. Little children pointed.

'I think there's one out back,' I suggested, knowing there wasn't.

I laughed at him when he came back. Small pleasures.

He was frantic, and I could see he was torn between showing his anger and getting to a toilet. Then he sussed it out. 'What did you put in that chocolate?'

'Razor wire. Jerk!'

With that comment, I think Daniel realized that he was at the vortex of all lost souls. His mind may have refused defeat, but his body had other ideas. A lost puppy could not have made a sadder face. His khaki shorts billowed as a loud showerhead eruption of gas and detritus erupted outwards. The tangy stench flooding from the growing stain in his shorts overwhelmed the entire restaurant.

As I left the table to move to the street, I pulled out the empty box of Maximum Strength Detox Chocolate, crushed the packaging and threw it into a nearby wastepaper bin. I'd have to buy more for Uncle Donald, but it was so worth the cost.

Within minutes, all the customers and staff had streamed out on to the streets, gagging as they went. The tinkle of a broken glass could be heard from the other side of the restaurant.

Round two to the good guys.

23

I walked over to the tattoo parlour shops, tempted. I looked through the window at a few of the examples. The Sarawakian tribal designs were sick. I wanted one. Then I noticed some of the dude's other work. There was a picture of a heart with 'Dad's Angle' written around it next to a 'Regret Nothng' tattoo on a shoulder. Perhaps irony's not dead after all. I was having second thoughts. Then I saw the decider. A portrait of Freddy Mercury on an upper arm about to be indecent to a microphone. It consisted of a scary set of giant front teeth framed by a mess of hair below tiny, beady-bug eyes and lips that resembled overcooked sausages. I'll find another place.

'You caused a commotion at the café.'

I recognized the voice instantly and spun around, beaming. 'Maya! It's great to see you again.'

'I know.' she replied with an elfin smile of her own. 'There's much I want to share with you today.'

There was a sense of excitement and stress. When you were still getting to know someone and you had invested emotion, there would be tension. Would it be better than before or would they have second thoughts now that they had time to process the real you?

Maya was weird, but in a 'I'm different, get used to it' kind of way. I wasn't sure what to expect. I said, 'Yes, me too. I feel different. And you look good too. Better than good.'

That took a lot for me to say. My Brit side is a shy person at heart.

'I feel good when you're with me. I feel much less than a hundred and eighty-seven years old.'

I didn't know how to answer that.

'Follow me,' she said.

Maya led the way along an overgrown path around the side of the shops to a small clearing at the back. There, we hugged like long lost friends.

'I saw you use your new strength against the motorcycle boy. How did you feel?'

'Great. I don't know where it came from. You should have seen me throwing palm bushels into the truck yesterday. And the look on the other workers' faces.'

'It was my gift. I'm pleased you are enjoying it. It will not last, unless—'

Maya's voice was soft, and full of thunderstorms, but I was still having trouble with the idea that a nibble on my lower lip could create such a change. I'll go along with the idea that one or two people have powers which science can't explain, but the vampires and zombies stuff? No. *Or am I just saying that?* Perhaps, deep down, I did want to believe that humans were evolving with new skills and abilities. If anyone was different enough, it was her.

'Show me what else you can do,' I asked, half expecting the answer to be a feeble excuse of why she couldn't.

Maya took out a small knife from her jeans pocket and opened the main blade. 'Give me your hand.'

'You serious?'

'Trust me?'

That phrase rang heaps of warning bells for me. I'd been conned too many times. I was also cornered. It was one of those make-or-break questions in a fledgling friendship, or whatever it was.

'You want to see, don't you?' she added.

Checkmate.

I held out my left hand. 'Not too deep,' I said with a furrowed brow.

Maya held my palm upwards and said, 'Look at me, not the knife.'

I looked into her magical eyes and watched with amazement as the gold specks within the rich hazel grew larger.

'Ow,' I said. 'I can feel that.' On instinct, I looked down to see a deep wound with fresh blood flowing down my fingers. 'Christ, what have you done? You're batshit crazy. I need to get to a doctor. Like now.'

I tried to pull my hand away but Maya held it firm.

'Wait. Trust.'

I watched Maya squeezed my hand to close the two edges of the wound. Then she placed a little saliva on the first two fingers of her other hand and ran them along the line of the cut. The blood stopped. She then brought my palm to her lips and used her tongue to tease the lesion.

I felt pins and needles at first, then a tingling sensation which was strangely nice. At the back of my mind, I was reassuring myself that there would be a doctor or two in town I could go to. When she let go, I stared at my palm. Apart from the drying blood around the fingers, I couldn't see where the cut had been, not even a scar. I looked into Maya's eyes again and watched them change from a golden-yellow with tiny shining black pupils back to hazel with wide black centres. They were mesmerizing.

'That's amazing; you're amazing.' Did I actually see that, or did she hypnotize me?

'It must be done with love. The chemicals are different.'

Okay, she's consistent.

Maya held me again and whispered into my ear. 'I want you to drink from my chalice.'

Okaaay, where was this going? I was not a chalice-drinking sort of girl. But the hedonist part of me wanted to swim with the current.

I said, 'Can we take things slowly first?'

I saw her smile. Her teeth were impossibly white, conically and beautiful. She alone could keep toothpaste manufacturing going.

'It is a real chalice.'

Oops. My bad.

'You will be able to see what is too painful for me to endure again.'

'Oh, yes. Of course. Wow.' I needed to shut up before anything more ridiculous came out.

With that conversation closed, we sat in the clearing talking and sharing. I told her about the thugs, the attempted landgrab, and the recent run-in with Abidin, the Zak imposter.

It was mostly me, but when Maya did speak, it was perfect. An hour passed like tropical snow.

During a lull in the conversation, she gave me one of her enigmatic smiles and said, 'Come with me.'

It was one of those statements where you knew you didn't have much of a choice and you knew that something exciting was about to happen.

A short while later we were walking back along the narrow path to where we had been before. This time we veered off to another small clearing where there was a small red shrine built on a concrete base. There was strange writing all over which I thought was graffiti but Maya assured me that it was part of a ritual to protect her chalice. Inside the centre of the wooden structure was the golden goblet. I was surprised it hadn't been stolen.

'Zo,' Maya began.

I liked it when she called me that.

'I'm going to share a story with you which will sound strange, but what I'm going to tell you is true.'

I was waiting for my mind to be blown.

'After that we'll figure out what we're going to do about Abidin. One dragon at a time'

'That's what I usually say.'

'I know'

Her smile morphed into a more serious face, and her voice was whispery and melodic. 'Most humans evolved from great apes. What most ethnologists won't tell you is that the apes evolved in different stages. It's obvious when you think about it, but not comfortable for most humans to talk about. In Africa, compare a Turkana with a Kamba, or a Western Kenyan with the Forest People of the Central African Republic. Then there are the Nordics, the Mongols, the Japanese and many others. All these from one species of ape? I don't think so.'

'Which one are you?' I asked, absorbed. She wove a good story.

'We are from Ranomafana, which, back then, was pretty much all north and east Madagascar. Like you share ninety-nine per cent of your genomes with bonobos, we share ninety-nine per cent with the Indri, a species of lemur. The difference is that, for millennia, we became more hominid without meeting or interbreeding with other similar species. We were isolated. When other hominid species first met us, we were already late to the party. We hadn't evolved. We were looked down upon, persecuted and even eaten, but also feared because we knew the secrets of the forest alchemy. We were more lemur than human and didn't mix with Neanderthals and *Homo erectus* and *Homo sapiens* until much later.'

'Seriously amazing. Incredible,' I said, enthralled.

'Our history begins several millennia ago. There was a ruling tribe, and all the other tribes had to pay tythe, a kind of money tribute, to their royal family. We didn't have to since we were still regarded as animals, even though, by then we had lost much of our tails and a lot of our fur. The law was clear: 'people'—which were not us—were not allowed to marry outside of their tribe, otherwise they risked banishment into the wilderness or death. It was the same thing since humans could not survive like we did. One year, when the fruit trees were barren in the orchards from successive droughts, a young viscountess wandered around the edge of the Dark Forest, the home of the Untouchables—us.

The trees there were always heavy with ripe fruit and the princess climbed one to enjoy a juicy *pibasi*, but she lost her footing and slipped. Luckily, one of us who had been watching her, saved her using his knowledge of the *Maizina Ala*. The lady was very grateful to the Indra and made it her life's purpose to learn our language and save the forests from destruction. They met in secret for many months and she integrated herself into our society. However, eventually her people found out about it and she was declared a traitor, captured and locked up. Before she was executed by her own father, she gave birth to a baby girl. The girl child was cast out into the forest to live or die as nature wanted. She was the first of my modern ancestors.'

While Maya had been talking, she had prepared a potion. She poured the clear liquid into the chalice and the whole jungle went quiet. It was beyond unnerving. Imagine you were at a crowded rave enjoying yourself when all the sounds stopped and everyone turned to stare at you.

Maya began singing in her language.

The birds came first, followed by clouds of insects, which stayed at the edge of the clearing. Animals and reptiles appeared together; all staring. It was unreal. *Détente.*

Maya picked up the chalice. There was no backing out now.

She said, 'We must wait.'

I had loads of questions but didn't know how to ask. More animals and birds arrived. A kaleidoscope of butterflies fluttered in the light zephyrs.

I was about to ask what we were waiting for, but Maya said, 'I will now compress time. Do not be frightened.'

Whenever anyone says, 'Don't be . . .', I know the smelly stuff and the fan are going to meet. Maya opened her mouth and bared all her teeth. They shone brilliant white. She had thin, sharply curved incisors I'd never noticed before. Without taking a breath, she began a scream that hurt at first but morphed into white noise and then mellowed to harmonics. It lasted an age.

A mouse deer moved to one side; other animals created a space. I heard heavy breathing. Along with Maya's soft chanting, it was the only other sound in the forest. A strong odour invaded my sense of smell. A musty, earthy scent laced with death. I sensed nervousness. Mine or theirs, I wasn't sure.

Through the undergrowth, a large tiger appeared. She was old and had vicious scars over her face and sides. Following her was her cub, barely weaned.

'We can begin,' was all Maya said. She took one handle and offered me the other.

I stood facing her. We each had our right hand on one side of the chalice. 'We drink together.'

That would be impossible because if I drank, the cup would tilt away from her.

'Put your lips to the chalice.' I did and saw the lilac liquid swirl anti-clockwise. Maya pushed her forehead to mine and placed her lips on the other side. Half the liquid swirled clockwise pushing the contents up to both our lips. We sucked on the water and I swallowed. Maya spat hers back out.

The last thing I remembered her saying was, 'The pain is too great for me.'

I panicked. If it was too great for her, how the hell was I going to cope?

The butterflies fluttered around me. They were exquisite. I looked down and saw the old tiger eating my leg; the cub had one of my fingers in its mouth, crunching down hard.

I tried to scream but found I couldn't. I wasn't breathing; it was the forest that was pushing air in and then sucking it out again. I existed at its caprice, its desire. Insects swarmed and bit into me. The birds, bats and other flying animals pecked at my flesh. A crow took out one of my eyes.

I felt my body being devoured, pulled and tugged each way until only the consciousness of the breathing forest was left.

Pictures began forming beautiful shapes in rich colours. I watched in wonder as the shapes combined into a dark and verdant forest filled with golden-yellow eyes.

I saw flashes of hideous things: destruction, repulsive and violent monsters, and torture. White pain burned into my mind.

I woke screaming, sobbing. Desperate. Maya held me tightly. Tears flowed from her eyes.

'I think I would die if I had to endure again the things you have now witnessed.'

I found I couldn't speak fast enough for the thoughts in my head and what I said came out as gibberish.

When I paused for air, Maya raised a long slender finger up to my lips. It was replaced with soft lips and a hug that had me shuddering from a tsunami of sadness intertwined with inner anger. I knew I'd never be the same again. Different. Complete.

When we unglued, I felt a contented tiredness washing over me. I said to Maya, 'When I saw you that time in the plantation. Your eyes . . . the same eyes . . . it was you. I saw a creature.'

'Yes. When we are . . . when we become aroused too much, adrenalin floods our bodies and our genetic systems can't cope. We start to turn back into what we once were.'

'You're like a drug. I want to know everything. How many more are there like you?'

Maya flashed a lemur-like smile 'I know they are there, but I've never met them. It's like sleeping with a friend in a pitch-black room when there's a huge storm outside your window. You can't see them or touch them, but you know they're there. It gives you a feeling of being complete.'

My phone buzzed its annoyance at me. 'Shit. It's the Hamsters. Wow. I can't believe the time.'

'Hamsters?'

'It's another story. I've got to go.'

She looked perplexed. 'Why not compress time?'

'I can't. It's impossible.'

'Of course not, people do it all the time. It's not a secret that only we know.'

'How?'

'Can you cut me a slice of time? Can you give me a piece of it?'

'No.'

'Then what is it?'

'It's created. We measure things by it.'

'How can you measure something with something which doesn't physically exist?'

'There is a general understanding of what it is which means we can use it to measure parts of a day.' I was happy with that answer.

'You mean today is now and tomorrow is the next day.'

'Exactly!'

'Then why is today the day you'll wish for tomorrow?'

I knew the answer to this. 'It's when people regret not doing more things in the past and remark that people should make the most of every day.' I smiled and raised my 007 eyebrow.

'Why don't they go there and change it, then?'

'They can't. You can't go back in time.'

'You can. You said time doesn't physically exist; it is a mental creation. Therefore, you can do anything you want with it. I will show you how next time.'

My phone buzzed again and I sent a quick reply. 'I've really gotta go and I don't want to. What you said about eating people, and what I saw in that dream, that's not true is it? I mean you're playing, right?'

'We love all living things, except those who wish to destroy us. That's all you're getting for now. I promise I won't eat you. But then again,' she flashed her tongue over one of her incisors, 'you *are* tasty.'

She smiled and my face reddened for the first time ever. I said, 'You know I'm struggling with this, don't you? Your weirdness can be different planet stuff, but I want you in my life.'

'I know,' Maya said. 'Your chemicals are changing.'

I was exhausted. I'd experienced an overload of new sensations. Most of it was illogical and I guessed Maya must have put some wacky stuff in that cup. I checked my fingers. They were all there. What a trip.

'We can share our secrets through the transfer of saliva and other fluids. Let me bite you again.'

'Have you ever been called a vampire?'

She laughed, 'They don't exist.'

'That's what I say.'

'I know.'

'You don't think there's any comparison then?'

'We don't drink blood. And it must be done with love . . .'

'The chemicals are different,' I said. 'I know.'

24

The sun poked bright laser strands through tiny, frayed gaps in the blackout curtains and pierced my eyes open. I rolled over into the face of a slobbering Rosmah.

Startled, the dog and I eyeballed each other.

'Eww. Rosmah. Get out. Go! You really are an ugly beast in the morning.' If the dog could speak, I'm sure she would have said the same.

The hound half-jumped half-fell to the floor on the other side of the bed.

The past few days had been relatively uneventful, which allowed me to fit in more with the Hamsters' lifestyle and write some articles for my blog and Instagram pages. But today was different. Today mattered.

I put on a smart blue top and knee-length red shorts, went to the kitchen and gave Aunt Margaret a morning hug. She smiled with her rheumy brown eyes, and pillow-stamped wrinkles lazily unfolded from her cheeks.

Out on the front deck Donald was in his favourite rattan patio chair with a tablespoon in hand, prodding, poking and staring with fierce intensity at a bowl of multicoloured gravel.

'Is that the sample Zak was talking about having tested?' I asked.

'Yes, although it certainly doesn't look like much. Here, what do you make of it?'

I reached out. 'There could be semi-precious stones in it, I guess.' My mind went to a picture of Maya's eyes.

I'd told him about who was involved with the landgrab: Daniel, the lawyer, and Chow, the Land Office guy who was being bribed. I thought about suggesting we offer a bigger bribe, but I knew Donald wouldn't go for that. He was too regimentally rigid with right and wrong to consider it. I didn't mention Maya. My tongue went to the tiny scar on the inside of my lip. Again, I wondered how she had performed that trick with the deep cut in my hand. It had to be a trick. I hoped she would teach me the next time we met. I wondered what other magic she could do. And I had to find out what that trippy liquid that I drank was.

'How's the knee, Uncle?' I asked. 'You seemed to be moving much better in the estates yesterday.'

'Yes, well, I thought as much too. Unfortunately, it's seized up a bit today. While I'd like to go with you to the Land Office to give that useless pork scratching a piece of my mind, I think it is best to rest it for the court case tomorrow to save our land. Good luck today, by the way. Everything sorted?'

All we had to do was evade the vicious thugs, convince the bank that Zak was the rightful owner of the safety deposit box, walk from the bank to the supposed shelter of the Land Office, then deal with Malaysian officialdom and register the land in Zak and Daud's names. What could possibly go wrong?

I said, 'We think so. We plan to take the busiest roads and stay in the crowds. After we file the deed, there's nothing they can do anyway, and we should be safe.'

'I'm sorry I can't do more for you both,' Donald said. 'Especially after borrowing all of Zak's harvest over the weekend. Of course, I'll sort things out with him when the money comes through from the sale of the kernels.'

Margaret poked her head around the corner. 'Zola, why are you eating dry muesli? Have we run out of milk already?'

Before Uncle Donald or I could say or do anything, Margaret rushed into the kitchen, retrieved a quarter-full carton of fresh milk, and poured half of it into the bowl. 'There you are, dear. It'll taste much better now.'

I was sure it wouldn't but was not in the mood to challenge my aunt's craziness. I put the bowl down.

'Onwards and forwards, Zola. Be a dear and help me get back to that spot which Zak told us about. We'll need to get him another sample.'

'Sure.'

Aunt Margaret glanced down at Zola's breakfast bowl and tutted, 'Well, it's not going to waste,' and put a huge spoonful in her mouth.

She immediately spat out the contents. 'Donald Junkett! You're feeding Zola gravel. Have you gone mad?'

The mad calling the mad, mad. It was a psychiatrist's dream come true.

'Well, my crunchy apple, you're the one eating it, not her,' Donald said sheepishly.

Luckily, the bowl missed him by a few centimetres.

Later that morning, Zak and I got off the train at Central Market and blended in with the crowds, our senses on hyper alert for any sign of trouble. We knew we were pushing our luck. They were sure to be waiting for us.

We made it to the bank and collected the deed without incident. So far so good. Ultra-cautious, we made our way back across the Klang River to the Land Office, sprinting the last two hundred metres to the government building.

We stood on the cool marble tiles under the stream of air-conditioning next to the front doors. 'Do you get the feeling like something's not right?' Zak asked, trying to catch his breath.

I had the same feeling and it wasn't just his English. 'I must admit, I thought they would make at least one attempt to get hold of it. Maybe they've given up?'

'*Ah Longs* rarely give up.'

'But we've made it. You said yourself, they wouldn't dare attack us in here.'

'True, but with the amount of money involved, they're not going to give up that easily. What am I missing?'

'Maybe they didn't notice us in the crowds. The ones in the alley weren't exactly graduates from the school for the gifted. Bet they didn't even have the IQ of a vegetable plot between them.'

Zak smiled. 'Let's file it and go for ice-cream.

We climbed the stairs and I remembered the doors leading to the vampire coven full of lawyers. I hated the place.

Zak knocked on a door marked 'Land Acquisitions' and we walked into the open office.

'You!' I hissed, staring at the clump of whiskers now running for cover

'Ah, er . . . Miss Zola, isn't it?' Vivien said, sitting behind a thick teak desk, startled with my venomous greeting. 'I wonder what brings you back here?'

You already know, don't you.

'I'm accompanying my friend, thank you,' I said sarcastically.

From my angry look, Zak must have worked out that the man was the official I'd had to deal with previously and intervened before I said something that wouldn't help his case.

We walked towards the desk. Zak knew officialdom and his manner changed to match it.

He spoke in a factual tone, 'I'd like to file this deed with the Land Office under my and my brother's name.' He pulled out his and his brother's National Registration Identity Card and placed the deed on the table.

Still sitting, Chow reached over to select a black plastic file from a pile of paperwork and opened it to a bookmarked page. 'Sign here and here, please. Then sign here on behalf of your brother. I'll also need certified true copies of your identification cards.'

Zak produced the required documents. I kept quiet, thinking of all the evil things I'd like to do to Chow.

Chow made notes then signed and stamped the deed. 'Good. That's all done. Now all we have to do is wait.'

'What do you mean wait?' Zak demanded, losing his cool.

Welcome to my world.

'We have to wait for a court date before ownership can be ratified.'

'What do you mean ratified? That land is now ours. There's the deed.'

'Yes, Mr Abraham. The problem is that there has been a police report filed to say that the land is stolen.'

'What! That's not right. The land was our father's and he left the deed to us.'

'The facts, I'm afraid, state otherwise. Mr So Ching Long has made the report. Do you know him, by any chance?'

I saw Zak's shoulders slump. 'Yes, I know him.'

I put a caring hand on Zak's arm 'Who is he?'

'He's the *Ah Long* who lent the money to my father. His son is the one we've been having problems with.

Problems? Is that what you call it out here? He was going to kill us.

Zak added, 'No wonder we didn't see them this morning.' He turned back to Chow. 'When's the court date, then?'

Chow looked at his nails. 'We don't have any notice for that yet as the judge's docket who specializes in these cases is particularly busy at the moment. I'll inform you when a date becomes available, but it won't be for another four months at least.'

I snapped and my Kenyan side made another appearance. I tore into the monotoned idiot, 'Then how come my uncle's court date is tomorrow? You organized that pretty damn quick, didn't you?'

Vivian pushed himself to the back of his chair which scraped on the flooring. 'They are different cases and er . . . therefore . . . er . . . come under separate courts.'

I could see he was making it up as he went along, but short of throwing him out of the window, we were stuck. His ridiculous whiskers were begging to be yanked out.

I slammed my fist on his desk with such force that it splintered the wood and everything jumped up. Even I was surprised at my own strength. I thought, go large or go to the shopping mall. I picked up the chair next to me to throw it across the room. Instead, it flew into the opposite wall and the legs went through. It hung there like the head of a dead animal. I could hear myself snarling.

Wow! I couldn't believe what I'd done and, judging by the expression on their faces, neither could they. Maya would say it was her present, but thin plaster walls and muscle build-up from hurling bushels into trucks was more likely. Or was it? I needed time to get my head around things.

'I want to make a complaint to your boss.'

Chow hesitated, still shaken. I thought we might be getting somewhere at last. Nothing like a well-placed threat of violence to stir the action up. How the hell had I done that? I had a newfound respect for my alter-ego Ms Shit-storm-thrower. She was cool.

'Certainly,' Chow said, composing himself. 'If that's how you feel.' He pulled out an old looking form filled with impenetrable legal jargon and requests for large amount of personal information.

Zak took one look and recognized what was going on. 'Come on, Zola. We need a lawyer.'

Chow gave a perfunctory smile as if to conclude the business. He also wanted me out of the room in case I decided to throw him at the wall. Tempting. I waved goodbye to the chair on the way out.

Outside, Zak asked, 'How did you do that? The chair thing.'

Now was not the time to tell him about shit-storms or Maya. So I said, 'I'm stronger than I look. Anyway, what's going on here with that Chow guy?'

Zak's head drooped in resignation. 'It's a fix-up. I bet the *Ah Long* has made a deal with him. They know I need quick cash for my brother's operation. The hospital won't keep him forever. They also know I can't afford a lawyer to get the case dismissed. All Chow needs to do is delay the court date until I agree to sell for a bargain price. They know I won't let him die so they will get the land for almost nothing.'

'Can't you sell to anyone else for a higher price?'

'It still has to go through the Land Office.'

'When will the money come through from the harvest?'

'Not for another two months. By then it will be too late.'

I had an idea but didn't want to get his hopes up and kept quiet. I didn't completely like it myself. Tomorrow was going to be a big day.

25

It was the morning of the court case. A lot was riding on today and I wanted to do everything I could to help. Despite all that had happened in recent days, I felt more and more that I belonged here instead of the UK. Yes, I missed Mum and Dad, and for different reasons, I would even be happy to see my brother. Even the perpetual heat was becoming more bearable; I still needed at least two showers a day for sanity or run the risk of ponging. More than anything, the Hamsters had given me space and still cared, even when I'd screwed up or said stuff I regretted later. I could see money was tight and that I was a financial burden, but the fact they tried to hide it from me showed caring on another level. I'd find a way to repay them before I left. My thoughts hit a dead end. Left to go where?

I'd been tasked to drive Uncle Donald to the courts in Kuala Lumpur.

'I've drawn a couple of Ls in large red letters to put on the front and back of the jeep. You can borrow Margaret's licence; the picture's too small for anyone to tell the difference anyway.'

I was about to raise the obvious difference in age and the fact that Margaret was a Chinese Malaysian, but you'd have to be crazy to try and rationalize with the crazy.

Getting to Serendah had been a doddle, having done it several times already, and my confidence was bubbling. Then we came to the end of the Rawang bypass and dropped on to the main thoroughfare. It was another world. Cars sped by both sides of the rickety blue jeep with horns blaring. I stuck frozen to the middle lane with the rest of the slower traffic, my hands clinging to the steering wheel like limpets.

I screamed, 'Why does everyone drive so close to each other?'

'Marvellous, Zola. That's the spirit. Middle lane, wise choice. Driving like a true Malaysian now. Carry on. Try to keep up with the traffic. Onwards and forwards.'

I was drenched in nervous perspiration with the jeep bouncing from one inglorious pothole to the next. I eased off the accelerator when more cars joined the main road. I didn't need the extra stress of overtaking in an underpowered, four-wheeled tin box.

Uncle Hamster kept up his periodic compliments. 'Excellent choice, Zola. We are in plenty of time. No need to rush, my dear. Doing splendidly, what?

A split second later, I felt the jolt from a solid object going under the offside front wheel. The jeep started veering left, the tyre losing air rapidly. I yelped. It was a loud one. Donald added, 'What the . . . Oh, dear. Lookout!'

I wrestled with the steering, but the car wasn't having it and pulled further towards another car coming fast on the inside lane. The sound of a loud, angry horn filled our car. I braked, which sent the jeep careening further left. The other car managed to swerve out of the way with its horn blaring and our blue jeep came to a stop as it bumped against the kerb on the hard shoulder. I was still clinging on to the steering wheel, staring into the distance. I never wanted to drive again.

'Grand job, pulling the car to a halt like that. First class indeed. I couldn't have done any better myself.'

'You're not angry?' I asked.

'Most definitely not. Splendid car management. There is the slight problem of the puncture though.'

'Onwards and forwards?'

'That's the ticket. Of course, I'd love to help, but I'm afraid my leg won't be having any of it.'

'We're going to be late. Why don't we call for a taxi, you go to court, and I'll stay here with the jeep?'

'I don't think that's a good idea. Malaysia's safer than many places, but Margaret would never forgive me if I left you here.'

'But the court case? That's way more important,' I tried to argue.

'Let's hope we can flag down a passing motorcyclist who wants a bit of extra money, although on this road I doubt people will want to stop.'

'Let's call a garage.'

'We're still a long way out. It will take too long to get here. That's if they have anyone to spare, that is.'

'Okay, what do I do first?'

Changing the tyre had been easier than I thought, with Donald expressing amazement as I girl-handled the spare wheel. I'm loving my new strength. At one point, I thought I'd cut myself on one of the rusty wheel nuts, but when I checked, there was barely a scratch. Maya's gift crashed into my thoughts. The next time I saw her, I would drag her out of her fantasy world and get her to be honest with me about the powers she has. But what if they were real? Was that why I liked her? Two peas in a pod. Two crazies in a bizarre fantasy to escape the real crazy world.

A good hour and a half later of studiously slow driving, we arrived at the courts' huge car park. We were cutting it fine.

'Zola, run ahead. It's on the second floor, courtroom number five. You can make it. Stall them for as long as you're able. I'll be along as fast as my walking stick permits. Here, take these documents. Onwa—.'

'Got it, Uncle. Never surrender.' I ran as fast as I could and within seconds reached the stairs and bounded up them three at a time. I wasn't even out of breath. Had I compressed time? An Olympic medal entered my thoughts. I'd check out my local athletics club when I went back to the UK. Whenever that would be.

I pushed through the swing doors to courtroom five.

It was two o'clock in the afternoon and, in the still courtroom air, the smothering humidity battled the air-conditioning for dominance. A heavy pause fell around the courtroom like a hung pheasant.

Sweat was forming under my skin, ready to burst from every pore. I felt like a walking water balloon.

'All rise for Justice Ada,' echoed around the chamber.

A small gathering of lawyers and paralegals in a cordoned-off area rose like the vampires they were.

Justice Ada entered from a side door. She had large pink lips, a square, boxer's jaw, which was supported by several chins that wobbled like excitable jellyfish. Large earrings swung on plump earlobes like pendulums from a grandfather clock. Thick mascara surrounded her piercing piano-black eyes. She sat carefully as if any quicker movement would risk a wardrobe malfunction. She had character. I liked people with character, but she didn't look happy. Someone was getting a death sentence. I hoped it wasn't us.

She rummaged through the papers placed neatly in front of her. A deep and crackly voice rang out from the court's speaker system, 'Be seated.'

I remained standing at the back and half hid around one of the pillars.

'Case number 3874A concerning the appropriation of the land parcel entreated to Donald Junkett commonly known as the Antara Gapi Estate. Will the representative from the Land Office please approach and state your case?'

I looked around and saw Chow from the Land Office sitting two rows down and to my right. He looked nervous. Good. Next to him was Daniel or Toilet Boy as I think fits better. He looked over and I bore my eyes into his with a hate stare. I can do those well. He got the message. I wished I had a roll of toilet paper I could give him as a present. He nudged Chow, who, I hoped, was still remembering the chair stuck in his wall. His expression said 'Yes.'

'Again,' the clerk repeated in annoyed tones. 'Will the representative of the Land Office please step forward.'

Chow stood and made his way to the front. He was visibly trembling. Two symmetrical brackets written in perspiration were left on the vinyl-covered bench seat. TB shuffled further away from them. Self-conscious little prick.

I was willing Donald to arrive before I had to say anything. Trickles of perspiration ran down my sides and back. I could feel my bra soaking up the small pool at the base of my sternum.

The lawyers and paralegals peered around columns of books and parchment, glaring at Chow like vultures at a wounded beast. I was starting to like them more.

Then I heard the rear doors furthest away from me open. I turned, expecting to see Donald. Instead, I saw a flamboyance of a man, who paused theatrically at the top of the rear stairs, sporting a hairstyle that had a slight Mr Whippy ice-cream effect. He was dressed in a pair of retro, crushed-red-apple-coloured trousers and a jacket which could only be described as very Dr Who. I noticed that Justice Ada's caterpillar eyebrows were escaping to the top of her head. Everyone in the courtroom turned to stare at . . . us. Oh, no. I'm not with him. I found the nearest seat this side.

The front part of the court rolled their eyes in exasperation as the visual catastrophe descended into the seating area, leaving a trail of incense and cleaning fluid in his wake, and parked himself next to Toilet Boy.

His father? No, the only thing that dude could produce would be a 99 Flake.

TB looked uncomfortable, but not as much as I'd like to make him. His lawyer? Had to be. They must be doing this on the cheap. Or he was on the take? Or both?

Justice Ada glowered at the snivelling Land Office being before her. 'Proceed quickly, Mr . . .' Ada looked for his name, '. . . Chow. We have wasted enough time already.'

I saw Chow wince, which reminded me to ask Maya how the pins into dolls trick worked. She'd know.

'Yes, er . . . your Honour, of course,' Chow began. 'The facts as we see them . . .'

At that point I started zoning out until I heard 'Which I have here, tabulated and ordered.'

'Let me see that,' Ada snarled. I liked her. I bet she threw shit-storms when *she* was younger.

The court bailiff handed the papers across. Justice Ada leaned forward, causing one of her chins to meld into another and scanned the documents. She then re-examined one of her notepads and then goat-eyed Chow. 'It also states that the landowner has the right to give justification as to the efficiency of its use and claim redress. I'd therefore like to hear from the landowner if he wishes to contest it, as I'm sure he will. Will Mr Donald Junkett please approach the bench?'

I panicked. *Where was the old hamster?*

The whole courtroom fell silent but for the whir of a few small desk fans and the rustling of a few sheaves of paper in their air stream.

An explosion of sound broke the hush as a heavy, leather-bound legal tome fell from its perch on to the floor. A stack of papers flapped down after it like the wings of a wounded partridge.

Justice Ada repeated the call with venom. 'Mr Donald Junkett, are you in this courtroom?'

Justice Ada glowered at the trembling tentacle before her. 'Can I assume, Mr Chow, that the Land Office at least had the courtesy to inform the landowner of this hearing?'

I watched Ada's words laser melt the flesh off Chow's scrawny frame. Her glare tore into him. I did the same.

'Yes, your Honour,' he said. 'I sent it *Pos Laju*, personally. I have the signed receipt with me. In fact, it states that the notice given must be not later than—'

'I'm well aware of the dates of notice, Mr Chow. Are you trying to tell me my job?'

'No, your Honour,' Chow bleated, his whiskers looked like they were running for cover. 'I apologize, your Honour.'

'Then please explain why a person who is about to have his land taken away from him is not here to defend himself.'

The silence that followed strangled Chow's next utterance into a submissive glottal stop. Paralegals and lawyers looked at their desks as if they had been caught cheating in an exam.

I wanted a chance to help. I've got one. Let's do this.

'Hello,' I called out, waving a tight circle of rolled papers. 'I'm Mr Junketts' assistant, Zola. Actually, he's my uncle.'

Justice Ada stared at me, as did everyone else in the room. I became aware of my ragtag appearance with oil stains on my hands and clothes.

Ada beamed a toothy grin that swept across her face and, to my surprise, and the rest of the court's, she chuckled. 'You seem to have had a bit of an accident,' Ada said.

I sensed Justice Ada was on my side and went down to the microphone on the other side of the room to Chow. I mentioned the story of the puncture and the fact it was the first time driving on the crazy roads of KL. I was halfway through before I remembered I didn't have a driving licence and that I should shut up. I finished with a description of Donald's bad leg and that he would be along any moment now.

'Well, young lady, welcome indeed to my court. I see you have some documents in your hand.'

'Yes, Madam Honour. These are the papers from him.' I pointed an evil finger at Chow.

'It says that the final amount of our last harvest must be at eighty-five per cent operational efficiency and that he has arranged with the Boustead Refinery to have the evaluation sent directly to this court.'

I thought I sounded pretty good. I had everything crossed. It would be close either way. Ada was still on my side and I was starting to like her a lot.

In the background, the hushed courtroom heard the faint cries of 'Onwards and forwards. Never surrender, what!' A few seconds later, the regimental figure of Uncle Donald burst through the back doors. He smiled courteously at Justice Ada. 'Donald Junkett, MBE at your service, Madam Honour. I see you've met my excellent assistant, Zola.'

Well, it was good while it lasted. Didn't know the old hamster had an MBE. I wonder what he got it for?

'Mr Junkett, I presume,' Justice Ada stated.

'Yes, indeed. A pleasure to make your acquaintance, Madam Honour.'

At my uncle's boldness, the rest of the court seemed to cower behind whatever they could find. Paralegals hid behind their books. There was the sense that a large firework was about to explode. I checked where the nearest exit was.

Ada chuckled again, much to the relief of everyone. 'Mr Junkett, do have a seat to rest that leg of yours I've heard about.'

Donald gave me a wink; I felt great. I also knew that in a matter of minutes, we could be out of a place to live in. I was happy with the Hamsters and didn't want to leave. I felt I was part of a family again. I didn't want to lose that twice.

Justice Ada asked the Clerk of the Court if they had received the tonnage and efficiency ratings from the refinery.

The clerk hesitated before passing the documents to Justice Ada, checking all his fingers were intact afterwards.

I saw her scrutinize the papers; her small beady eyes devouring the legalese. We were on tenterhooks, hanging like animals heading for slaughter.

I saw Toilet Boy grinning like he'd won the lottery. I wanted to smack that grin.

Ada's face dropped. That wasn't good. She was on our side. *Please lie.*

'This court,' she began, 'wishes to pronounce that the efficiency rating regarding the Antara Gapi Estate, currently owned by Mr Donald Junkett, is running at eighty-three per cent . . .'

I looked at Donald, who had aged in seconds. His despair was plain. TB was bounding on his seat like a child in a bouncy castle. I wanted to bounce him on my foot. His lawyer was clapping his hands like one of my gay friends does. It's cute when he does it. Not cute at forty.

'Therefore, this court finds for the Land Office, unless there are any other extenuating circumstances.'

Ada dragged out the last two words. She wanted us to come up with information to help her find facts in our favour. I could tell she was biding time. Uncle Donald was sitting, shaking his head, but still thinking. Never surrender, Uncle. Appeal.

I asked, 'Is it possible to appeal?'

Ada gave me the same smile I used when I had to give bad news but showed there was nothing I could do. I knew what was coming next.

'I'm sorry, Ms Zola. In this particular case, no. The figures don't lie and cannot be changed. There are no errors that *I* can see and I have no other choice but to rule in favour of the Land Office. What I can do is agree to the maximum period of three months before handover of the land begins to get your affairs in order. It's the best I can do.'

Her words train-crashed into my memory. What's not right? Think, Zo, think. I had a wrecking ball of questions swinging violently around the inside of my head. What's wrong?

I could see her about to bring the gavel down, sealing the order.

I saw Daniel smiling at me as if he'd already won. His lawyer was also grinning with savage glee. Screw you, TB.

'Wait!' I shouted.

Everyone was looking. I felt like a solitary prawn in a bowl of fried rice. Ada was staring at me, the queen of her court. I felt her willing me to come up with something for a different ruling.

TB was doing a pretend yawn. Chow was trying to sneak away.

I was blank. It was there. It had to be.

Ada raised her gavel again.

'You said,' I began, not fully aware of what I was going to say next. 'You said that "there are no errors".'

Got it.

'But there is a margin of error. He said so.' I pointed to Chow, who was halfway back to his seat.

'He said there was a margin of error of three per cent. If we add three per cent to eighty-three, it's enough.' I was guessing. It had to be enough.

'Mr Chow. Is that true?' Ada demanded.

A meek 'Yes' was heard through the speaker system.

'In that case, you should have said as much instead of wasting the court's time and scaring these poor people into believing they had to give up their home and livelihood.'

Ada used her phone's calculator.

'The figure of efficiency is within 3 per cent at 85.49 per cent. This court therefore rejects the Land Office's claim.'

I thought I heard TB say, 'That's impossible.'

Suck on it, jerk.

Ada shifted her gaze across to the other aisle, where Chow stood halfway up the stairs in rigid disbelief.

'Do you not think, Mr Chow, that it would have been a good idea to review your documents before wasting the court's time with all this nonsense?' she snapped. 'I sincerely hope that the Land Office will offer Mr Junkett and his assistant a full and unreserved apology in writing at the earliest opportunity. Further, you should consider cases more carefully before bringing charges which have no merit to this court again or I will hold you in contempt. Case dismissed!'

The gavel came down with a wonderful crack.

Justice Ada breathed deeply, regained her composure, and turned to my uncle with a smile, 'I'm sorry if your court appearance has been an inconvenience to you, Mr Junkett. I do hope that it has not affected your opinion and trust in the Malaysian courts.'

'No problem, Madam Honour. An absolute pleasure to have met you.'

Don't say it here. Not here.

'Never surrender. Onwards and forwards.'

He said it. Mad old hamster.

At least Ada was smiling when she got up to leave.

I collected a hastily made copy of the documents from the clerk and helped Donald walk out of the courtroom in the direction of the car park.

'You were marvellous, Zola. You saved the day.'

'I did, didn't I?' I was well pleased.

26

My mind began to surface from the depths of prosecco-laced dreams to curious murmurings in my right ear and a soft breath caressing my cheek. I kept my eyes closed and let my imagination drift while my earlobe was gently nibbled. A warm nose brushed against my cheek, and I felt heavier breathing over the nape of my neck. Still luxuriating in the half awake, half dream state, I felt soft lips move down my upper arm and then sensed a delicate tongue tickle the wispy hair around my armpits.

'Armpits?'

I shot awake and looked down at the large bulge under the sheets now surfacing from the heat of the bed. Two dark eyes peered mischievously upwards.

'Rosmah! Get out!'

Rosmah half-slithered and half-fell over the side of the bed and trotted through the slight opening in the door and into the hallway.

A kaleidoscope of images came streaming into my mind from the previous evening at the Royal Selangor Club, where we had all gone to celebrate our courtroom victory. Memories of Maya flashed in my mind. It seemed like ages since we'd last met. There were still many questions I needed answers to. For every one question she answered, two or three more were created. Did she really have special abilities or was she full of horse poo? I didn't care. I liked her either way.

While Aunt Margaret cooked toast with Donald's blow torch—the ancient toaster malfunctioning again; I should get them a new one as a present—I joined Zak and Donald on the front deck.

'Ah, morning, Zola. I was sharing with Zak, here, that we're unlikely to get the payment for the bushels of palm nuts we took from his land to add to ours for at least another month. And then there's the issue of hiring a lawyer, who may or may not act in Zak's interest given the influence and reach of the *Ah Long*. The problem remains and time is running out for his brother.'

I had the answer but was hesitant to mention it because I had an uneasiness about the whole idea. My creative imagination usually got shot down anyway. It would also put more stress on the Hamsters, and my trust of Zak was nowhere near 100 per cent. In the end, Donald came up with it himself.

'Therefore, I've decided that the best way forward is to use our land as a guarantee for a short-term loan that Zak can use for his brother's operation. It'll take a couple of days to get approved, but there shouldn't be any problems.'

'That's great,' Zak enthused. 'I'll let the hospital know and make arrangements with the specialist today.'

To be truthful, I wasn't all that happy and had to speak up for the sake of my own conscience. 'Are you sure, Uncle? No offence Zak, but what happens if the *Ah Long* comes up with a scheme to take away *your* land and you can't repay uncle's loan?'

Everyone knows that 'No offence' means 'I'm going to offend you but I wanted to be nice about it.' How else do you say 'I don't trust you?'

My uncle was his usual understanding self and, as he pointed out, he was caught in a choice between being a complete bastard or doing the decent thing and said, 'Yes, you're right to point these things out, Zola dear. Nevertheless, without Zak's help, that court case would have taken *our* land away. It's the least we can do.'

I remained quiet. He was right. Nevertheless, the seeds of mistrust were starting to grow.

'Right then,' Donald stated, 'Zak and I are heading to the hardware store in town. Zola, you're driving please. I want to rest my knee as much as possible after yesterday. Anyone want anything?'

Margaret finished the half-eaten slice of watermelon she had been using as a facial toner. 'Yes, Donald. I want to pick up a few necessities.'

I parked under the shade near the SGR, with everyone piling out as soon as the car had stopped.

An apprehensive tingle ran right through me. I could almost feel Maya's presence. Since our last meeting, my stress levels regarding my UK home situation had descended to a worry-about-it-later attitude. I was sleeping like the dead every night. My nails had grown back and the skin at the sides had repaired itself. Also, the inside of my lips had less craters from nervous chewing with one exception: the place on my lower lip where Maya had bitten me. It was a small hard line which still tingled when I ran my tongue over it, as if it still needed to heal.

I heard buzzing on the back seat and looked around to see Zak's phone flashing.

I guessed it fell out of his pocket when he scrunched up to get out of the two-door jeep. I picked it up and was about to run after him when the screen flashed again. It was urging me to find out what that message was. I looked at the screen and saw two pop-up notifications. I knew it was wrong of me to read them but was glad I did.

'Managed to get that mat salleh's plantation?'

'Damn you're gonna be rich, bro.'

WTF! What's going on here? *The traitor.*

How could he do this to us? Uncle Donald had even agreed, no, insisted that he loan Zak the money and put his plantation up as a guarantee. I wanted to put my hands around his scrawny neck and squeeze until his eyes popped out. But what could I do? Because of what I had said earlier, anything I said now would sound like sour grapes. I had to find the right time. Now wasn't it. I guessed I had a couple of days max before the loan was approved. Tonight would work, after Zak had left. I pulled out my phone and took a pic of the message, then left the phone on the back seat. No overactive imagination excuses.

That compartmentalized, my thoughts were all focussed on Maya. Sure enough, she was waiting at the top of the stairs at SGR. Her face looked cuter than ever and her elfin half-smile was so kissable. Her eyes sparkled with mischievousness. She was dressed in a white stretch top which looked a size too large, and baggy, blue-grey, stretch gym bottoms. And there was I thinking stretch stuff was supposed to be tight. In any case, she made them look good. She could make anything look good. Today was going to be about straight answers. And I wanted to learn how to do that trick with the cut hand. That was cool.

We said our greetings and gave each other a self-conscious hug—we were visible from the main street and I was a bit afraid that the Hamsters wouldn't understand.

'You are wondering why I'm wearing these clothes?'

'Yeah. What gives?'

'I've been lonely for too long. Society's changing and becoming more accepting, but I will never be accepted. And I believe you still don't believe or understand what I am.'

'About that,' I said. 'There are one or two things which don't make any sense.'

'Which things?'

'The hand cut trick and the compressing time thing. The things I saw with the drugs you gave me, the stories.' Then it dawned on me that I was actually describing everything. I rephrased, 'Maya, I don't understand anything about you, but I know I want to try.'

We walked and talked. I wondered how she managed to take time off from the café when she felt like it. While I spouted all my doubts and concerns, she listened and asked a few questions. When I'd finished, she was silent and I thought I'd offended her.

We were on the now-familiar jungle trail which led to the clearing at the back of the café. 'Don't hypnotize me this time,' I said as sternly as I could to a person whom I liked a lot. I wasn't ready to use the other 'L' word yet; too cliché.

She said, 'I understand you have problems accepting. It is why I do not usually make friends. You are different. It is more than attraction; I have empathy for you. And I think you feel the same. We relate. We are becoming the same. And you are a good person.'

I didn't know what to say to that. Yes, I thought I was a good person too, but when other people said so, it felt nicer.

Maya seemed to need to get stuff out in the open, and I thought that after today, we would either be friends forever, or she would disappear from my life. And I'd do almost anything to stop the latter from happening.

She said, 'Yes, I helped you go into a trance the first time, because I wanted to eat your heart. Now I want your heart to accept mine. All I have said is true. There will be no tricks. Do you trust me?'

'My instincts tell me you're telling the truth.' I was still cagey.

'That doesn't answer my question.'

'Then, yes.'

'There is one last thing to show you. It is painful and risky, but afterwards you will know everything.' Maya gave me an eyebrow raise the same as I do and a cheeky smile which was begging for a kiss.

I gave her a big hug.

'Are you ready?'

Ready for what? I said, 'I guess so.'

'To truly understand someone, anyone, you must see their other self. To love one, you must love both.'

I didn't have an answer for that.

'If humans saw what I am, they would lock me away in a facility for tests. They would cage me like an animal. I would never run free in the forests and jungles ever again. The café owner and other staff believe I have a rare form of epilepsy. They leave me alone.'

'That explains things,' I said.

Maya stared at me and I sensed she was offering me a last-minute bail option. I wasn't backing out now. There was no dreamy, super-relaxed state. I was lucid. Her eyes changed colour to the golden-yellow I'd seen before. They were beautiful.

Her legs collapsed first and she sat on the ground. Red tears fell from her eyes. I saw she was in incredible pain.

This was not what I expected and I shouted, 'Stop, Maya. You don't have to show me anything. I believe you. I do.' I went to hug her, but she held up her hand and snarled at me with teeth bared.

I watched in horror as her skin sagged around her frame and her muscles atrophied with sudden age. Rheumy eyes stared blankly into the distance, waiting for the inevitable. A whiff of decaying matter pervaded the air around her while she withered to a dried husk. Her breathing stopped and she collapsed in a heap.

I was crying with shuddering sobs.

The grass around Maya's body dried up, blackened and died. Nearby flower petals fell. A thick tree branch released its leaves, shrouding her with the fallen verdure. The jungle went silent.

Waiting.

Two energy atoms shattered into each other in the labyrinth of decayed arteries, releasing the lifeforce which governs all living creatures.

The foliage covering her exploded, which scared the hell out of me.

Muscles grew, then tightened and twisted; her whole body was consumed by a flameless fire. Maya's arms fractured first, then her ribs and legs as more and more mini explosions raged inside. Powerful energy spasms of wracking pain pulled at her physical shape. Her raw powers interweaved into bone and sinew, wrenching her into a new appearance. Black and white hair pierced through her skin. Burning white hurt screeched through her nerve endings.

Maya was screaming from the inside. Her jaw and throat were already changing, morphing into the cursed being she was born to be, to endure, and the existence from which she would never escape.

The jungle burst alive with noise and pulsated as if in reverence to the creature before it. Cicadas once again strummed their wailing call to mate.

Her clothes were now tight and had stretched. Her structure was lythe and muscular; a beautiful form oozing primacy. A jungle matriarch.

She needed to stabilize, to feed. She looked at me, breathing heavily. Each breath had a deep rumble to it.

I was reeling from what I'd witnessed. The creature stared and turned its head to me. Rows of perfect, white conical teeth glistened. The two top incisors had grown in curvature and length. Below them were two larger shark's teeth which sat on the inside. I felt like I was lunch.

Her slender fingers and sickle-sharp nails scratched around in her pocket. She removed a tin about the size of a mobile phone but with three times the thickness. She depressed the vacuum pump release on the side and opened the lid. An aroma of fresh meat and the energy it contained filled the air. Inside was a slice of fresh liver, which she devoured.

Thunder growled from the creature's mouth, and it took a moment for me to realize it was trying to speak.

We were meeting for the first time. I rushed forward to give her a hug. Her fur was soft and had the scent of herbs. She was taller than me now and, of all the bizarre things to think of, I thought she'd make a great pillow to sleep on. I heard her heart beat a slow rhythmic cadence. Her arms wrapped around me like a warm blanket. We stayed like that for a long time.

27

When we drove back to the bungalow, it was Donald who noticed the open patio door first. 'Lord's lapwings and lobsters, Margaret. Intruders! Where's my gun?'

'Wherever you left it, Dear.'

I pulled on the stiff handbrake and suddenly remembered giving the gun to one of the plantation workers. I thought it best to keep quiet. Besides, I had more important things on my mind such as Zak taking away my uncle's land, and Maya. It had been less than forty minutes since we'd last hugged, but it felt like years already. Was what happened real or did I imagine it? I'd been conned too many times and had been lied to too many times by pretty much everyone to not have a cynical outlook. Then again, the other part of me always wants to believe that there were special people with special abilities. I never thought I'd come across one. I had acres of wisdom to learn from her and tomorrow couldn't come soon enough.

Zak went over to his bike to make sure it hadn't been tampered with and hurriedly rode off without even a 'goodbye' or any concern about possible intruders. He was up to something, and it was up to me to find out what it was. But right now I had other things to deal with.

I helped Donald hobble up to the patio, where we saw the receipts we received from the Boustead refinery detailing the two deliveries of oil palm we made: one from our plantation and the other from Zak's. They were scattered on the floor as if the thieves had to leave in a hurry. He called out to Margaret who was waiting by the car, 'It seems they were after finding out where I obtained the extra palm bushels. Perhaps those property people are not giving up so soon. We may still have a fight on our hands.'

Aunt Margaret added, 'Oh well, if we're having guests, I'd better put the kettle on.'

Donald whispered to me 'Take no notice. Help with the shopping. Mad as a tin of termites, that one.'

He added, 'While I was in the hardware shop, I had a call from a Mr Saravanan from the refinery, who said that there were three people asking a lot of questions about our oil palm harvest. One was a teenager, one was from the land office, named Chow, and one smelled like temple incense with hair bouncing like shampoo advert.

'They were in court just yesterday,' I said, and then noticed Rosmah carrying something in her mouth. She barked a muffled welcome.

'Rosmah. What have you got there, huh?' I bent down to examine the large strip of black cloth clenched between her teeth and, after a few playful tugs, she released the fabric. She sat back with front paws extended, wearing what I could have sworn was a proud grin on her face.

Donald came over and examined the blood stains. 'I say, old girl, well done indeed. First in your class, my faithful hound,' and called Margaret to see Rosmah's good work.

As the sun's lemon-yellow slid into a deep orange, Rosmah dined on choice cuts of a succulent roast lamb with a drizzle of mint sauce. With the shank bone to take away for later, she curled up in her favourite chair with her prized cloth and dozed in the knowledge that, at least for tonight, her master's chair was hers.

After dinner, when Donald was chuckling over the local news in the paper, I tried to tell him about the text Zak received.

The response I got was what I'd feared: he wouldn't have any of it. He said that everything was under control and that I shouldn't worry. He even suppressed a laugh when I showed him the evidence. It was as if it was a joke. I made up my mind to convince Maya to join me and pay Zak a visit. And if she wanted to snack on his heart, I wasn't going to stand in her way.

28

High in the updrafts, two Brahminy kites shrill-called each other. They had been working nonstop on a suitable nest in the forested area next to the aging oil palm plantation which supplied much of their food and nesting materials. Neither paid any heed to the heavily laden pickup truck making its way up a rough, dusty trail that formed the boundary between the forest reserve and the Junketts' estate.

Rosmah nosed the mosquito-screened door open and pushed her way through to the front deck. With monumental effort, she pushed herself up and into Donald's rattan chair. Then, with several roundabout movements to secure the best position, she laid on her back with her front paws hooked skyward, curl-tongued a monstrous yawn, and let her rear legs fall flat to say good morning to the world.

I woke up to a knock on my door and a cheery shout of 'Tea?' followed by the sound of Donald being chastised for trimming his ear hair with the scissors Margaret reserved for descaling fish.

Hamsters? I love 'em to bits.

I put on one of my growing choices of shorts and Ts and went to find Donald on the front deck, enjoying his morning crossword.

'Ah. Good morning, Zola. You might know . . .'

'What's that, Uncle?'

'Six down, nine letters, "Politician's campaign promise", fourth letter is an "r".'

'Guarantee?' I offered

'Hmm. Possible. I'm going with "excrement".'

Margaret called out, 'I've made some fresh bread. Anyone?'

'Marvellous!' Donald exclaimed. 'A couple of large slices for me please; tie them to the yard arm and give them a good lashing with butter.'

'Zola?'

'Yes, please.'

Donald leaned over. 'Mad as a chocolate teapot, that one. Can't even find herself in the mirror. Love her to bits though. Don't know what I'd do without her. What are your plans for the day?'

He got me thinking of Maya. Sharing Maya's secret was like sharing her life. We didn't have to talk if she didn't want to. We were good to be silent with each other and still feel happy, like best friends. Being together was enough.

'Going into town to update my Insta feed and chill.'

Donald raised a 007 eyebrow at me. It must be a family trait.

'I'm not sure what that is, but onwards and forwards then. In fact, if you can hold off for a short while, you can drop me off at—'

'At the hardware shop, Uncle? What do you do there?'

'It's a surprise for my Margaret, you see. Can't say more with the old dragon about.'

Hamster

'I haven't mentioned before what I'm about to say now, Zola, and I'm not one to linger on the emotional . . .'

What was he getting at, I wondered. I hoped I wasn't in trouble again.

'. . . but I would like to think you're happy here. Because we're happy with you being here. Margaret and I agreed last night that we are having more fun in our lives with you around. Margaret always wanted a daughter. I suppose what I'm trying to say is that Margaret and I love you very much and you don't have to go back to the UK if you don't want to. We can find a school here for you.'

There was a tear welling in my eyes. God, it was so good to feel wanted. I tried to say how much his words meant to me, but I hesitated when aunty walked in and missed the chance. Later then.

'Ah, Margaret, my splendid shorn sheep, Zola's driving me into town to . . . err . . . wants me to help feed her Insta and chill it. Need anything?'

Back to the craziness, then.

Aunty looked understandably confused. 'I'd like to go with you, but I need to collect a few more wildflowers for my afternoon herbal tea. Also, Rosmah's starting to whiff and needs a bath, and the washing machine is on the blink again.'

I hoped they were two separate things, for the dog's sake.

I looked across and saw Rosmah's ears prick up at the sound of her name and wondered if she'd gnawed through the cable at the back. She uttered a limp whimper and then gave an evil stare at aunty.

'You two go ahead.' Margaret said behind Donald and mouthed the words 'hardware shop' at me. 'Oh, and Donald, before you go, I'd like you to give me a hand to fix the toaster and the washing machine.'

'Certainly, my persuasive persimmon. I'll get my tools and be with you in the twinkling of a jiffy.'

Rosmah jumped up and sniffed the air. She barked at the plantation and went off in that direction.

'Take no notice, Zola, she does that when the boar get close to the house.'

Donald went into the house to begin his repairs, and I went to check on Rachel's clutch. It was starting to leak, but to be fair, she'd had a lot of wear. Although my knowledge of engines was growing, thanks to Donald, she really needed more than my limited skills offered.

The growing reek of chemicals in the air was bothering me and I decided to investigate. Enola Holmes to the rescue.

The further into the plantation I rode, the stronger the stench became. I had to unwind the red cotton cloth I used as a headband and wrap it around my nose and mouth to make the stench bearable.

It was barely midmorning, but the temperature was already thirty-two degrees centigrade. Dust devils span around the dusty trails as the trade winds roused themselves. Hot, dry air swirled in ever-rising thermals in a pastel-blue, cloudless sky. Most fauna had already shut up shop and burrowed in the shade of a burrow or lair.

I thought I saw movement about three hundred metres away and rode around until I was upwind of the stench.

Laying on the ground was a large, blue metal drum with a black skull-and-crossbones on a yellow background. 'Hazardous Materials' was etched on the side. Foul-smelling chemicals were pouring out. Sitting astride Rachel, I pulled out my phone to take a short video for evidence later.

Then I saw another figure rolling another barrel about 200 metres away. I zoomed in for a short clip.

'Give me that,' a deep voice said from behind.

A wave of shock ran through me as if I'd been caught doing something I shouldn't have. I spun around and re-focussed to see a tall overweight thug, four metres away, wearing rough baggy trousers and an old grey T-shirt with an oil stain on it. He came out from behind a tree. He reached down to his side and slid his shining machete out of its sheath like he was gutting a fish.

Screw you. I put the bike into gear and revved the engine. The revs built but the bike went nowhere. *The damn clutch.*

Before I could get off and run, the thug rushed in front of the bike to block my way and raised his machete to strike. It was instinctive. I shifted to one side as his blade sliced through the air, missing my face by an inch, and embedded itself in the back of Rachel's padded rear seat.

While I was focussed on the knife, I missed his left fist which caught me smack in the centre of my forehead and knocked me off my bike.

I staggered to my feet. My jelly limbs were struggling to keep me upright. I felt the strong grip of the gangster's left hand around my throat, pushing me back against a palm tree, his thumb pushing deeper and deeper into the soft V above my collar bone. I smelled his sweat and determination. Was this it? The end? When I'd finally found a place where I was accepted. I wanted, I needed to tell Uncle Donald that I loved him too.

I saw sunlight glint off the steel blade as it flashed towards my head.

Oh, crap and a thousand hedgehogs.

29

The female Brahminy kite, circling higher in the updrafts, saw it before her mate: the perfect anchoring branch for their nest. She folded her wings and careened down, her sickle-sharp talons thrust forward and, with split-second timing, she had the bough in her left claw, but slipping badly. With the weight too heavy to lift, she dropped it back to the ground.

Donald's rifle skipped on the ground like a forest hare before hooking on to a parched banyan tree sprout that pulled the rifle to an abrupt halt, firing the mechanism in the process. A bullet exploded from the barrel and rose to enter Rhammar's rear ribcage and lodged itself in his aorta.

Autonomic reflexes from the bullet's impact threw Rhammar's arms upwards, the machete leaving his hand. He toppled backwards and lay rigid in the middle of the track. Dead. The machete fell on to a stone which spat a fierce, angry spark into the dry undergrowth. With the chemicals in the bush and the parched topsoil, it was an ideal storehouse for the fire of all fires.

Despite his hand leaving my throat, my vision was narrowing with sparkles at the edges. I couldn't get air back into my lungs fast enough and my throat was raw and swollen. My balance failed and I slid down the palm tree to the ground. The last thing I saw were blue and orange flames racing through the dry vegetation, pausing occasionally as trees tried to resist the inevitable.

I woke with a searing pain screaming along my right arm and saw a flame dancing on it. I pulled my shirt over the flames to smother them. The fire was dancing all around me. A flare from a tree licked my leg and sizzled the fine hairs on it. I wanted to scream but I had no oxygen. Black smoke swirled all around. I tried to gulp in some air but filled my lungs with toxic fumes and woodsmoke instead. I coughed hard and tried to stand again. I had to get out. I staggered a few feet gasping for cleaner air, but fell back to the ground. My hair and eyelashes were sizzling in the heat.

In the end, it was not the pain from the riotous burning in my throat but an ever-increasing tiredness that begged me to give in to the struggle of breathing, to relax into the deepest of sleeps.

What I would give for one breath of clean air.

A nearby oil palm sent a sizzling flame across the path where I lay. The blaze was all around me now. I looked around for an exit but found none. I saw the thug's body already engulfed in flames, his face melting.

Thick black smoke covered me and I closed my eyes to dream of Maya and the shared happiness we'd had.

I was at the bottom of a warm black ocean, underneath the ledge of a large overhanging rock.

Stationary.

Floating.

I couldn't remember how I had got there, but that's where I was.

My place.

The order of things.

I felt an innate urge to push away from the shelter consuming me.

To get out from my eternity.

I pushed as hard as I could against the rock to try and escape from the eddy I was trapped in. Clamouring, grasping kelp and thong grass twisted around my body, pulling me back from the power of the tides.

Fight. Exist.

Breathe. *Fight the pull.*

Filtered light.

Go to the light.

The sucking water pulled at me.

Get to the light.

I was swimming now. The higher I got, the easier it became. The light at the surface was clearer, brighter. Each push felt good, each shove a success.

Close now, very close.

I broke through the surface into a world of pain.

Two bright, golden-yellow eyes stared down at me.

My throat was on fire from the fumes. My head had icepicks clattering around inside. My whole body screamed with the relentless burn from the flames.

I was alive.

A soft growling voice said, 'You were dead. Now you are not. You feel what I feel. You are me and I am you.'

I was in a thin but deep irrigation ditch in Maya's strong arms. The still-flowing, thin stream of water with cool sand at the bottom was glorious on my legs. Overhead, a wall of flame sped past.

The wind changed direction again, pushing the fire away from us.

'Maya,' was all I could manage to say. She rubbed her saliva over my arms and legs, healing them.

'Fire is our greatest fear; it kills without soul.'

'I love you . . .' The three words sapped all my energy.

'Humans must not see me as I am. I sense danger. Your house. The flames are near. I need to feed.'

Maya blew on my face and it felt like pure oxygen. She kissed my nose, then bit my lower lip. 'It must be done with love: the chemicals are different.'

I knew.

She sniffed the air and listened. Then she was gone.

I scrambled to my feet, unsteady at first. The heat was intense, but I had to get to the house to help save it. I started to run, slow to begin with, then faster until I was leaping three normal strides in one with regular breathing.

The fire was raging ahead of me and I was racing towards it. Less than ten minutes later I was at the house. It was engulfed in flames. An empty barrel was nearby, blackened with fire.

I saw that the patio doors were closed and that a piece of wood had been jammed against the railing to stop it from being opened.

I panicked. 'Aunty! Uncle!'

I tried to get closer but the heat was too intense. I was screaming.

Then my whole world collapsed.

I saw two figures in the middle of the lounge surrounded by flames. A piece of the roof disintegrated and the smaller figure fell into the flames.

A face came to the window. Despite the heat, I ran towards the house. The blaze licked the walls. I could see Donald's face now. His hair and clothes were on fire. He was covered in flames. I screamed, tears evaporating from my eyes before they fell. He was shooing me away. His hand made a phone gesture. Then he fell back into the furnace.

I ran to the road screaming and crying. A fire truck zoomed past me towards the plantation. Moments later another raced towards the house. They must have seen the smoke. More fire engines arrived followed by an ambulance.

I walked back to the house. I didn't know where else to go. I was too broken to cry anymore.

30

Firemen dressed in what looked like deep-sea diving outfits pulled thick hoses along the ground and focussed on what was left of the house and nearby trees. Two other fire engines went further into the plantation. The heat was intense and the billowing smoke thick and disorientating. Two helicopters, carrying boxes of water gathered from the Klang reservoir, emptied their load at the edges of the estate to stop it from spreading into other plantations and the outlying housing areas of Serendah.

Urgently mobilized heavy equipment arrived to tear down trees and dug trenches at the unburnt extremes of the estate to halt any spread of the inferno. The blaze could not be stopped; at best it might be contained to one estate. Now it had to run its course.

I sat in the back of an air-conditioned ambulance. The cool air was wonderful. Cold cream had been applied to my burns, and bandages to my cuts. They weren't serious.

I was lost. Margaret and Donald were gone and I hadn't been there to help them. I did nothing. I should have pulled away the wood jamming the patio door. If only I'd stayed with them. I could have saved them. I couldn't look at the house and I didn't want to see when they brought the remains out. I wanted to have memories of how they were. Why hadn't I told Uncle Donald that I loved him too?

The inferno continued to rage throughout the estate, engulfing everything in its path. Thick black smoke rose in industrial columns from the plantation as the fire intensified. Trees exploded with the ferocity of a munitions dump. Singed wildlife ran and flew across the dirt road to the jungle reserve opposite, which had been spared the worst of it. The rest of the fauna, who had neither the speed nor the ability to escape, dug deep until they could dig no further. Many were lost.

'Zola, my dear. I would've brought sausages if I'd known we were having a barbeque.'

I was hallucinating again. It had to be the smoke.

The vision spoke again. 'Jolly quick on getting the fire brigade here. Well done. Onwards and forwards.'

'You're not real, are you?'

'Yes, quite real, thank you. And you are lucky not to have gotten more serious burns. Horrible it was.'

'I saw you. You were on fire.'

'Yes, absolutely. Never surrender.'

'And I saw Aunt Margaret collapse to the floor in the middle of the flames.'

'Yes, she does tend to make a fuss of things.'

Margaret walked around to the back of the ambulance where I was still sitting, confused. 'Did I hear my name?'

'Yes, my sizzling hotplate. Zola's here and she's fine.'

I had to do a double take. Aunt Margaret's freshly applied make-up looked like a cubist painting.

'Ah, there you are Zola. We were worried about you.'

'You were both on fire. How did you manage to escape?'

'No, Zola, it was Donald who was on fire. I was fine, thank you. We had a nice cup of tea.'

'I'm dreaming, aren't I?'

They looked at each other. 'No.'

I jumped down from the ambulance and gave them both a big hug. 'I love you both so much.' Joyful tears fell down my cheeks.

Donald spoke first. 'Yes, well, err, carry on then,' he said in his usual reserved manner.

'How did you survive the fire?'

'Elementary, Zola. We have a trapdoor and tunnel. I dug it years ago during the communist revolution when us farmers were under attack. It leads to a small track at the back of the farm. I thought we'd mentioned it.'

I didn't remember. 'Must've been the jet lag,' I suggested. Margaret nodded in agreement with my sage conclusion.

'Margaret went down first, to put the kettle on—we have a battery down there for the lights—while I covered myself in wet towels. I tried to get out, but the door was jammed. That's when I saw you. The fire evaporated the water on the towels and mop and they started to burn. But I was fine underneath. I threw them off and then I joined my summer snowdrop there in the basement.'

Margaret added, 'We took a little while to get out as I needed to adjust my make-up for those dreadful evening news chasers with their mobile phones who we knew would be coming. I'm not getting caught in anyone's photo with my make-up half askew, you see. The trouble was that I forgot to take a mirror with me and I had to use the reflection in the teaspoon.'

I had no answer to that.

'Right,' Donald said. 'I'm off to have a word with that fireman chappie. Not to put too fine a point on things, the insurance company will be analysing my claim closer than the hairs on a gnat's bottom. Carry on, everyone!'

A monstrous clap of thunder punched the air as Donald found a tallish man supervising the other firemen.

Rosmah barked a welcome, and Margaret fussed about how her fur was hot and singed at the edges. 'Poor thing, Rosmah.'

Rosmah looked up at her mistress's new make-up design and, for a brief moment, I thought she was going back into the fire.

There was another thunderous explosion from the skies.

Donald came back to where Margaret and I waited. 'Let's hope that that storm comes over here. If it doesn't, the firefighters are in for a long few days.' As he spoke, a dazzling sheet of lightning punctured the cloud and lit up the sky around us. 'Look, we're just going to get in the way here. Onwards and forwards to the Club, methinks.'

Donald stared thoughtfully into the plantation for a moment. Then his shoulders dropped and he smiled. 'Marvellous!' he exclaimed.

Margaret and I looked at each other, wondering if he'd finally lost the plot.

At that moment, a large blob of rain hurtled into Margaret's face as influenza clouds spat huge globules of rain at us, scoring murderous hits on our clothes that blossomed into large wet flowers.

'Come on everyone, we can't stay here.'

Three more large spats of rain hit Margaret squarely in her mascara.

Rosmah wagged her tail.

I whispered in the dog's ear, 'Early Picasso?'

Part Two

He who fights with monsters might take care lest he become a monster.

—F. Nietzsche

31

For the first time since the fire, the four of us stood in stunned silence as we surveyed what was left of our home. The happiest was Rosmah, who was again allowed to roam free after being chained up around the back of the Club's annex. She sniffed the air for anything other than a charred scent and trotted off.

I was wearing a soft-cotton long-sleeved top and a light-yellow summer skirt. I had plans to visit Maya later and wanted to look nice. I'd bought her a present. Nothing could repay the fact that she had saved my life, but I wanted to give her a gift from my heart. I hoped she'd like it.

We looked over the remains of the house and the plantation. The land had almost been completely cleared. A couple of charred, leafless trees remained in the distance.

'Oh dear,' Margaret stated in regal tones. Her face carried a stoic expression while the fine hair on her upper lip carried the crumbs of digestive biscuit she'd eaten earlier. Her hair was sprayed into a wild fashionable tangle. 'This will not do, Donald,' she said, waving her arms towards the devastation in front of her. 'Zola and I cannot stay here, but we also can't stay at the club forever, even if the insurance does pay out.'

'Not to worry, my luscious ladybird,' Donald intoned. 'I have it all in hand.'

'What you have in hand,' Margaret scolded, 'is your car key. And wipe that inane grin off your face. You have the wherewithal of a person going for a haircut in a bikini-waxing studio. You look as though you've won the lottery rather than lost our home. Please apprise Zola and myself of exactly what it is that you have planned.'

Ouch, I thought. Mind you, he was acting a bit strange even for him. Like my aunt, I also noticed the strange half-smile on his face and wondered what the old hamster was getting up to. Although I was becoming fond of his eccentric ways, I was also worried that he was living in another time zone and was a bit gullible. Had losing his home pushed him over the edge? I could relate to that.

Before he could answer, the sound of a motorcycle riding up the drive got our attention.

An unusually cheery Zak put the kickstand down and greeted us.

'Hiya,' he said to me. 'I heard you were in a serious condition. I can't see any serious burns.'

I was starting to find Zak fast becoming an annoying jerk. *Mouth breather.*

'Whatever,' Zak said, waving his hand dismissively.

He turned to my aunt and uncle. 'I have good news. Daud's operation is scheduled for this coming Saturday. The hospital is waiting for the money transfer. Have you sent it yet?'

Half listening to me was one thing; I was used to that. But being demanding of my uncle was not acceptable. He should be grateful that my uncle was prepared to help.

'About that,' Donald said with an intense seriousness. 'I'm afraid the bank called earlier and has cancelled the loan. The fire you see. I'm dreadfully sorry. There is . . .'

Zak cut in. 'But . . . you guaranteed . . . you promised. What about your insurance money?'

He was being way out of line. I should speak up. But, I thought, I should also trust that my uncle knew what he's doing.

'That will be available and you are most welcome to it, but they say they'll need to do a thorough investigation and not to expect anything for about four months. You know what insurance companies are like. There's more chance of the money from the harvest coming sooner.'

'How long?'

'In about a month and a half.'

'That will be too late. Can't you get a loan on that money?'

I felt my anger rising. He was using my uncle's good nature and bullying him into committing to expenditure that he couldn't afford. Especially since *he* needed to build a new home for Margaret and me.

'As I was saying, Zak. There is good news. Never surrender.'

'What?'

'I was talking to a lawyer friend of mine, Horsit Singh.'

I raised my 007 eyebrow. I bet he had a rough time in school.

'He agreed to take up your case and receive payment later. He agreed with me that the counter claim by the *Ah Long* would not hold up in court, and that the land would be put in your name. He also said he could arrange a loan with minimum interest from the banks based on the forthcoming ownership. Onwards and forwards, then.'

'But they say they can delay the court date for as long as they want,' Zak protested.

'Actually, he's arranged it for next week. It's fixed. If Daud can hold on till then, the land and the loan will be yours.'

Uncle saved the day. I knew he would. Never doubted him.

Aunt Margaret put her head deep into her handbag and rummaged around as if she had suddenly remembered something important. A few moments later, she was wearing a pair of reading glasses the shape of small rainbow trout. And then, with the softness of a pat on a baby's bottom, she handed Zak a small rectangle of white card. 'There you are dear,' she said, as if it would solve the world's problems.

Aunty, you sure are a lip gloss short of a make-up.

Zak also looked quizzically until he realized it was Horsit's business card with his address and telephone number.

'I'll call right away.'

'Excellent, well that's settled. Onwards and forwards,' Donald said and pointed to the bungalow. 'But first, let's all salvage what we can from here.

We split up, but I noticed that Zak was already occupied in sending texts. Curiosity may have killed the cat, but I was a Kenyan mix, my ancestors also killed cats, big ones. I wondered if I was starting to sound like my aunt.

Moments later I saw him heading towards my uncle in the toolshed, leaving his phone on a half-burned chair.

I didn't trust him; I had to take a chance.

I went to see what messages Zak had been sending and receiving. I got to the passcode screen and wondered what numbers he'd use. I didn't have much time, but I had a hunch. I traced 1235789 and the phone unlocked. 'Z'. Obvious really.

I saw Zak backing out of the tool shed, finishing his conversation with Donald. I had to be quick and just managed to skim through the last couple of messages. What I saw confirmed that I'd been right about him all along.

Happy to know the Junkett's land will be yours, bro. What about the matsalleh girl?

I looked down and saw Zak's reply and my stomach heaved.

The girl's gonna die, bro.

I'm "gonna die," am I? I don't think so.

I put his phone back on the chair and waited until he was on his own, walking back towards me.

When he got within speaking distance, I asked, 'Zak, can I have a word? In private, please.'

He picked up his phone and followed me around the back of the bungalow. With my anger more focussed, I felt stronger than ever. I put both hands on my hips and sized Zak up. With my increased strength and speed, he would not be a problem. We were in the back garden since I didn't want my aunt and uncle to hear what I had to say. I wanted our little chat done my way, no interference from my overly-trusting relatives.

I looked him in the eye. 'I'm gonna die, am I?'

'What? Where did you hear that?' Then he remembered. 'You saw my phone, didn't you?' It was his turn to go on the offensive. 'You have no right . . .'

I wasn't about to listen to a whinge and cut him off. 'Shut it. It was a good thing I did. I'm giving you one chance to tell the truth before I take your phone to my uncle.'

'Yeah, sure. Go ahead.'

I wasn't prepared for that.

'You don't understand, do you? I tried to be friendly, but you think you're better than us because you come from the UK. You don't know how we live out here. You always think bad things of other people when you don't know the crap we have to deal with every day. Parents breaking up? Poor little girl. Yeah, whose fault was that? At least you have them and can make things better, but no, you can't coz you're so selfish.'

Ouch. He was getting nasty.

'Take whatever you think you have to Uncle Donald and see what he says. Nothing, because it's already done. I tried with you, but you can't accept other people doing better. You suffer and we all have to suffer your misery with you.'

I didn't like the way he called my uncle 'Uncle'. I had the rights to that.

Zak pointed his phone at me. For a moment it reminded me of the machete I'd had brandished at me and I rushed forward. I got my hands over the one he was holding the phone with and then squeezed hard.

A strangled cry like a cat came from Zak's open mouth.

I let go and the phone fell on the soft grass. Zak grabbed his wrist. White indents stood out like bright white nail paint where the edges of the phone had been pressed into his skin. Zak fell to his knees in pain as the blood tried to make its way back into his fingers.

'You bitch,' he squealed,

'You had it coming.'

He got me thinking, though. Was I really like that—a bitch?

'I'm letting you know that I will not be "dying" anytime soon. And, while we're on the subject, what did "*Happy to know the Junkett's land will be yours, bro*" mean?

'Because it's true,' he said angrier than I expected.

I had no answer to that. I kept my stare. It'd become superb since Maya taught me how.

'Look, I know you won't believe me; you need to see what I mean. Maybe then you'll understand.' He rubbed his fingers until the white lines finally faded. 'Come to Ulu Yam to see what I've done with my land.'

I was suspicious, but I'd heard enough for me to question a bit more before bothering the Hamsters. I needed proof.

'Why?'

'Because it will explain everything. "The girl's gonna die" means you won't believe what I've managed to achieve with your uncle's money. It was a compliment.'

'What money?'

'The money I've been using to build a lodge.'

'Why would he give you money to do that?'

'It will be his when it's finished.'

'Why? He has—had—everything here.'

'Come see for yourself. Or are you such a chicken shit that you'll carry on judging me without the facts like usual? My hand still hurts, you know.'

Donald walked around the corner. 'Ah, Zola, there you are. I've been looking for you. And Zak, what are you doing on your knees? A bit soon for the old marriage proposal, don't you think? Anyway Zola, I've found a replacement motorcycle, sort of. It's not too bad, I suppose. The plastic has melted a bit, that's all.'

Zak didn't say anything. I was grateful for that. Perhaps he was still waiting for my answer. He'd have to wait a bit longer.

I followed Donald down towards where the drive met what was left of the oil palm. Leaning next to a charred fence post was another of the workers bikes. Its front mud guard had melted and warped until it stretched to the ground. The grips on the handlebars had liquefied and dried at the ends and warped in the middle. The side mudguards and plastic engine cover were deformed too, although not by much. The seat and tyres were surprisingly okay, but the rear mudguard had melted off. It was a two-wheeled Salvador Dali clock painting.

Donald pressed the starter and the bike fired into life. 'Incredible, these new bikes. Ultra-reliable,' he said.

I wondered what my uncle would consider old.

Donald kicked off what was left of the front mudguard and said, 'There, almost good as new.'

I brushed my hair out of my eyes and took a new headband out of my pocket. The choice between following Zak to Ulu Yam or going to see Maya.

No choice at all.

32

It was with much anticipation that I rode down the dirt track to the main road with Maya's present hot in my pocket. I'd had it specially made in Kuala Lumpur and hoped she'd like it. It was unusual, but perfect for her. I was excited to see her reaction and I wondered what incredible secrets I'd be shown today.

It was with a happy eagerness I turned into the main road and picked up speed. I was aware of a white van coming up behind me and I pulled in closer to the verge for it to overtake. It still waited for a car coming the other way to pass. Then, once the road was clear of any other traffic, it pulled out and came alongside. I paid attention to the road for potholes and other dangers but could not have predicted what would happen next.

The van then came in towards me and pushed my bike on to the grass verge.

'Asshole!' I tried to hold on to the bike as best I could, but the rough grass concealed hidden bumps and crevices. My front tyre went deep into a rut and stuck there, sending me flying head over heels into a thick bush. I was grateful that it cushioned my fall and saw only a few small scratches and cuts, but my skin was still sensitive and stung. The van stopped beside me and I was about to give the driver a full opinion of his driving, when a side door slid open and four large men got out. One had a white cloth in his hand. When I heard 'Hold her', I knew they weren't about to invite me for tea and biscuits and I lashed out with fists, palm heels and groin kicks. They were strong, but so was I, and I was faster. I was holding my own until the guy with the cloth put it over my nose and mouth. Fade to black.

When I woke up, I was in the van with a raging headache that hurt every time I moved. My hands and legs were tied together, both with Ziplock plastic bindings. I stayed still and used my eyes to take in where I was before screaming for help. Sitting on the floor opposite was the person I hoped I'd never see again.

'I expect your head is hurting like hell now. Let me prove my point.' He reached over and slapped my face hard.

Shiny white stars floated in front of my eyes while bolts of lightning struck behind them. I refused to yelp and give him the satisfaction of knowing he'd hurt me.

'What are *you* doing here?' I snarled.

'To see you,' Abidin said with sincerity. He was dressed in grey chinos, brown leather loafers, and a loose, off-white shirt—smarter than usual and I was sure it wasn't for my benefit.

'Go screw yourself.'

'You've no idea what you've gotten in the middle of, have you?' His voice was calm and calculating; it chilled the air.

Then I noticed his hand and smiled. I would have laughed, but my head hurt too much. 'Your Precious?' I asked sarcastically.

Abidin's hand was lightly bandaged where his ring finger should have been.

'The pain was excruciating. It still is. I should be resting it in case the infection decides to spread again,' he said in an emotionless tone. 'But it helps me focus on you.' He glanced down at the space where his finger had been. 'This is nothing compared to what you're going to experience. I begged my father to allow me to finish you. And guess what he said?'

An offer I couldn't refuse. 'Stick the finger you had cut off up where the sun doesn't shine?' I wanted a better come back, but it would have to do for now.

Abidin gave a condescending half smile. 'He said I could do anything I wanted with you, but I had to promise him that you would feel more pain than when I took my own finger. I can see the question in your eyes. Yes, I cut off my own finger. I had a choice. Would I make it to the hospital before the poison spread? Or cut out most of the poison first. The decision was easy. I've seen what cobra venom can do. I put my hand on the concrete, then slipped the knife underneath the little and middle fingers but over my ring finger and then stomped on it. I got a packet of ice from a nearby shop, but I knew the limb would be lost. Better that than a hand or an arm.'

'Poor snake. Did it suffer indigestion?'

'I ate it.'

I cringed but remained defiant. I was facing a one-handed enemy. The bindings, though, were painful.

'You got what was owed. Now leave me alone and crawl back to whatever disgusting hole you came out of before I crush that stump of yours.'

'And there we go again. You don't get it, do you? You think that because you are a foreigner nothing will happen to you. It doesn't work like that out here. The funniest part is that I could tell that you had fallen for me. Oh, Zak. I love your voice,' he mocked me. 'Oh Zak, you have such beautiful eyes.' He made a retching sound.

I raised both hands and pulled back my right index, little and middle fingers with my left hand to leave my ring finger standing proud. 'Appropriate, yes?'

'You're going to die, painfully. You do realize that, don't you?' Abidin reached around to the small of his back with his good hand.

I was about to sneer at his pathetic attempts to scare me. But when I saw what was in his other hand, I went rigid with shock. For the first time, I knew I was in serious danger.

'I keep my promises.' Abidin nodded to the pistol in his left hand. 'It is too kind. And, even in Malaysia, murder matters. And while no one gives a shit about you, if I used a pistol, it would leave a signature. Even your dumb uncle would figure things out. It has to look like an accident. Too many fingers would point towards me and my father otherwise.

Despite the real threat, I couldn't resist. 'One less than you might think.'

It took a moment for the sarcasm to hit. 'Ha-ha. Hilarious,' he said sarcastically. 'I can't wait to see if you can smile in a short while.'

As far as I could see it, I had a choice. Should I wind him up in the hope that he would lose the plot, giving me a chance to escape, or should I pander to his ego and create an opening that way? What would Maya do?

'Whatever. Get lost, go screw yourself. You're pathetic. Go on, run along to daddy's scary moneylending business. Jeez, what a sad prick you truly are.'

I could see he was fuming inside. Now what? I wished Maya were here. I wondered if she would be able to sense that I was in danger and come save me again.

'Maya's coming and she'll rip you apart. You know what she's capable of. Think about that for a while.

'No-one is coming to save you.'

Abidin slid open the panel door. 'Here, you can get a good view from here. See, no-one.'

The empty road reinforced the hopelessness of my situation. Maybe it was that more than anything else that brought home the idea that this really might be the end. A thousand things I wanted to do ran through my mind. I was expecting myself to breakdown and cry and could feel the tears welling, but the hate was still there and once I'd found it again, it consumed me.

Abidin looked at me and saw the fury in my eyes. He was enjoying himself.

I was on an emotional roller-coaster and snarling like a wild beast, until he spoke again and brought me back to a scary reality.

'Now it's your turn.'

33

Abidin was fidgeting. 'He's late. Again.'

Whoever was coming was making my captor nervous. I thought I should be too, but my anger was still bubbling like hot mud underneath. I'd been here before. In my bedroom, the moment before my synapses collapsed.

The sound of a four-by-four pick-up truck coming up the road, kicking up dust, had everyone's attention.

The truck stopped opposite the open van door and a small, bony man covered in tattoos got out of the passenger door and walked over. He was dressed in long dark trousers, leather shoes and a string vest. Whatever image he was trying to project, I hadn't seen that film. He looked a bit like a wannabe yakuza, but the tattoos were amateurish. I thought I knew the parlour.

'You look prettier than I was led to believe.'

He made the compliment sound like an insult.

'I'm So Ching Long, Crazy Green Dragon.'

I did a 'Ooooh, scary.' Well, what did he expect with an introduction like that? *Thrope!* My comment didn't faze him, which actually was scary. I reminded myself to be on better behaviour. He overruled snake-boy.

'Your presence in my country has been like a poison-tipped dagger inching its way into my skin.'

Articulate. I wonder what books he reads. I guessed not rom-coms.

'Each of my son's failures has been a twist of the blade and a squeeze of lemon juice in the festering wound.'

He'd rehearsed his speech. I tried to guess what was coming next. 'Has your hatred of me been fermenting like Icelandic shark meat?'

He gave me that 'You're a weird bitch' look. I get that a lot. His tattoos looked like they were angry.

'These?' He pointed to a particularly large indistinguishable blob of black ink on his forearm that could have been a decomposing Freddy Mercury with a microphone.

'These were done in prison.'

I'd never have guessed, duh. I was getting bored. I wish he'd get the 'I'm a scary dude' stuff out of the way, then we could get to my release and revenge. I wanted to wrench his joints from their sockets. I noticed Abidin was fidgeting even more. Either he wanted out of the crime scene, or he was worried that daddy and I would do a deal without him.

'I want that land your uncle is buying from Zak Abraham. And you are going to help me.'

'What land?' I played dumb. I do it almost as good as yelping.

He grinned—but it could have been disgust—and then pulled a Swiss army knife from his trouser pocket and opened the largest blade. 'Do you want to live?'

It was high on my agenda. I said, 'Yes please,' as nicely as possible. I was not going to mess around. He *was* a scary guy. My stomach squeaked its agreement.

'I loaned that money to the Abrahams for a precise reason. For my retirement. It's perfect for boar hunting and the old palm and rubber will provide a modest income until it reaches unprofitability, and then I'll replant with a mixture of hardwood and faster growing saplings. I never had any intention of collecting the money. I had it all planned until your uncle got in the way.'

'Uncle Donald?'

'He's made a deal with the Abraham brothers to buy the land and has been building a nice eco-lodge there. It will become mine.'

That explains why he was spending a lot of time in the hardware shop. That must be the surprise he'd been building for Margaret. Maybe Zak really was telling the truth. Enola Holmes cracked the case again. Or did she?

'He doesn't have enough money to do that.'

'He won't have to pay until the money comes through from the bushels he sold and the insurance money. And he's giving the Abrahams his land as he won't be able to own it much longer. The soil contains Rare Earths.'

I remembered the sample I had collected. Wow, word travels fast. My Enola Holmes brain now understood Zak's text. It all made sense. Uncle would retire to a beautiful eco-lodge with Margaret, and hopefully me; and Zak would make a fortune with a piece of already cleared land.

'Only a *Bhumiputra*, a Malay, can own that land. Even I can't, officially. The younger Abraham wants to mine it. He'll make a mint. I'm pleased about that as I'll make sure he shares it with me. He planned to give a share of the profits to your uncle, but I'll have to see it comes to me instead. Your uncle will be rich enough from the insurance payout and the last harvest.'

Abidin cut in. He was not in a good mood. 'We should get going. The police will come soon.'

'Let them. They can earn their "coffee money" for once. I've paid a lot for information and their assistance. Now, I want my land.'

I saw a frown on the old man's face. Maybe Snake Boy wasn't as much of a favourite as he thought he was. The knife was a concern. My guts thought the same and squeaked again. It was followed by the first stomach spasm. I needed the loo.

'Where do I fit in? I have nothing to do with your plans.'

'But you do.' The old man's voice grew softer, and scarier.

'A finger, please.'

He imitated my voice with the 'please'. The situation had quickly turned a lot worse.

'Abidin. A finger for a finger.' Mr Crazy handed over the blade to Snake Boy.

'Whoa,' I shouted. 'I never did that. He did it to himself.'

'Your finger will remind your uncle to persuade Zak Abraham not to go to the court case next week. The ruling will then go in my favour and the land will become mine.'

What? Next week? When did that happen? I thought the date hadn't been set yet. I knew I had to ask the next question, but part of me didn't want to know the answer.

'What if my uncle can't persuade him?'

'You die. You will be of no use to me. Your death will remind him that I'm serious about our business together.'

Another stomach spasm hit hard.

'I need the loo.'

He looked at my bindings. 'Then go. I'm not stopping you.'

A large pocket of gas made its way out. Brussel sprouts and sambal prawn curry.

'You stink.'

'I need the loo, duh.'

'Abidin. Get it done.'

Snake Boy got closer and reeled from my newly released fragrance. He grabbed my hands and I snatched them back. He was strong, but I felt stronger.

He got one of the big boys to try and hold my arms. It was still easy to move away from the hovering knife. I released another fragrant message.

Blunder boy gagged his way away from the van. If I wasn't in such a serious situation, I'd find it funny.

'Hold her still,' Abidin said through clenched teeth.

'Cannot boss. One arm, can.'

He grabbed my right arm as firmly as he could.

Abidin cut the Ziplock binding with one slice and used all his strength to hold my left hand. The knife hovered over my index finger.

My last fragrant message left the house. I wouldn't be able to do it again without releasing more than I wanted to.

The thug let go of my arm and held his nose.

Something clicked in my head. I had a chance. Take it or die.

In one move, I smacked Abidin as hard as I could on the side of the head, grabbed his knife hand and pushed it back towards his chest. The blade folded inwards, cutting deeply into his other fingers. His screams filled my ears and drove my rage further. I put my hand over his and crushed the red handle against the blade, making sure it sunk deeper into his flesh. I felt a crunch of steel going through bone. I could hear myself snarling and my teeth snapping above his screaming. Then I yanked the knife away, opened the bloodied blade and cut off my leg binding. In a split second, I leaped out of the van, slashing wildly at the other nearby thug who quickly backed away.

Before anyone else had a chance to react, I ran as fast as I could towards a small game trail in the adjacent forest while Abidin shrieked in horror behind me. It soon became thick undergrowth. I heard bullets zipping past and I crouched low to move faster through the scrub.

There was shouting in the distance and, in addition to Snake Boy's screams, I heard, 'I want her alive.' Moments later, there was a crashing behind me. It was either a fat wild boar or the thugs. They had to get me alive. That would cost them if they caught up with me. Claws and fangs would come out.

I was making slow progress. But the people following were slower still. If the bush got any thicker, I'd be stuck. My thoughts jumped to Aunt Margaret. What I'd give for a nice cup of tea and a Hamster's hug.

There was movement to my left. I guessed they were the rest of the thugs who were moving much faster and must have found a better trail.

A large bee buzzed around my head and I hoped I hadn't disturbed a swarm. I was getting scratched all over, and the scent of crushed vegetation was strong. Thorns ripped into my clothes and lianas wrapped themselves around my shoulders and legs.

The trail I was on was moving left and getting narrower. The thugs behind had an easier time of following me, but they were still slow. If I maintained my speed, they wouldn't catch me before I would reach a better path where I could use my speed to outrun them. The thugs on the left were more of a problem. They had caught up and were running parallel to me. If a gap opened, I'd get caught. Abidin would want to carve me up like a roast, although I supposed he'd been rushed to a doctor. His father, though, would want his pound of flesh.

A clap of thunder exploded nearby. A loud hissing sound came from the right and, within seconds, heavy rain fell. I was glad. The sound of the deluge would cover my tracks. I pushed on as fast as I could. I felt the bite and sting of insects as I clawed my way along. It was a snake's paradise. I hoped it was true that they would move out of the way. The rain was getting heavier. It was harder to make things out, even blinking fast didn't help much. I managed another five metres and came to fork. Straight on or right? Straight on was wider and would be faster to get through, but there was a risk that I'd run into the thugs on my left. There was a good chance the trails would connect. The right fork was narrower but looked like it was moving further away from danger. It also looked as though it was heading into thicker, thornier bush. Panic. *Which one?*

I took neither and doubled back three metres to where a sizeable boulder bordered the path. I squeezed myself between the roots of a giant palm with spikes which scratched at my skin and the rock. I hunkered down at the back. I barely made it. Three thugs had been following each other. The first two came to the fork with the third on the other side of the boulder. I could hear their lungs wheezing for air.

The rain was easing off and I heard a soft metallic clatter behind me. I twisted my neck to see a huge, black hornet the size of my thumb hovering less than a metre away. I knew from YouTube videos that hornets, unlike bees, can sting multiple times and the large ones carry a heavy dose of venom. They are also meat-eaters and have powerful mandibles which can slice through flesh like steak knives. If I moved away, the thugs would get me. If I stayed still, I would have to risk getting stung. A sting around the throat would result in the windpipe closing and death. More than three stings anywhere on the body would send most people into anaphylactic shock and death. Death or death: not my favourite choice.

I could hear the thugs arguing. They split up.

The hornet darted forward and landed on my shirt and I strangled a yelp. It walked up to my neck, its legs pinching the soft skin as it moved further up. I felt the brush of its feelers stroking my mouth. One of its feet slipped between my lips and I felt the other legs clasp tighter to pull it back out. It moved on across my face, dragging its pulsing abdomen behind it. I understood at that moment how an animal feels before it's slaughtered.

It reached around to my ear and then it left as quickly as it came.

I was dripping from sweat and the rain.

Maya once said that if you couldn't defend, then attack. I took her advice and went back along the trampled and now wider path towards the cars. Abidin would not be there, a thug or the *Ah Long* would have driven him to a hospital. They might have left one thug to guard the remaining vehicle. One on one. I could manage that.

I made it back faster and exited the jungle cautiously. There was no-one around. I checked the van. The keys were still in the ignition. Thrope. Although it was much bigger, it resembled Donald's jeep more than the other truck that Crazy Green Dog Turd had arrived in.

As I drove off, I looked in the rearview mirror and saw that the thugs were still in the jungle and that I would make it out. But something else also caught my eye. For a moment I thought I saw Maya staring back at me in the rearview mirror. I turned my head to check the back of the van, but it was empty.

Part Three

Be careful, lest in casting out your demon you exorcize the best thing in you.

—F. Nietzsche

34

The previous week seemed like a lifetime ago. I'd heard that my parents were getting a divorce. Maybe it was for the better. I wasn't in a place where I cared much anymore. I was a changed person. I felt harder and more resolved not to let people in so easily in future.

I did care about the Hamsters, though. They had been brilliant to me and tremendously supportive. Instead of the usual criticism, they enjoyed with relish the story of the escape I'd made and the chase that followed. There were pauses for tea, of course. Uncle Donald offered his opinion of what he would've done, with Margaret shushing him, which sounded more like an Inspector Gadget cartoon than real life. I can't remember when I'd felt such a feeling of belonging. So, when the date for the court case came up the following week, I wanted to be there. We all needed this triumph; the beginning of a new life. Zak would get the money for his brother's hospital care. The mining concession he had signed with had the advance ready. The land would be signed over to Donald and Margaret who would then sign the burned and cleared estate to Zak. For once, all the jigsaw pieces were fitting together. The eco-lodge was coming along well with the small cottage next to it almost completed and waiting for us, the Hamster family, to move in while the rest of the lodge was finished.

I was fourteen and had already decided to take a year out and help Aunt Margaret with the marketing and getting the lodge ready for guests. They wouldn't need the money anymore, what with their shares in the mining concern, but it gave them focus and the excitement of a new adventure. I wanted to be a part of that. Besides, they needed sanity in their crazy world. Never thought I'd see myself as the sane one.

Another piece of news that had put a vengeful smile on my face was hearing that Daniel the Toilet Boy had been arrested for being an 'Accomplice to Arson'. The evil side of me wanted to send him a box of extra-strength detox chocs, the better side of me was indifferent. He wasn't worth the energy of my thoughts.

We were sitting in courtroom five, the same one in which Donald and I had been in before. Margaret was dressed in a low-slung black and scarlet number more suited to an evening in the town for a twenty something than a retired plantation owner. Her lipstick had been generously applied and baton-rouge ready for battle. I was worried it might crack if she smiled. Donald sat comfortably in an old lounge suit which had a whiff of mothballs to it. I was the sensible one, dressed in a smart yellow, notched cotton blouse and navy skorts.

Zak was dressed in a green batik shirt and black trousers and deep in discussion with his lawyer. They both wore expressions that did not fit victory.

Then I noticed the weird lawyer from before enter the court. His dark pinstriped suit gave him an air of respectability and his starched white-collar shirt with a dark-mauve tie suggested professionalism. His bright purple handkerchief overflowing from his top jacket pocket like cheesecake topping did not. There was a faint scent of cologne wafting in spirals around him. He was also wearing the vampire robes that the rest of the lawyers had on. What was he doing here? I felt a small wiggle of unease creeping in.

Then I saw Snake Boy, Abidin, enter.

My anger rose and I felt my heart pounding. Fight or flight. Then I saw his hands and felt more composed. The right was unbandaged and missing his ring finger. His other hand was covered in white gauze with two splints where his index and middle finger should have been. A battle won. I smiled at him and got a nod of approval from Donald. Margaret took out a flask of tea for us.

Abidin and his lawyer joined Zak and his lawyer. Their faces bore fury.

Donald leaned across and said, 'Something's going down, Zola. Check with Zak, will you?'

I was about to go over when the Clerk of the Court announced, 'All rise. Justice Ada presiding.'

With a fierce expression, Justice Ada took deliberate steps to her throne and settled herself like a mound of quick-drying cement. Her eyes looked with architectural precision over her battlefield. She leaned forward to better read the papers laid before her.

Out of the corner of my eyes, I saw Donald give a clandestine wave.

Is he flirting?

Can't be. But . . .

I watched Judge Ada. Blink and I would have missed it. She smiled. Then she looked at me and I thought she was peering deep into my soul. I got a small nod. This was good. If ever I was caught in a war, I'd want to be on her side.

Seeing the Justice in a good mood, Abidin's lawyer thought he'd try his luck and made an elaborate bow. What I saw next was scary. She gave him the evil eye with a force that could have melted wax.

So far so good.

With a cursory wave of Ada's hand, the court deputy began,

'Case number 4212 concerning the ownership of the land parcel with deeds presented as being owned by two independent parties.'

Ada reviewed the papers in front of her. I thought I saw her sigh. 'What is this?' she asked, as if the whole case belittled her status. 'This land is in the ownership of family Abraham. The other claim is irrelevant.'

Brilliant. She does it again. I watched the gavel rise.

'If it pleases the court,' a high, monotoned voice called out. 'We would like the court to note that the Abraham family includes Abidin Abdullah, the son of Mr So Chin Long and Siti Abraham. I have the DNA evidence here.

'Bring that to me,' she let the words stretch out like warm plasticine. You could hear the proverbial pin drop in the silence which followed.

Ada reviewed the papers before her. 'Lawyers to the bench now.'

When both parties stood next to her throne, Ada hissed at Abidin's lawyer. 'Do you think I don't know what's going on here? Sort this out privately or get an arbitrator. I have no time for family squabbles in my court.'

'We would like a ruling, Judge.' Abidin's lawyer requested.

'Very well! Now, go away and let me think on this.'

Justice Ada went through the papers on her desk and consulted the library on her phone. Without any warning she left the room, leaving the rest of us wondering what would happen next.

Zak came over to Donald and explained. 'It seems to be true. The DNA suggests my mother had an affair with So Ching Long, and that bastard is the result. I have no idea why, if she was blackmailed, or what.'

For the first time I felt sorry for him. Shitty news. And made public too. Well bad.

'What's going to happen?' I asked as politely as I could.

'Up to the judge.'

We sat there waiting, not entirely sure if the Justice was coming back or not. Twenty minutes went by. The tea flask was empty.

'All rise,' the clerk shouted as Justice Ada bulldozed her way to her chair.

'You and you,' she pointed to both lawyers. 'I hope there is nothing you want to add before judgment.'

'No, Your Honour,' they harmonized.

'In that case, this judgment is based on a similar case "Hassan vs Hassan, 1960" and the ruling will be as follows.'

Everyone in that room held their breath.

'Ownership of the Abraham parcel will be by percentage. Daud and Zakariah Abraham will own 45 per cent of the land each. The remaining 10 per cent will be owned by Abidin Abdullah. Case closed. Court dismissed.'

Just like that it was all over. We'd won and lost at once.

We traipsed out of the courtroom leaving Zak and his lawyer to negotiate with Abidin. Donald wanted to get involved, but Margaret and I persuaded him that it was not the right time. We walked along the long narrow corridor to the lifts, passing a newsstand on the way. The headline story was 'Taxi Driver Eviscerated by Wild Animals'. I wasn't sure exactly what 'eviscerated' meant, but it sounded just like we all felt.

Later that evening, back at the RSC, we showered and changed for dinner and were in a better mood than before. We again dressed in a rag-tag mixture of clothing which we had saved from the great fire. Donald wore a dinner jacket with a yellow open-necked shirt and khaki shorts with black leather shoes; Margaret wore a trouser suit made up from two different patterns—it somehow suited her; and I wore a comparatively sensible pair of patched jeans with a patterned white blouse and sandals. I was still trying to wrap my head around what had happened.

'So, you intended to sell your plantation all along?' I asked.

'Yes. Onwards and forwards, never surrender.'

'What, even before the fire and the fact they found Rare Earth mineral deposits?'

'Oh, yes. As soon as I saw Zak's land with its potential for an eco-lodge, I was hooked on the idea. We're not getting any younger, and running a plantation is a young person's game these days. It was to be a surprise present for your aunt. It's why I spent so much time at the hardware shop, and most of my savings too. It didn't matter that my land had to be owned by a Malay. I was going to sell it anyway.'

'But, Uncle, you sold your land for 1 Ringgit. Even with the trees all gone, the land must be worth more than that?'

'Most definitely. But that figure was just for convenience and legality, and the fact that Zak was desperate for cash for his brother's care. We also agreed that your aunt and I would receive a 10 per cent share of the mining returns, which will be substantial.'

'What about the two million you paid for Zak's land?'

'That's about a fair price. But I know what you're thinking. Where did I get the money from? And why didn't Zak use it for his brother's care? Well, I don't have it, not yet anyway. It was a promise. No money has changed hands; it will come out of the dividends of my mining shares.'

'But I thought that whiskery idiot from the Land Office put a hold on the land sale?'

'He had. But he soon changed his mind when I told him that if the land wasn't transferred immediately, I was going to the police to hand over some evidence of the theft of the bushels with his name on it.'

Donald started chuckling, which turned into a deep guffaw.

'You don't have any evidence, do you?'

'No, not a shred. Only a motorcycle baffle with Rhammar's name on it. Useless really. But he didn't know that. His guilty conscience did the rest.'

'So, you've done okay out of this after all?'

'More than okay. What with the insurance payout based on the last harvest—and let's hope they don't investigate that with too much thoroughness—and the actual payment for the bushels we sold, Margaret and I are going to be quite well off.'

'But I didn't trust Zak after the texts I saw.'

'He knew you were being protective of your aunt and me but also wanted to keep it all as a surprise for Margaret, my fawnest of deers.'

Margaret heard her name and put down the *Alchemist's Monthly* magazine she had been reading. 'Yes, Donald, you old hamster, what is it?'

Yes! Finally.

'I was saying to Zola that we are going to be quite wealthy.'

'It's all karma, you know,' Margaret tried to explain. 'What comes around, goes away.'

I didn't say anything to that. Now was not the time. 'So, what *are* you going to do with all the money? Any plans?'

Margaret sat in thought with an expression so vacant it could have been listed on Airbnb. Then it turned into determination. That or it was gas from earlier food.

'Travel,' she blurted, and then grinned with joy at the espresso topping on her ice-cream of an idea.

I'm sure I come from her side of the family.

'I've always wanted to go on an African Safari or visit Japan to see the cherry blossoms there. We've been running around like a pair of hamsters in a wheel, and it would be so nice to get away.'

Yay, they're admitting it.

'Which reminds me,' she added. 'I must ask one of the staff to exorcize Rosmah later.'

'Don't you mean exercise, Aunty?'

'I know perfectly well what I meant, Zola.'

'Drinks?' Donald asked, changing the subject. 'The usual, my plum peach? Zola?' He called over a passing waiter.

'One Tiger, poured correctly this time. One Manhattan Iced Tea, and . . .'

He looked over to me and I mouthed the word beer.

'. . . and a Shandy, please.'

'Actually Zola, there is something we would like to chat with you about.

Okay, it was good while it lasted. Here comes the shitty bit, like always. Back to the UK, I guess.

'We would be most happy if you would join us on our adventures. We could tie our travels to the school holidays. Or when convenient.'

'Yes, Zola, you must consider,' Margaret supported, nodding like a bobbing Buddha in a novelty store. 'We do so love having you around. You make our lives so much more exciting.'

I thought I should pinch myself to check that this was real. So many strange and wonderful things had happened to me here. I really wanted to stay. At least for a while longer.

'Yes! And yes again. Thank you so much! I love you both.'

'Excellent! That's settled then.'

I saw my uncle take a breath, but I beat him to it. 'Onwards and forwards.'

35

It had been a tough couple of days with everyone coming to understand what the ruling meant and what the future held. On the bright side, Daud was going to get the operation he desperately needed, and the Hamster family—that's me too—was moving into the cottage on the Ulu Yam estate in a week's time. This all came at a cost. Abidin became a shareholder of the mining concession in exchange for agreeing to sign that his 10 per cent of Zak and Daud's eco-lodge and land would be transferred to my aunt and uncle for the rest of their life. There was still more than enough money to go around, but the idea that he was still involved was like a large festering thorn that, when you tried to squeeze it out, dug in deeper. I hoped his fingers still hurt. I should practise my Vulcan salute for when I next see him.

Donald and Margaret were keen to see how the mining was changing their old estate and had tasked me to go to see my new home, the cottage, in Ulu Yam and make a list of all the things I'd need in my room in the immediate future. It would be the first time I'd seen the place, so I was more than a little curious. We'd then meet up back in Serendah at the SGR Café. And I had so much to tell Maya. Perhaps she would be okay with me introducing her to the Hamsters. A pang of guilt twinged in my conscience. There had been so much going on that I hadn't made much effort to get back to Serendah.

I had no choice but to follow Zak, with whom I still had trust issues. And the revelation that he was related to Abidin and Crazy Green Dog Turd had me wondering if his loyalties would change. I wanted to take my new, as yet un-christened, old wreck of a bike instead of riding pillion on Zak's. It gave me options. Abidin hadn't been seen for a while, but I was sure he'd love to get his revenge if he found the right moment. And I wanted to ensure I could get out of trouble if needed. I wasn't expecting any, I mean what can a guy with a missing finger on one hand and two splinted fingers on the other do? I hoped they had rotted and fallen off.

We, the Hamster family, first turned up at our old plantation, or what was left of it. The cleared land, which had already started to look like a mining concession, was a hive of activity with bulldozers and other excavation equipment throwing noise and other pollution into the air. My bike had been rescued by one of the plantation workers the previous week and was waiting for me near the piling stones of where the old bungalow used to be. The key was still stuck in the ignition.

Within fifteen minutes of my arrival, Zak turned up looking as weary as ever, but I wasn't going to let him spoil my mood. I was curious about my new home and excited to see the new lodge. A new beginning.

After riding through the small township of Ulu Yam with its many bric-a-brac and repair shops, Zak turned north past the police station and turned right at the edge of a pretty little stream. I followed as fast as I dared and was grateful when he slowed down at the second narrow bridge. We crossed over the stream and rode for another 500 metres deeper into the forest until the track became rutted and the undergrowth thicker. I noted the differences between this and my uncle's ex-plantation. There were far fewer navigable tracks for cars and there was a greater variety of trees. The undergrowth looked wild and unkempt. It was cooler too. I had to swerve to avoid a litter of cute, light brown and speckled wild boar crossing the track. The mother would be nearby and not so cute.

Then, following a sharp right-hand bend around a clump of tall trees, the landscape opened up into manicured lawns with clusters of brightly coloured garden flowers. On the left was a small cottage, and next to it a large resort style structure was being finished. Between it and a small, gravelled car parking area, a crystal-clear stream meandered lazily under an old-looking bridge. Bright green vegetation swayed as it flowed in the current, and polished rocks reflected the sunlight like shining gems. Further up the stream, towards thick reed beds, there was a marshy area which created a home for wading birds and other fauna. Beyond that was an oil palm plantation with the tallest palm trees I'd ever seen. Between them were fruit trees and a whole host of other smaller plants.

We parked our bikes in front of the lodge next to a beaten up four-by-four truck, which I assumed belonged to the construction guys.

I thought I'd try being nice to Zak. 'This so cool. I'm sure Donald and Margaret will love it here. I know I will.'

'They're lucky to get it' was all I got back. So much for being nice. He added, 'Wait here while I check on something. I can't see any of the building workers.'

I looked around at the structure. It was about 80 per cent finished, but needed paint and inner furnishings. The cottage was beautiful and, like the bridge, had an aged look built into it. Then I saw Zak's golf bag resting against the side wall. In it were three clubs, and his rifle.

I walked over. It was light brown, old, covered in dents and scratches, and heavier than it looked. An inner voice told me to do something about it in case he was mad enough to use it again. I reminded myself that he was aiming for the imposter, Abidin, but he could have hit me. Would he have cared? And he was way too unpredictable after finding out he was Abidin's stepbrother.

I heaved it out and fumbled with the small cartridge clip. It wouldn't budge. Then I remembered what they did in films and pulled on the bolt action. A cartridge pinged out on the floor. I made the same movement until there were none left, picked up the shells and threw them back in the bottom of the golf bag. I was not a thief and besides, he might need it to scare off crows or other pests later.

I texted Donald to let him know that I'd need a bit longer than the hour I'd been given. Then I realized that he probably wouldn't read it until 6 p.m., which was his scheduled time for texts. He called it anti-social media. I pressed call and briefly heard a ringing tone, which then went silent. I looked down and saw that there was only a single bar signal. I listened again but didn't hear anything. Didn't this country have relay stations?

Zak came over and I put the phone back in my pocket.

'Weird. None of the workers are here. I specifically asked the foreman to make sure that there was always someone here to make sure none of the equipment gets stolen.' He said some words in Malay which sounded like swearing.

The crackling of a fallen branch underfoot got our attention.

'At last,' Abidin said. 'You know you've both been a real pain.'

Zak went to his golf bag and took out his rifle and pointed it at the middle of Abidin's chest.

I saw that the splints were missing, and he had two bandaged stumps on his right hand. Maybe there is a God.

Trying to get you away from other . . .' he paused, searching for the right word, 'witnesses, has been quite a waiting game. And you,' he pointed to me. 'Why won't you just die?'

Nothing to worry about, I convinced myself. Thanks to Abidin's missing fingers, I was way more capable than him and I could smack him into the ground. Maya would like that. I'd do it for her.

'You're right about one thing, Abidin. There are no witnesses. And, as you can see, my rifle is itching to be used.'

Oops. I guess I was wrong about blood being thicker than water. *At least I'm saving him from murdering anyone.*

'Before you do, I want you to know a little more about your parents' car accident.'

'What do you mean?' Zak asked.

Abidin paused, then smiled. He was enjoying the tension. 'It was no accident. I've been wanting to share this little gem with you for a long time now. And today is perfect, the anniversary. It took my father a long time to set up, but then all the best unsolved crimes take time. Like this.' He gestured to the surroundings. 'As soon as I was informed you were coming up here, I organized a staff holiday. They didn't need much convincing—you should have paid them more. And don't expect your brother, Daud, to survive either. The anaesthetist for his coming operation has a gambling habit which is currently being fed with my father's money.' Abidin arrogantly jutted his chin out towards us. 'Put the rifle down, Zak. We both know you're not going to shoot me.'

Oops. He must've been watching.

'You don't know me.'

'Don't be so sure. Your family has always been a bad risk. Why do you think my father gave yours that money?' Abidin began a cackling laugh. 'When your mother came begging my father for the money, she said she'd do anything. And she did. Screwed like a rabbit, he said. Then, *plup*! And there I was. We were always going to get this land. It's just that the money's more important for now. Your father never found out, but we always had that hanging over her, in case my father needed the occasional servicing.

'Click.' Zak pulled the trigger.

Oh, crap with a hedgehog.

'Well, well. Didn't think you had it in you.'

Zak rapidly used the bolt action.

Click.

He kept trying until he understood.

Abidin saw the confusion on Zak's face. 'I watched from the truck. She'—he pursed his lips at me—'took them out. They don't come much stupider, do they? I didn't even know you had the rifle hidden there.'

Zak looked at me and said, 'You bitch,' then threw the rifle down.

I had just saved him from a prison sentence or worse. He should be thanking me. I reminded Snake-eyes, 'You won't get this land. You signed over your 10 per cent. It's in the agreement.'

'Ha, until they die. An accident will happen. Old people tend to make a lot of mistakes. The police won't even investigate. It'll happen soon after you shoot each other.'

'I don't think so, Stumpy,' and watched him wince at the cruel moniker.

Abidin used his left hand to reach around and whip out a revolver from between his belt and the small of his back.

A troop of small-faced monkeys barked and screeched high up in the canopy as they jumped from tree to tree. We all looked towards the jungle.

'Monkey's bothering you?' I asked.

'No, insects like you bother me.'

'If you shoot us, they'll know it's you,' I argued. 'You may have some of the police in your pocket, but even you said that "murder matters", and you'll spend at least the rest of your life with a lot of real insects in jail.'

'Or they'll hang you,' quipped Zak.

'Not if you two have an argument, and you shoot her. Then, realizing what you've done and the heartbreak you've caused her aunt and uncle, in your grief, you shoot yourself. Don't worry, the note I've typed will explain everything for the police. I'll make sure you get some great scratches from her nails and a few other bruises. It's not ideal, but for the police, it'll do. That and a generous donation.' He then pointed at me and then at the rifle. 'You! Pick it up and pass it over. Then collect four bullets from the golf bag.' I complied but as slowly as I could get away with. There was no choice. The best I could hope for was that my aunt and uncle would worry where I'd got to and come to help. The longer I could hold things up, the better.

Abidin cradled the rifle in his left hand, the pistol moving wildly, while he tried to put the cartridges in with his bandaged right hand. Each bullet took time to load using his thumb, ring and little fingers. I saw the pain he was in and would have laughed or rushed him if the revolver wasn't pointing at me. I was hoping Zak, who wasn't in the firing line, would do something. But he was his useless self.

Shit! If this is it, go out with a bang, not a whimper.

Fight!

Abidin held the rifle in his bandaged hand, his ring finger near but not on the trigger. He went to put the pistol in his front pocket. The rifle swung between me and Zak. A chance.

I was strong and fast and fancied my chances. I had to do something. I rushed forward and reached out for the rifle now swinging towards me. I managed to touch the end of the barrel when my ears were filled with a loud explosion. I felt myself being rammed backwards, but I managed to stay upright. I looked down at my stomach in disbelief and watched a bright red bloom appear and grow. Then came a monumental pain as though I'd been slammed in the guts with a sledgehammer. I dropped to my knees. My vision narrowed and I gasped for air.

36

The sound of the shot reverberated through the jungle. Insects rasped their hindlegs in warning. Birds and monkeys screeched a riotous alarm. I heard Abidin shouting, 'Why don't you just die?'

I was squirming in pain on my knees.

The shot galvanized Zak. He was next. He also needed to get me to a doctor—he owed it to my uncle and aunt.

Abidin was distracted by a troop of pale-faced langurs and looked at the edge of the plantation.

Zak saw his chance and rushed Abidin.

Abidin swivelled around, keeping the rifle at his hip and shot Zak in the chest. He collapsed in a heap.

Abidin turned back to me. 'Two bullets left. Let's finish this mess. Where would you like it? The heart? No, too small a target.'

I tried to say the worst words I could think of, but my Ki-Swahili came out in whispers.

Abidin wanted to rant. 'Why do Malaysians think *matsallehs* are special? You're so screwed up that I could have done anything I wanted with you. It would have been easy. You liked me; I could tell. And you thought I was in love with you!' Abidin made a mock retching noise. 'But you're ugly and your character sucks. Take those words of wisdom to your grave. You're a messed-up ugly bitch.'

He paused for a moment. 'I suppose the story has to change now: he shoots you and I manage to wrestle the gun from him while he's trying to reload and shoot him in self-defence. It's his rifle and he brought it to the party. You're a real idiot, you know that? All I wanted was for you to leave. That's why I arranged that text message from your father's number. But now you'll leave in a wooden box. Your choice. Shit. Now I think of it, I should've finished you earlier and saved my father and me all the trouble you've caused. You chose this.'

The jungle suddenly went quiet, the air still.

Abidin looked towards the oil palm, his face a picture of confusion.

'She's coming, you know.'

'Who?'

'Maya. She will destroy you.'

'Who? You're really fucked up, you know that?'

A large branch fell and landed with a thud.

Abidin swung around and fired in the direction the sound came from.

'I can almost taste your fear,' I hissed. My vision was blurring again and it felt like I was leaving my own body.

'Shut it. You're not going to get in my head that easily.' He loaded the last bullet into its chamber. 'Whatever you're hoping for is not going to save you this time.'

'Before you do—' I said in a detached voice and moved my eyes to look behind him. Then I smiled.

'Nice try. Too late.'

I heard another distant explosion, but my vision had already faded to black with brilliant shining stars, each glittering with excruciating pain. I felt an immense force lift me backwards and the feeling of flying. As my eyes closed, I caught a glimpse of a magnificent creature with sharp claws and scimitar fangs racing forward. Then everything was quiet. In my heart I carried the memory of a beautiful elfin-faced girl who had bright yellow-and-gold eyes with shining black irises. They were the most beautiful eyes I had ever seen.

Part Four

Become who you are.

—F. Nietzsche

37

My insides were on fire. *What?* If I'm feeling pain, I must be alive. *How is this possible?*

I opened my eyes to find I'd been intubated, with more tubes coming out of my arms and wrists. I had a plastic clip attached to my index finger with another wire feeding into a beeping machine to my left. I wanted the tube out of my mouth and started to panic. A nurse passing by saw my flailing and rushed into the room to help calm me.

Moments later, a doctor entered and removed the uncomfortable tube from my mouth and several other wires. My throat was burning. He listened to my heart, took my blood pressure and asked several questions related to memory. I'd been awake for no longer than ten minutes when a heavy tiredness, like a giant wave, crashed over me. All I wanted was to sleep.

The next time I opened my eyes, I saw Aunt Margaret and Uncle Donald peering at me like I was something from a biology class.

'Hello,' was all I could manage.

'Zola!' my aunt said with such enthusiasm that I thought the whole hospital probably heard her.

I smiled as best I could.

'No need to say anything, dear. You're in shock. That's what the young doctor said. Such a nice man. You've been in a comma, so I've brought a nice flask of tea.'

'Coma, my luscious lily, it's a coma.' Donald added.

'How long?' I managed.

'Today is the third day,' Donald said. 'They found two bullet holes in you, one in the stomach and the other in your shoulder. The bullets went straight through and you're healing nicely. Incredible luck they didn't hit anything major.'

'What about Zak? It was So Ching Long's son, Abidin. He was the one who shot us.'

'Relax, Zola. Relax. Zak will make a full recovery. When Abidin shot you, the kickback from the rifle must have thrown him backwards and spun him on to a pointed tree stump. He has a nasty wound in his chest and vicious scratches on his face. The police assume that's why he couldn't escape. He's in a secure hospital until he can be transferred to prison. My phone recorded everything on voicemail when you called me. I came as fast as I could and found you already unconscious.'

'Yes, dear,' Margaret added. 'We were quite worried and were going to let your parents know tonight, but now that you're awake, we'll leave that up to you.'

'Thank you,' I said with grateful eyes.

'Righty ho. We can see you need more rest, so we'll leave you for now and come visit tomorrow about the same time.'

'Yes,' Margaret added, 'I'll bring some fresh tea. You can't trust the hospital stuff. Soon have you right as a tortoise.'

I must have drifted off again because the next time I woke up, the curtains had been closed and I could tell it was dusk outside. The subdued lighting in the room made everything look peaceful. I felt much better and noticed most of the wires and tubes had been removed. I was still on a drip and the plastic clip on my finger was still there, but it felt reassuring rather than intrusive. I had an urge to get out of bed as my legs were itching to move and in need of a good stretch. My stomach still hurt like hell but was better than before. The thick padding to one side, front and back, felt soft and spongy. I looked around the room and noticed there was a mirror by the door. Curiosity had me wondering what I looked like in a hospital gown. I walked over, being careful with my steps and dragging the drip with me. I saw myself in the mirror. It was me, but something looked different. It was like seeing a school friend after the long summer holidays; they were the same but oddly different.

To be honest, I thought I looked better than I remembered. My nose looked smaller, and my eyes were clear and sparkly, maybe even a little larger. Weird.

I'd lost weight but, having been fed liquids through a tube, that was to be expected. Yet I felt great and powerful. Apart from the entry and exit points in my stomach and shoulder, strangely, I had another pain in my jaw. My teeth couldn't have been brushed and I scraped my nails over the front ones expecting to find a furry coating. No, they felt clean. I gave a false smile to look at the rest of them. They looked slightly different, more rounded than I remembered them. I hoped I wouldn't need to get braces. I pushed my face closer to get a more detailed inspection. Then I froze. I slowly stepped back from the mirror.

Maya was staring back. My eyes refocussed and she was gone. I stared again at the same old me. Sort of.

A powerful scent got my attention. It was overwhelming. Food. I was starving. Living on a liquid diet couldn't have been good for me. I was salivating. Wow, I needed to eat.

The door opened, and a Malay doctor came in with a concerned look on her face.

'What are you doing out of bed? You just woke up from a coma. Your arms and legs need time to rebuild muscle. Slowly, okay? You can't expect to be at hundred per cent in a few hours. Physio wants to work with you tomorrow to ensure you practise the right exercises.'

'I feel fine,' I said, feeling ravenous. 'I want that yummy smelling food.'

She put on a condescending smile. 'Well, appetite's a good sign. If you get back into bed, I'll ask the nurse to get you something. What would you like? Porridge would be the sensible choice.'

'The food I can smell.'

'Really? I can't smell anything up here. The kitchen is on the ground floor.'

'What are they serving?'

'I can't be sure as they have two or three main dishes every day. But judging from when I walked past about an hour ago, I wouldn't be surprised if it was chicken curry.'

'I want liver and bacon.'

'We're in a hospital. Regulations don't allow for those types of food. And why are you making those strange growling sounds? It must be your medication. Now get back into bed, or you'll get nothing.'

After the reprimand, she helped me climb back into bed, fluffed my pillow and let me know that one of the nurses would come up with some porridge. Yuk, but she was probably right about it being the best thing for me. I didn't remember growling. Perhaps she was also right about the medication.

I lay in bed listening to the rhythmic thrum of hospital machinery punctuated by a soft distant beeping. I was bored already. The wire in the back of my wrist was beginning to annoy me.

I thought I heard someone call my name; must be the medication; *I should rest.*

'It's not the medication. I'm here to say "hello".'

Am I going crazy or what? 'Who said that?' I bit my lip and felt it.

The familiar voice spoke again. 'I've missed you.'

'Maya? Where are you?'

'Over here.'

I looked over at the mirror and thought I saw it shimmer.

I pulled the sheets back and wished I hadn't moved so quickly. A bolt of shooting pain surged up from my stomach to my shoulder. I sure didn't imagine that. I paused to get my breath back.

'Take your time. I'll always be here for you.'

'This is a dream, isn't it?' I said aloud.

Maya's voice, soft as a distant thunderstorm, said, 'I am as real as you.'

With slow baby steps, I made it to the mirror. It was a great relief to see me. Just me. I turned my head sideways slightly to try and understand what was glinting on my chest in the low hospital lights. Hanging around my neck from a delicate chain was an anatomically perfect, solid gold heart—my present to Maya.

I sighed heavily and again looked at my familiar button nose, pointy ears, and golden eyes with small black irises. 'Wait! That's not me. You're not me,' I growled.

Maya spoke tenderly but there was anger on her face, 'I'll never leave you.' Then she shook her head violently as if she were ripping a piece of flesh from a carcass. I watched in horror as her teeth grew and fur sprouted. Her hands stretched into grasping claws. Her body ripped through its clothes. Her face became half elf, half creature.

'No, no. I'm not you. I'm me,' I challenged, my fear rising.

The creature in the mirror growled, 'I am whatever you want me to be.'

Its hand exploded through the mirror and seized my arm. A surge of emotion punched a hole through my chest. My head started spinning. Images pulsed in my mind. I saw pictures of when Maya and I first met in the plantation, but this time I was saying the words that *she* had said.

Another image streamed through—of when I saw her at the SGR Café and ordered the avocado toast. But as I watched the movie play out in my mind, it was me who went up to order, not her. And when I saw her holding my glowing pendant and telling me that my heart was fast, the image merged into me holding my own pendant with my other hand gripping my own arm tightly. My head snapped back, and the picture changed. The images came faster now. I wanted them to stop, but they forced their way in. I was hurtling bushels of palm nuts with a pitchfork over the collection lorry and laughing at my own strength. But every bushel always had another pitchfork in it, one of the other worker's pitchfork, also heaving the same bushel as me. It was his strength, not mine.

The creature's other hand burst through the mirror, seizing my other arm. 'Come to me. I'm all you will ever need.'

I heard a disembodied wailing echo around the room.

I felt my legs starting to buckle but the creature held me up. The mirror glass turned opaque and shivered. The creature's face strained against the obstruction until it made its way through. Its eyes were bloodshot red. Behind pointed front teeth and the two scimitar-like side fangs, its breath reeked of rotting flesh. Skin and fur dripped down the side of a face wracked with intense pain.

It howled a long wailful cry, 'Heal me . . . love me.'

I tried pulling myself free, but the creature's grip was too strong. Like quicksand, the harder I pulled, the more my feet slid towards the mirror. The creature's jaws opened wider and its lips peeled back from its mouth. With a vicious snarl, its teeth closed over my neck and dragged me through the glass.

I was on the rise in the plantation covered in loose cloth. In front of me were two thugs. One was on his knees sobbing wildly, blood dripping from his face. His friend was by his side trying to close the wound around his eye with a scrap of dirty cloth. My hand was no more than a claw, and in it was a machete. Behind me was a half-open door I felt compelled to walk through.

Everything was still and silent. Perfect.

I turned around to see myself standing alone under a large rain tree near the entrance of SGR Café. The girl I saw looked like she would give anything for a friend. *Was that really how I looked?*

I floated over, took the girl's hand in my claw, then ran a sharp talon across her palm. Blood flowed freely. My long tongue curled around the wound, sealing it. The girl looked amazed and laughed. We walked through the entrance and were transported to a small clearing at the end of a small path by a small stream where a discarded porcelain bowl lay on the ground. The girl who looked like me was singing and talking to herself. Then she took the dish, filled it with stream water and drank from it. Moments later she stopped talking, turned pale, and vomited until there was nothing left. She then lay down in the grass, crying, and rocking herself to sleep. Alone.

I was in hell. Vicious red and orange flames danced with plumes of thick black smoke. I floated over burning coals to where a man was melting in the heat. Away from the flames was a brown-haired girl with a red headband lying in the middle of the path. The smoke had gotten to her and she was giving up. I wanted to scream at her to run, but nothing came out of my mouth except a low growling. I was willing her to get up and get away from the burning plantation. A branch fell nearby, throwing sparks over her bare arms. She moved and pushed herself up, disoriented. She got to her feet and ran down the trail to an irrigation ditch where she lay for a long time in the cool water. She'd been lucky. Her burns were minor. When the fire had shifted away, I watched her climb out of the ditch, sobbing dry tears and stumbling back towards the plantation bungalow.

A ball of flames exploded around me and I felt myself being transported to Zak's farm and the pretty cottage I had been looking forward to moving into with the Hamsters.

I saw myself sitting on the ground next to Zak, who was motionless in the dirt with a bloody patch on the side of his chest. I had a growing red patch around my ribs.

Abidin was there, waving Zak's hunting rifle at the girl who looked like me. Her face was filled with pain. I saw Abidin fumble as he loaded the next round into the chamber. I wanted to rip his heart from his chest, but I continued floating. I watched myself rushing forward towards Abidin, clawing at his eyes, and being shot again. It must have been pure adrenaline flowing through my body since I kept moving. Abidin fell back and I saw myself pick up one of the small, uprooted tree stumps, recently cleared from the construction site, and ram it into his chest.

I felt the creature's face I was trapped in and felt wetness around its eyes. I looked down at the monster I had become. For the first time in the dreamworld I was trapped in, I felt something: a massive pressure crushing me—a momentous desire to belong, to feel wanted.

The sky opened and a huge vortex filled with all the other lost souls of the world swirled around me. The wind roared like a jet turbine, sucking me into it.

A face appeared in the churning clouds and I heard a voice through the noise. 'Zola! Never surrender.'

The whole sky cracked and the creature I had become shattered into a thousand pieces.

Brilliant golden light pierced my eyes and I heard myself shouting and growling in the hospital room like an out-of-body experience.

A screeching white pain filled my whole being. White coats were around me. I was covered in blood. My limbs were pinned down and I saw a large needle go in my neck.

On the floor, the hospital mirror had shattered into tiny pieces, each containing a fragment of the creature I never wanted to see again.

37

There was brilliant sunshine outside when I woke up. I was me again and I felt exhausted. I lay there for about twenty minutes before one of the doctors peered around the corner and asked how I was. There was no heart monitor attached and the drip had disappeared. That had to be good. The bad news was that I was covered in plasters and bandages from the broken glass.

He let me know not to worry about any more nightmares since they had confirmed that I'd had a reaction to the medication and they had changed it. He also told me that in a short while I would be moved to a general ward. I would be under observation for a couple of days before I would be discharged to re-hamster myself into my new family.

Mentally, I wasn't sure where I was exactly, but I felt I was back in a good place. My aunt and uncle were all the crazy I would ever need. I wondered what time visiting hours started.

Hesitantly, I got out of bed and took halting steps to the window to see the view outside. I pulled back the blinds and the sun glinted off my necklace, which made my eyes refocus. My reflection smiled back. I flipped the heart-shaped pendant over and saw some scratch marks. I peered closer and, after my eyes had adjusted, saw that they formed a message: 'Done with love.' There was the beginning of another letter, possibly a 'T', but I already knew what it would have said.